Manhattan Mayhem

ISBN-13: 978-1-7377620-4-1
ISBN-10: 1-7377620-4-8

First printing: December 2022

Cover design by ThomasMax

Front cover photo by Vlad Alexandru Popa, used courtesy of pexels.com

Published by:

tm

ThomasMax Publishing
P.O. Box 250054
Atlanta, GA 30325
www.thomasmax.com

Manhattan Mayhem

A. Shane Etter

ThomasMax

Your Publisher
For The 21st Century

ACKNOWLEDGMENTS

Most of all, I would like to thank Lee Clevenger and Robert Preston Ward of Thomas Max Publishing for believing in *Manhattan Mayhem*. To all the friends and extended family who have given me their support and encouragement during this literary journey, please forgive me for not mentioning you all by name. It would take more space than I have here. You all know how important you are to me. Thanks to my sister Amy Etter Mills, for your support and love. And to Bonni Newberry, my primary and first reader, for everything.

All mistakes in settings or timing are completely my own and I take full responsibility for them.

For my late brother, Chief Warrant Ret., and U.S. Army Aviator, Kevin Andrew Etter. You left us way too young. The world is worse off without you in it. I will never forget you. I'm happy you were proud of me because I was really proud of you, and still am.

OTHER BOOKS
BY A. SHANE ETTER

Bottom Dwellers

Mind Dwellers

Trail Dwellers

A Brain in Third Person

A War in The Bronx

A Brain in Third Person II
– The Return of The Bad Penny

Devil's Sympathy

World of Rage

The Prosaist and The Unholy Ghost

Chapter One

Detective Rossi and his NYPD informants, Bookworm and Reefer, were still basking in the veneration of apprehending the most prolific serial killer of the past half-century, the vicious sharp-edged murderer known as the Unholy Ghost, more than six months previously.

At Bookworm's insistence Rossi had convinced His Imminence The Reverend Lieutenant and the NYPD's even higher-ups to keep Bookworm's and Reefer's vital assistance and more importantly, their pictures and their given names, John and Danté, even though few people were aware of them, out of the local papers, or their value as informants would certainly be diminished if not completely destroyed. And they were too important an asset to the department to allow that to happen. Even so, word about the heroes was still finding its way out in some quarters.

Summer was about to arrive in all of it's hot and humid glory, and after packing away their winter clothes, those who were able to were beginning to pack Coney Island beaches, or were off to the boardwalk in Atlantic City, or the AC, as locals referred to it. That's not unusual.

That didn't include Bookworm and Reefer, however. Bookworm found Coney wearying. Besides which, summer was the city's busiest time of the year for violent crime; probably because the heat was oppressive and tangible and escalated tempers that were already on edge and over the precipice; likely because they'd finally had enough of whatever shit it was that had pissed them off in the first place.

And so they would not be thought of as a one-trick pony, he and Reefer were in the street not solely for a constitutional, but also for doing what they did best—keeping their ears to the ground. The hot afternoon sun beginning to bear down. Anyone paying attention to them might have thought Reefer was Bookworm's younger brother. With skin the color of milk chocolate, a slim build, and gentle delicate hands. Indeed, Reefer, though thirty-two; looked like he was barely out of his teens, if that. Blessed with high metabolisms and good genetics, both had skin the color of lightly toasted bread and looked like they could stand to eat a cheeseburger or two.

Reefer was almost a head shorter and that wasn't allowing for Bookworm's vast Afro as high as the proud curly black hair on a standard poodle's head compared to Reefer's shiny shaved head that he joked he shined with Turtle Wax. Reefer had Māori-ish facial ink similar to boxer Mike Tyson. Young and angelic except for the facial ink which gave a permanently pissed off look to his otherwise aesthetic face, people tended to shy away from looking directly at him. So probably no one paid that much attention. The main reason he had the multi-colored facial tats.

Life can be difficult for brothers. But even though they were as close as, because they weren't brothers nothing was difficult for Bookworm and Reefer. They had all of the advantages of being brothers but without the usual accompanying layers of problems; showing affection, complimenting one another, and the like. It was easy because they both had big hearts. And they felt everything that blood felt.

And even though Reefer was as congenial as Bookworm he didn't mind people thinking he wasn't. Walking the sidewalks of midtown, they passed a black-market peddler. A seedy-looking brother with long dreads wearing a cheap tux jacket with worn out jeans. He was propped against a wall behind his bargain-basement table and selling watches.

To hear his spiel describing their features they'd have to sell for ten thousand dollars apiece instead of ten bucks each. And the latter was likely, a somewhat close to fair price for bogus Rolexes and Breitlings. During the short wait on the sloped concrete corner at the next stoplight, side by side, Bookworm grasped his shorter young friend's shoulder in an intimate brotherly gesture and said, "Reef, what's the matter, my man? You're sort of quiet."

"Nothing, not really. You know, just want to make a difference and nothing be's happening." Bookworm understood. Reefer only looked puerile. In truth he was a striver, an achiever. He had matured in their role of assisting the NYPD. And the change hadn't been an ephemeral one. But even after changes upon changes he was more or less the same.

They both had been indispensable in stopping the Unholy Ghost's genocidal rampage, and though it wasn't by design, they sort of felt put out to pasture. A funny euphemism given that they both were native Knickerbockers of and a part of the street, and therefore, didn't really understand the ancient saw regarding old horses.

"I get it, brother. That means we gonna have to take the proverbial Wall Street Bull by the horns." Bookworm was referring to the massive sixteen-foot-long bronze sculpture of a head down, snorting bull—a beloved artistic treasure gifted the city by the Italian artist, and Ellis Island Medal of Honor awardee, Arturo Di Modica—the massive piece appropriately titled "Charging Bull," on permanent display in Bowling Green Park, the oldest park in New York City, and one of, if not *the* oldest, in the country. It had been designated as a small public space in 1733 and the site of the original Dutch fort of New Amsterdam.

Reefer didn't respond but the confused expression on his face showed that he had no idea what Bookworm was talking about.

"Hey, how 'bout a beer? It's five o'clock somewhere," Bookworm said. He'd always liked that old saying. And he felt like his young friend could use some quality time to talk.

"I could stand a cold one."

"That's my man. Let's do it. One of the best bars in midtown is right around the corner."

Shakespeare @ the William was one of the few places left in the city where one could still get a draught for five dollars. The look and feel of a true British pub in every sense of the word. In fact the bartenders preferred it if you referred to a beer as a pint. Felt it lent to the authenticity. Not that they were putting on airs. Not much, anyway.

The wide plank dark wood floors covered with old world brocade rugs, dark wood tables, dim light and scarlet-painted walls would look right at home in the most authentic of centuries old pubs in the venerable U.K. city of Oxford. And the stamped dark copper low ceiling gave it a coffin-like sense. Bookworm liked the feel. Made him feel comfortable and relaxed him. He thought he could sleep forever in the place. Although that was probably not the designer's intent.

The large space at the rear with the gigantic stone fireplace was especially welcoming, but they made their way to the bar, instead, nearly empty at not quite three o'clock on a week day, although closer to happy hour it would start filling up. The long dark bar with small jars of salted peanuts placed sacredly on top in front of every third backless wooden stool was cool to the touch under the air conditioning's thankless job, and ready for the happy hour crowd, ran down the right side of the long narrow shotgun space.

Although Bookworm almost never drank the stuff he liked the smell of the bar. Its smell beery. They picked a spot almost to the end. A few stools down the way from a slender professionally-dressed woman about the same age as Bookworm, somewhere in her venturesome mid-thirties, who was either a regular day-drinker, or was drowning her sorrows. You could see that she had a taste of attitude about her. A typical New York Italian female. But this was no dago-wop-skank. This chick had class. Anybody could see that.

The wall opposite the bar had a long shelf at which one could stand to offload patrons from the bar proper if it got too crowded.

Uber-cool, and taking it too seriously, like it was the most important thing in his life, the inked and pierced, late-twenties bartender looked at them with disdain, for they were interrupting his life-altering chore of polishing heavy cut glass beer mugs. Even so, he acquiesced to take their orders. A moment later he returned with the icy gold liquid in a pair of the perfectly frosted schooners, which, the bar lights reflecting off them enviously, were bigger than typical beer mugs. But before he could even set them on the bar, he sloppily splashed a small amount worthy of a refreshing beer commercial on tv onto their napkins.

In an attempt to get Reefer to open up, Bookworm said, "Man,

I know whatchu talkin' about. Last November we knew we were helping the city, helpin' the peoples, even if no one else knew it."

Reefer said, "yeah bruh, never thought I'd care about that shit. Recognition was for other kinds of peoples. But turns out I liked knowing I was making a difference." Then he blew off some of the frothy head and took a pull of some of the beer from the huge glass.

"I get it bruh. I get it. But what're we gonna do about it?"

His stare woeful, and his shoulders sagging under the unseen burden, Reefer shook his head unknowingly. "Fuck if I know," he eventually said.

"I hear you. So let's quit wasting time, and do something 'bout it."

Chapter Two

Bookworm and Reefer decided that he, Reefer, should do what he does best; work the streets.

The main problem was that if they weren't working on a specific case they weren't getting paid by the NYPD. So they needed to rustle up something fast, to make it a paying gig.

The good news for them, if not for the people of The Big Apple, was that apparently there was a new killer terrorizing New Yorkers. So, Reefer needed to do what he did best. Find out what he could.

After each took the first healthy pulls from their pints, and continued to drink, Bookworm's phone buzzed. Detective Rossi calling.

"Dude, I need your help. I'm quite certain you've heard about the Swordsman," and without taking time to wait for acknowledgment, and with a presentiment he didn't realize he was offering, Rossi continued, "this new guy might end up being worse than the Ghost was. But, believe you me, he's no phantom. He's a mere mortal. Albeit one with a vampire's taste for blood." Rossi's Italian soul sometimes tended toward the melodramatic.

"We're ready," said Bookworm, excited about Rossi's timing. "When and where?"

"Now? Where are you?"

"Lucky for you, you got both of us. Coincidentally, my man, Reefer and I are having a pint at Shakespeare @ the William, discussing business."

"Good; cool. I know the place. I can be there in an hour if you guys can hang out."

"We'll be here." Bookworm knew he could speak for Reefer. He sensed that this was exactly what his man needed to perk him up. Bookworm explained to Reefer what Rossi had told him. Immediately energized, Reefer squared his shoulders, and his eyes suddenly seemed alive again.

And Bookworm was glad to hear from Detective Rossi because even though he loved Reefer literally like a younger brother, he didn't get many chances to use his Princeton and Wharton education and the accompanying vocabulary with him. In all reality, Bookworm agreed with the noted Samuel Beckett quote, 'Words are all we have.' And even if Rossi didn't have an advanced education, he tended to be somewhat more than a little garrulous and had an extensive vocabulary that he constantly worked on improving.

He and Bookworm had bonded over their mutual love of words and got a kick out of trying to one up each other. They tended to speak volubly with each other when together. In addition to his Merriam-Webster size vocabulary the best thing about Bookworm's Ivy League education was it had been free due to the scholarship he'd earned after being named an all-conference wide receiver at a Bronx parochial school where he had been the famed university's annual charity case since his mom couldn't afford the steep tuition.

Otherwise he wouldn't have been able to matriculate at one of the most elite, and expensive, universities in the country, before continuing to Wharton for his MBA mostly because he just enjoyed the crap out of going to school and he thought that being a highly educated black man would help to piss off white people; or at least some of them. And by way of matriculating at Princeton and then Wharton at least he didn't go to Yale and become a fucking Connecticut Yankee. They were almost as bad as the ones from Harvard, in his mind.

But even with his scholarship, his education, in a manner of speaking, did cost Bookworm. Some, most typically those of his own race, would say it cost him his blackness because he didn't arbitrarily side with African Americans on every issue; political or social. And even though he had good white friends, like Detective Rossi, neither did he try to be white. It wasn't that Bookworm didn't see color, he did; he wasn't egalitarian about it, but it didn't control his thoughts or decision-making. Color was merely something that was present. And he dealt with issues and people; not color.

He'd earned his undergrad degree on time in four years. And, he had to admit to himself if no one else, that the many seasons of football contributed to his predilection toward occasional violence even when it might be somewhat less than required or justified. He still had the lean hard body corded with sinews and muscle. And even though he was New York City street born and raised, he sometimes found himself missing the agrarian New Jersey setting in which the internationally renowned school sat.

It didn't mean he thought New York grim; quite the contrary, in its own way he found it beautiful. Every yellow taxi, every beauty salon, every bodega, dry cleaners, and even though they were out of place in this century-every undertaker's parlor, sorry-ass tv repair shop, every dingy little no class tavern, every little fruit and vegetable sidewalk stand and even the OTB parlors. All of them part and parcel of the spell of New York and all beautiful.

Although he had to wonder how many Chinese restaurants the city really needed. But they had their places, too. A Knickerbocker through and through, Bookworm had enjoyed his scholarly time spent at Princeton with his classmates, most of whom were from far posher backgrounds than his own, but now that he was back in the city that never left him he knew he'd never leave it again.

Although some would feel trapped, Bookworm never felt freer, than when he was in the Bronx. His body, his soul, his spirit; all free. Most would never understand it. An earnest student, he'd gotten his education even if it had been merely for his own satisfaction since it would never be used, at least not in the traditional sense, and he had everything he wanted, so why would he leave? It was more than a rhetorical question. Why, indeed?

For Reefer it was a question never to be considered. He didn't know that people like him could leave. The answers worked for each of them. Reefer didn't understand that if one had the means to travel; whether by wheel, rail, air, or foot; there was a different world to be experienced—a world of food, drink, culture, language.

For a young man it could be an enlightening experience, but he lived in the city that many considered the capitol of the world and many of those different things could be experienced in the twenty-two square miles of Manhattan, alone. In truth, one could sate one's wanderlust without spending their fortune or committing themselves to a military life, in Manhattan itself, an exclave surrounded by an indifferent country. The borough being the end goal for diasporas of Asians of various sorts; a polyglot of languages-Japanese, Chinese, Hebrew, Italiano, Irish, Puerto Rican, Spanish and others groups literally representing all corners of the globe.

Chapter Three

Bookworm and Reefer were deep into their second round when the archetypal wooden door with the classically British pointed arch top creaked open. Rossi entered and looked around warily. Checking out every nook, every cranny. A cop on guard with every calculated step.

He spotted his good friend Book, and Reefer, and a sudden warm smile lit up his inscrutable face that usually resembled a clenched fist. Bookworm had that effect on people. And he knew it. He was no Narcissus, thinking he was beyond handsome, but he knew his personality was attractive and attracted people to him. Even people like the eternally vexing and irascible Rossi.

So they, Bookworm and Rossi were alike in that way. Rossi made you care about what happened to him. No, not only him, but about what happened to everyone he loved—his wife, his kids, his grands—for him; so he would be okay. You wanted Rossi to be okay.

"Detective, how are you, my friend?" Said Bookworm, glad-handing him. He was happy to see the man he thought of as more like a close friend than a business acquaintance. They hadn't seen each other since the Unholy Ghost's murder trial. Three months past, now. Somewhere between too long and way too long for them both, but neither would ever see the Unholy Ghost again, given that he would be incarcerated in a steel-barred cell at the infamous and disreputable Sing Sing Correctional Facility for the rest of his natural life.

Or even worse, Atlanta Federal Penitentiary, a massive grandiloquent classical block structure similar in style to the more infamous Leavenworth. The Atlanta Prison, the third oldest in the nation and where Al Capone, Vincent Papa and even Frank Abagnale of the film, *Catch Me if You Can* fame, with Leonardo DiCaprio starring as Frank Abagnale, spent time. One of the toughest and most notorious prisons in the country. Where everybody in gen pop was as bad as the Ghost and he could get shived at any minute, possibly making the rest of his natural life not overly long. Needless to say it would keep one sprightly and on one's toes. And he didn't want to think about what could happen in the showers. Unless, understanding himself and what a troublemaker he could be he might be locked in solitary confinement or whatever other name it might go by at that facility and sequestered there for the duration. Of course, even Sing Sing wouldn't be as bad as the Vernon C. Bain prison barge, the more than a New York City block long, eight hundred bed, large flat-bottomed boat which would never be confused with a luxury cruise ship, that was docked on the Bronx shoreline at the mouth of Long Island Sound, where every day in prison might make one seasick or other maladies too obscene to even think about.

"Ah, you know how it is. The lieutenant's all over my ass. His favorite place to be, it seems."

"Well," Bookworm said, "what we gonna do about it?"

"Let me tell youse what's happening." Even though the traditionally southern colloquialism y'all was overtaking the country, Rossi was old school and one of but a few mature Knickerbockers, those set in their ways, who still said youse. "We're trying to keep the details out of the papers, but what we think we got us is a copycat."

"It's a good thing you're giving us the 411 then, since my delivery person keeps throwing my copies of the Daily News in the East River so I never know what's going on anymore," Bookworm said cleverly, while making a throwing motion trying to demonstrate how well he thinks on his feet.

"Well, anyways, it seems that our new asshole has a bro crush on the Unholy Ghost. In fact I'm betting the primary difference in these two is that our new guy knows what he's doing—and as you remember, Cole was in a fugue state when he committed his murders. But anyways, I intuited who better to catch the copycat Ghost than the men who caught the real Ghost."

Rossi got the bartender's attention and with an over-the-top cool movement subtly pointed at his friends' mugs, indicating two more, and one for himself. What brand he got wouldn't matter as long as it was wet and cold, since he was mostly an Italian red wine drinker anyways. It wasn't like he was a beer connoisseur; and when it got down to it, was anyone?

"And with summer coming and the temperatures rising, as you well know, the Big Apple will soon become a baked apple, and with it, tempers rising. And given that full moons bring out the crazies, the asshole, whoever he is, will probably be more active, so we need to try and nip it in the bud sooner rather than later." He took a mournful breath. "Otherwise this could be the worst summer in Gotham City since the summer of Sam. His real name was David Berkowitz, you remember.

"That was one sick son of a bitch; said his neighbor's dog told him to kill all those people. A talking dog, goddamnit. The .44 Caliber Killer—he was known by both nicknames, son of Sam, and the .44 Caliber Killer—summer '77. He was in Attica for years, one of the worst prisons in the world, before they transferred his worthless ass to Shawangunk Correctional Facility upstate which is almost as bad. Worthless piece of shit got what he deserved; unless they fried his ass in Old Sparky. But they would've had to send him to Sing Sing for that.

"The problem that sticks in my craw is that His Imminence The High Lieutenant wants me to call some of my recent parolees, find out if they hear anything. But I don't trust felons, current, ex- or any kind. And to be honest I think it's a slap in youse guys' faces. So, instead, I'm gonna not and say I did." The way he said it was sturdy. Obviously meaning it. "And youse guys will have to help me keep the secret. As long as we get this motherfucker we'll be fine. The high lieutenant won't care." The lieutenant, a Latino two-thirds Rossi's age with half the time in that Rossi had was primarily motivated by success and how he looked in the process.

Rossi sounded, and looked, fierce. A look of which he was certainly capable—he got it from his mother. God bless her hot-blooded Italian soul. And although that wasn't his usual manner, tracking down parasitic serial killers became so tiresome, and could cause one to become frumious. That's not unusual.

"I recall reading about Son of Sam. But, I'm much too young to remember him." Bookworm got a kick out of reminding the detective of that point. "You give us too much credit, Sal, but we're fain to help. You remember what I told you the last time you called me for our assistance, right?"

"No, what?"

"Your timing is perfect, because I'm just about out of piasters is what I said then. But it's worse this time because it means my man, Reef, is too."

"I need to hook youse up, then. So, since you reminded me, I'll tell you now the same thing I told you last time. I hear the NYPD's crime stoppers fund is chockfull of piasters."

"Smartass."

Recalling that that was what Book had said the last time, Rossi asked rhetorically, "Why does this conversation sound familiar? We figure we need youse guys' ears to the ground so to speak. If you recall last time, Reefer's old running buddy Spike told him the Unholy Ghost was somebody famous. Turned out he was right, after you recognized Cole's author pic on the back of one of his books. Too bad it wasn't on the back of a wine bottle; then maybe a Manhattan socialite woulda recognized him sooner. I'm just sayin'. *In vino veritas*, and all that shit, you know. Maybe we would have caught his sorry ass sooner. But I digress; I'm guessing, or at least hoping, youse guy's contacts will know something again."

Rossi paused, "Are you okay, Reefer? You seem a little down."

Bookworm patted his man on the back and said, "He'll be fine. This is precisely what the doctor ordered."

Reefer perked up in agreement and his dark eyes shone alive for the first time in quite a while.

Rossi said, "That's good. I have enough to worry about already without having to worry about my men."

"We're good," said Bookworm. Truth was, until Rossi called he'd been worried about Reefer too.

After one pint, Rossi stood and said, "I promised I wouldn't keep you long, and I want to keep my word, and since you guys are on the payroll now I don't want to have to pay you overtime, anyways. So, here's your down payment," and handed Book five crisp one-hundred-dollar bills. "Keep your receipts for expenses, except for bagels or beer. Those are on you"

"Damn," said Book, wishing Rossi hadn't mentioned those, because he could eat the crap out of some toasted garlic bagels slathered with real butter, none of that margarine shit, but only if they were crunchy; unless he was in the mood to go sweet, then he was all over crumbly blueberry ones with some cream cheese from the city about a hundred miles south of there with the same name as the brand. "But as long as we're here we might as well have two more cold ones. But only because we're strategizing, you understand. It's always easier to strategize over a couple of icy ones."

Reefer looked at him skeptically, but was nonetheless happy for the chance to be relevant, once again…and to have another beer.

"Suit yourself," said Rossi.

So, to a greater calling, they bent over their pints and huddled. Much like before with the Unholy Ghost they would start working their phones bright and early the next morning. Because it was more efficient than beginning on foot. And if they needed anything it was to be efficient.

Chapter Four

The next morning at nine Reefer rang the doorbell of Bookworm's thirtieth floor condo in the nearly fifty-year-old Co-op City. No more than ten minutes away from the Happy Land social club, the site of New York City's third deadliest fire of all time, set by an unhappy ex-boyfriend of a female employee, where eighty-seven people lost their lives in the spring of 1990, now the site of a tax preparation business. Minutes away from Bookworm's condo but he didn't know about the tragic event since he wasn't much more than a toddler when the tragedy occurred.

Reefer entered his friend's home where he'd been many times, but still taken aback by the books lined up like the uneven tops of buildings of the NYC skyline on belabored shelves, the worn and torn dust jackets of the books long discarded. Mostly classic fiction and works reprinted in English by ancient philosophers, including Voltaire and René Descartes along with his personal faves, John Locke and Immanuel Kant.

Unless Bookworm wanted a trifle lighter reading, in which case he'd choose Dante Alighieri, colloquially known by his Christian name, Dante and also Reefer's proper name. Especially his 14th century epic poem, *Divine Comedy*. The books accompanied as they were by inexpensive framed reproductions of nevertheless recognizable prints possessing the walls.

The thirtieth floor looked down on the flat curbstone gray roofs of lesser buildings' firmament dug deep into the granite schist and stone far below the surface, parking lots and debris-strewn ribbons of concrete running both parallel and contradictory to each other and thingness.

Even though Bookworm made a substantial non-taxable income from his a little less than reputable career calling, he was happy for New York's rent-control laws. About the only thing he wasn't crazy about living the high-rise lifestyle was if he needed to use the bathroom in a hurry but had to ride up thirty floors in an elevator before he could get to his. And it was even worse if the lift happened to be full and was stopping at other floors along the way. But at least he didn't live in one of the city's many old-law walk up tenements; the at most eight story buildings that had been built over a century before with four large apartments per floor. Before they were cut up to make each individual room an apartment with one bathroom per floor. That could certainly make for some interesting late nights.

"Reef, come in. Come in. I can't wait to get started. How 'bout you? I want to get this son of a bitch even quicker than we did the Ghost. Save some lives. Let's have some caffeine and get started," he said, pointing to a shiny red Keurig coffee maker plugged in and gurgling on the counter. On a roll, and getting louder, Bookworm sounded like he'd already had a whole pot, black, himself.

Chapter Five

The Swordsman wandered South Street Seaport, the shopping mall that juts out on a wooden pier piercing the esplanade, into the dun-colored serpentine East River pointing to Brooklyn and its factories and plants with their billowing smokestacks on the other bank and across the street from the open air Fulton Fish Market which most people remember from the movie *Home Alone 2, Lost in New York* and the famous scene when the two criminals played by Joe Pesci and Daniel Stern, stowed away in a fish truck.

The air around the market always has the strong smell of fish even though it's open air where the fishmen slam the fish against a wall to stun them then cut off their heads with long knives, and a short one-half block away from Fraunces Tavern, the site of General George Washington's farewell address to his officers when he left the military to become the first president of the United States. The killer wasn't carrying his preferred blade with him in open daylight, so he wasn't really on the hunt, but what he was doing was reconnaissance, bloody preplanning, as it were.

And ruminating. Indeed, with his keen sense of self-worth and if he knew more of history, he would have felt certain that had he been born of a different age; the Roman Empire, say, he would have been a respected brave praetorian guard. Or even better, their mortal enemy in the famous Colosseum, one of the former slaves- a courageous gladiator.

A hundred yards out on the pier, he leaned against the wood railing and stood gazing at the inspiring iconic skyline of lower Manhattan, the blinding sun ashine in all its shimmering glory, reflecting off the glass of the tall towers, while enjoying the warm breeze sweeping the East River, which actually wasn't a river at all, but a brackish tidal estuary, the water almost still except for gentle rising and falling with the capriciousness of the Atlantic Ocean's current never changing more than a fathom in depth. Always the same, summer or winter, little change. No current, only tide. Brody loved educating people with that bit of biological minutiae of which most weren't aware. Especially the upper middle-aged privileged white douchebags who thought they knew everything because they have a fat bank account.

Different from The Unholy Ghost who was gifted his name by local newspapers then splashed on headlines of each of the city's major print publications, Gage Brody had self-bestowed his nickname, in a letter to the Post, his preferred New York newspaper, because of its tabloid style of writing. Which was the same reason the so-called intelligentsia didn't care for it. He wished now he'd come up with an even cooler and deadlier sounding nick, maybe something like The Broadway Executioner— of course he felt like he'd seen that somewhere; he wasn't usually that keen, or even The Fifth Avenue Executioner or if one preferred alliteration, the East Side Executioner—alas, too late for that now.

The other main difference in the two killers was that Grayson Cole had a clear case of dissociative multiple personality disorder, as defined by the DSM3 manual, the unquestioned bible of psychiatry published by the American Psychiatric Association, and no knowledge of the other side to himself, another self, who was committing the heinous homicides. And within that disorder his superego was underdeveloped-lacking in moral restraint, remorse, empathy and integrity.

Gage Brody on the other hand was a manifestation of evil that was producing pure cold depravity. No schizophrenia, no apparent psychosis, no one else he could blame. It would be easy to call him an amoral psychopath, but even that would be oversimplifying it. Because in the end, all New Yorkers, in some way or another, are psychopaths. That's what you get in a city of over ten million people. That's not unusual. And as everyone knows New York isn't home to anyone, even if they're from there and that home without the usual trappings of a place where they belonged had an effect on people.

And so he was The Swordsman. He might have given himself the name Katana after the curved Japanese sword carried by the samurai, and even though he thought it was a cool name it had already been taken by the Asian chick in the movie Suicide Squad and he wouldn't be accused of being a copycat or having a chick's name. And although an ugly looking hori hori knife, about a foot long typically used for digging in a Japanese royal's garden, with both serrated and smooth edges, was his preferred weapon, he was willing to utilize whatever sharpened blade might present itself. And of course, his was a replica—even though the sign above the shelf on which it awaited him said the hilt was of genuine dragon bone from the seven kingdoms, when in truth it was neither—he'd picked up at a Wal-Mart far out on Long Island for thirty-five bucks since there weren't any of the massive discount big-box stores in the city proper. And he definitely didn't have the low four figures that an actual Japanese nobleman's dagger fashioned of fine Japanese steel would set you back.

What he really would have liked was a bejeweled short sword like the Chinese killers wielded in *John Wick Chapter 3 Parabellum* used in assassinations, but he couldn't afford the price of one of those either. Not on a blue-collar worker's meager—at least for a New York City lifestyle—wages. Especially when he was paying alimony and child support to an ex-wife. He couldn't wait til the little shit turned eighteen so he wouldn't have to pay the child support no more. As long as he didn't go to college, and so far his namesake had shown no propensity toward that lofty goal at least as yet, at twelve years old.

And he'd love to know if the kid was really even his. There was some question, at least in his mind, since they had had a short separation shortly before the time she announced the pregnancy. He remembered she got as big as a cow. Even though memory tends to be temperamental or contrary. And the baby was anything but tiny at more than nine pounds. That was another reason he'd questioned its paternity, since he himself was at best, an average-size man. Psychologists, studying Brody in the future, would invariably deduce that his relationship with his former wife, as with most killers, who are quite ordinary, familial relationships being the biggest influence on his becoming a homicidal maniac.

But he enjoyed his recently acquired avocation. He found it thoroughly fulfilling. Every time he killed somebody he felt like he was getting even with those mother-fuckers who'd bullied him and picked on him in high school; the ones who caused him to hate everything about school—the building, the people in it, especially the people, the dusty smell of chalk powder settling on everything, the cafeteria that smelled like stale food and lunches that sucked— all were part of the reason he dropped out and couldn't get a better paying job.

He only wished he could get paid for killing. Instead of just doing it for fun. Because it amuses him. If it weren't for supplementing his income by teaching sword technique at a Bronx martial arts dojo to feed himself he'd be even thinner than he was. And if he didn't start sleeping better he'd soon be driving a cab at night, like Robert De Niro in the noir Gotham City-set film, Taxi Driver. Of course most of the cabbies were Haitians nowadays, and he certainly didn't want to associate with them. Like anybody except himself would think they below him.

***

At the same time Gage Brody was in the dispatch office of the air conditioning maintenance company where he worked. The job was decent. He'd never be wealthy, or even unworried about dollars, but people couldn't live without their recycled conditioned air, so he'd always have a job, even such as it was. The only part of it he disliked was paying the goddamn HVAC union membership dues. The fuckin' bloodsuckers.

He probably oughta kill a few of them sons of bitches. That's who he oughta kill, but then no one would care, except the union. But what else was he going to do with only a high school education and as a reserve army and regular army enlistee where he got his HVAC training. And ironically, as well Brody felt like the rest of the army's training and insinuated aggression contributed to his avocation as The Swordsman.

The other blue-collar workers were having their morning cuppa, probably their second, and passing around the morning's edition of The Daily News and discussing The Swordsman. He couldn't remember, or didn't know, most of their names. It didn't matter. They were losers; in his estimation, not up to his measure. And since they trended toward facile, they thought Brody the most intelligent among them, and so they waited for his erudite opinion. He himself had cultivated that view of himself. Though truth be told, even to himself, he knew he wasn't long on good sense. If he had been that cunning and knowing, he would consider that his extracurricular activities were Faustian in his hoped-for achievement.

Of course, if he were that intelligent he would be studying the sacred Hindu treatises, written between 800 and 200 BC, or playing the violin like Izthak Perlman or playing doleful Russian baroque nocturnes on the viola, but he wasn't so he wasn't. In fact, his dearth of education and lack of nous, combined with learning disabilities, primarily dyslexia, meant he was dumb as an eggplant and wasn't destined to be a follower of Herbert Marcuse's teachings; rather he was destined to be what he was; a blue-collar worker barely eking out a meager existence—those being the main ways he differed from a lot of serial killers, many of whom tested for high IQs and were fairly well-educated.

Although unlike most, who suffered from inferiority complexes, Brody had a higher than realistic opinion of his keenness and in fact, had a superiority complex. Or at least he knew he wasn't like the killer mental patients on Shutter Island in the great Dennis Lehane novel of the same name. He was somewhat cunning, but even he recognized that it was an unsophisticated cunning born out of sheer meanness. He did, like the majority of like-minded killers, follow the profile of overuse of alcohol, drug abuse, anti-social behavior, an alcoholic father, and follow the paths of Albert DeSalvo infamously known as the Boston Strangler; Jeffrey Dahmer; and David Berkowitz, better known as the Son of Sam, for whom animals were their first victims, by torturing small animals, a morbid example of serious anger issues even as a child.

The fact was however, Brody wasn't even sure he fit the classic definition of the term serial killer as first coined by FBI agent Robert Ressler in the late seventies, as someone who kills at least three people and takes a cooling off period at sometime during their spree. And he certainly didn't believe he was as evil as Dahmer, usually considered to be the most evil of all, keeping heads in his refrigerator and cannibalizing the bodies and using them for necrophilia. Brody thought that was just sick. And Brody had never had the cooling off period since he felt the overwhelming urge to quench his need as often as possible.

He wasn't a ritual killer; it was just that he had his preferred methods. Hence, his doubts about him fitting the term's proper definition. And he was sure his main motivation for killing was simply the desire for power and control over another human being; unknown to him, however, a common thread that runs through most serial killers. That and the notoriety for the Swordsman and ultimately Gage Brody as well when his vile escapades came to their inevitable conclusion.

What he knew he was doing was living a double life—one seemingly normal, the other he chose, in which all of his friends, of which there weren't that many, since serial murderers, by their very nature tended to be loners, and coworkers would never believe or even suspect him him capable of such gruesome acts; it extraordinary.

Anything but mundane, his after-hour pursuits were in counterpoise to his boring as shit job. They didn't have to wait long for his answer. He had big balls if nothing else. Answering not evasively, but choosing his words carefully like he didn't have many to spare. And that made him appear more intelligent to his audience. And the set of his jaw told them he would brook no argument; even of the most facile sort.

And he was nothing if not succinct. "I hope they get the motherfucker and get him real quick-like. He's ruining the reputation of this fine city. The summer tourist trade will die if that son of a bitch isn't caught and caught soon, and that hurts all New Yorkers." He said it emphatically with the idea that his verbosity carried as much weight as what he said to make him seem even more pedagogic. Or at least that's what his self-consciousness told him. Of course Brody was not one to be hindered by paranoia. He believed he would never be caught. And as long as he wasn't stupid, he wouldn't be. Even so, somewhere deep inside himself he wanted to be exposed, recognized, feted even, for what he had done and what he knew he would continue to do.

A vulturine-featured bone-thin man in his fifties with bi-polar hair that stared in all directions over his tiny chinless head, and appeared to have had a rough life, wore a permanent look of perturbation on his unattractive face and even though he didn't appear to be paying attention, over his mug of steaming coffee nodded knowingly, as if Brody had voiced what he'd been thinking. Or at least that's what he wanted the others to think. Feigned, passive-aggressive intelligence. The other technicians near-deified Brody with their reactions. After all, he was the cleverest of them all. Of course that wasn't saying much. Most of them high school graduates at best. Some of them not even, their frayed blue collars on obvious display. It wasn't like any of them were grads of the Choate School, the high-end Connecticut preparatory boarding school; that followed by Yale or Princeton.

Chapter Six

The Swordsman plied his evil trade in Manhattan. It was his killing fields. Except when he occasionally ventured north to the Bronx, which he almost considered an extension of Manhattan, except for being made up primarily of the Puerto Rican and Dominican families. But never Brooklyn. You never shit where you sleep to mix metaphors. His numbers might have climbed faster had he chosen to brave the other boroughs, but they wouldn't have been as newsworthy as staying in Manhattan made them. The center of business, culture and arts for the world.

And he had to think of his legacy, it more important even than the number of kills. Although, he had to consider how to increase his numbers so as to cast his viciously bloody pall over the city. To ensure that the city that never sleeps, couldn't. From fear and worry. To make citizens afraid and the NYPD nervous. Not that he hoped to exceed the great Ted Bundy in terms of total kills, that would be next to impossible. And although Bundy wasn't the most prolific in terms of the highest number, his movie star looks and the aplomb with which he performed his kills, made him paramount in the minds and eyes of many and so, incomparable. But the outer boroughs were too pedestrian for The Swordsman's image.

After all, he was an artiste with a sword. And presentation was of ultimate importance. Similar to the sushi chef slicing raw fish at high speed in front of a mesmerized crowded table of watching strangers.

***

Places where tourists congregate were The Swordsman's preferred areas for finding victims. Tourists, by their very nature, less cautious and more vulnerable while oohing and aahing over the big city sights, made for easier targets. He wasn't one to go to yuppie pubs—he was self aware enough to realize his blue collar and red neck wouldn't fit in, so he wouldn't find much in the way of opportunities in those. And being at least somewhat gainfully employed he usually had to wait until weekends to fulfill his sadistic needs.

Saturday had finally arrived and he chose somewhere different. A beautiful but ordinary late spring day and Washington Square Park, built in 1871, should be teeming with heaving crowds of unsuspecting *touristas*, as he derogatorily referred to them, given that they weren't New Yorkers.

Brody waited in the shadow of the white marble arch conceived of and designed by the internationally famous Stanford White in the manner of a Roman arch, and across the street from the narrowest house in Manhattan. The three-story house, formerly owned by both the great writer Edna St. Vincent Millay and afterward the famous actor, Cary Grant, was built in a narrow 1800's era carriage alley. Not that Brody was aware of any of those esoteric facts.

He had guessed right, because the park was full of families, locals and tourists, retirees recently-returned from their annual migration to Florida for the winter months, laughing, playing, accompanied by children's shrieks of laughter, all the while enjoying themselves because life was good, as good as it was supposed to be.

The blue of the covetous sky was unreal in its truest sense. A large bouquet of helium-filled balloons got away from a blonde-haired child and he started screaming his head off as they floated upward to be captured by the sky. Passenger jets on final approach at Kennedy International not high enough to produce contrails, would probably report seeing a UFO. There were always a lot of the airliners in the sky above New York even if it weren't a Sunday, the biggest day of the week for air travel.

The morning sun was bright and beginning its rise to hang high in the sky over the East River; like the first time, the very first time. The shadows long. There would be a lot of burnt shoulders and florid faces today. Brody liked daylight savings time and how the days were much longer. In the goddamn winter the city would be full dark before five o'clock. A working man would have no sunshine, neither actual nor metaphorical at the end of the day.

Now to the task at hand; finding an unaware, unsuspecting and vulnerable victim. And unlike most multiple killers he didn't have a preferred type. Most would want Asian women or Latinas, or Caucasians. Very specific. A certain sex, or age range. The Swordsman didn't give a shit; men, women, white, black, Asian, old or young. He wasn't a racial bigot in any way. He couldn't care less. To him, people, others, were no more than mere shadows and dust.

Whatever God was inclined to send his way, he was thankful for. But first he needed to take a leak. A single car garage-sized cinder block building on the other side of the park that housed both the men's and women's facilities was a five-or-so-minute walk, unless one walked leisurely, in which case it would take longer. But if one needed to answer the call of nature, did one ever walk leisurely?

As Brody sauntered near to the building a bereft looking hummel homeless man ducked behind its rear wall and with Brody's practiced perception of these things, he sensed an opportunity to get his ninth victim, and quickly became the hyper vigilant Swordsman. The man aged, infirm, gaunt, and chinless with watery eyes. The Swordsman felt like he'd be doing the sad excuse for a man a favor by ending his depressingly bleak existence.

In fact this was his favorite part of a kill; when he knew it was about to happen only because he loved what he did. And even if the loser of life's lottery were capable of cogent thought, the sorry little man had no idea that his pitiful life wouldn't last five minutes longer, and indeed he might be grateful that his sorry existence was coming to an end if he'd seen the killer designated his terminator nearing. Or it might only be unthinkable confusion that shadowed his face in his last moments on earth.

Killers used blades for a number of reasons. Perhaps because a knife is easily concealed, or it's quiet; or there aren't any bullet casings to pick up at the scene, or because it's impossible to be traced to the registered owner like a gun, but probably most importantly of all, because a knife instills more fear in the victim than a firearm.

The piss would have to wait. The Swordsman peeked around the corner and watched the man as he unzipped and a warm stream began to splash on the green new vernal grass. From this close proximity he could smell the pungent odor of the warm urine even over the rank smell of the man's unclean body and his filthy clothes. Those smells made the public facilities smell like spring roses by comparison.

The Swordsman wondered why the man didn't piss in a toilet in the restroom like a normal human being. Likely only because he was accustomed to pissing outdoors.

The Swordsman knew it would be a bold act, killing someone on a bright sunny Saturday in one of the city's busiest parks; and he had nothing personal against the unfortunate loser of life's lottery, but his bloodlust was getting the best of him, becoming an impossibly insatiable need, and so he didn't concern himself with much worry about the risk of being caught. But with the large number of people enjoying the park on a beautiful early summer Saturday it wouldn't be long before the body was noticed so he needed to make a hasty exit.

This particular victim didn't appear to have a tooth in his head, so it would be unlikely that the police would be able to identify him since dental records for him most likely didn't even exist. The Swordsman glanced around one last time and then slipped the concealed trenchant hori hori knife from a sleeve, and with his martial arts training coming into real world use, he took a deep calming breath to slow his rapidly pounding heart then crept stealthily one sure step at a time, like a ninja, insidiously twisting and scuffing his feet on the ground as he did in the event an NYPD Forensics team attempted to get impressions from his shoe prints. The ground was dry and grassy but better to be safe than sorry. He hugged the rear side of the dreary block building, being careful not to touch it with his hands. As he drew nearer he could hear the derelict's phlegmy breathing. The unsuspecting victim, calmly relieving himself, never saw, or heard, his assailant approach.

The Swordsman quickly grabbed the man's filthy oily hair with his left hand and yanking him backward exposed the unhealthily pale wrinkled skin of his neck, as white as a clown's face, and without a word and feeling no empathy, used the knife in his other to raggedly rip the unsuspecting derelict from the left jaw to just under his right ear, through the throat, feeling the resistant ridges of the esophagus, jugular, and spinal cord to the sound of an unholy gurgling in mid piss, utterly alone at the end of his miserable life. The pain too torturous, indeed too exquisite, but no anguished cry escaped his mouth, instead, only the plangent bloody gurgle came unfettered from the craggy rent in his throat. Copious amounts of blood in an arterial exodus joined with the urine on the park's verdant lawn that was anything but inviolate.

The Swordsman was fortunate that he had a strong stomach since the vagrant's head, tendrils of gore hanging from the vicious wound, and now unattached from his torso, grievously flopped unceremoniously to the fresh summer grass, a large halo of rust-colored blood staining the ground, before his spasming but nevertheless limply falling body did in a ghastly scene. D.O.A before his body hit the ground.

The man to thrive no longer; if indeed he had ever. In a defiantly uncooperative final physiological act of biology, his urine stream continued to pour after his heart stopped beating. The deed done, even for Brody the psychological temperature dropped precipitously. Pigeons feeding nearby fluttered loudly away. In the warm summer sun decomposition would be fast.

Now The Swordsman's biggest challenge was to return insouciantly to join the crowd of Saturday afternoon revelers before making a hasty exit. He knew the body would be discovered shortly in the crowded Saturday park and would not come close to beginning the putrefaction process.

Deep in thought as he walked. He knew that most people in the uneasy comfort of their luxury suburban homes or their exclusive high-rise penthouses, what New York City realtors call sky mansions, wouldn't give a shit about the homeless, smelly, loser victim, as long as it wasn't them. But to focus on his unfortunate lot in life was to miss the point. The Swordsman gained something with every kill. Experience, increasing his lack of empathy, to ignore even more the visceral and tactile sensations of blood and gore. All noteworthy occurrences that couldn't be overlooked in their magnitude. As it was, he considered that they were similar to improving one's job skills.

His latest kill had been even easier than he thought it would be and on a lovely early summer Saturday afternoon in the park, in New York, he even looked forward to returning to the despondent room he called no more than the place he stayed that he rented from an elderly widow in the three story red brick townhouse in the Bedford Stuyvesant neighborhood of Brooklyn that would have been described as stately in a different era—and watching the reports on the late night news about The Swordsman; probably New York One, with the hot blonde news chick that was on the eleven o'clock newscast.

He had to admit it was cool that the whole city; no, probably the whole goddamn country was in an uproar over him, even if they didn't know who The Swordsman was. He knew. And in the end that was what mattered most. In fact he hoped the whole country would never know him because that would mean he had been apprehended.

It was the place where she'd lived for longer than he'd been alive, bought when she was a newlywed and the nabe was affordable and before it became cool.

It was a shitty room where he had to live, but the only thing he'd found that he could afford anywhere in the five boroughs.

And since it was such a lovely early summer afternoon he decided it would be a pleasant stroll across the wooden plank pedestrian and bikeway level of the Brooklyn Bridge and its glorious gothic arches, while enjoying the fresh air and sunshine, even if the air was a bit fishy smelling, instead of taking a stuffy sweaty smelling and overly packed train. As once said, it's the little things in life…and death, that are important. And of course he'd changed that saying somewhat more than a little for his own twisted beliefs and to suit his own sick needs. And his personal mantra was to remember that live spelled backwards is evil. So to live was evil. So he'd made the decision to help people out with fixing that.

Brody hiked the short distance to the plaza entrance of the bridge, passing a huge housing project and fenced-in basketball court with steel chains hanging from the hoops in place of ropes— they lasted longer, but didn't swish when you drained a three. They sort of clanked. Not the same affect. He paused a moment leaning against the chain link fence watching a pickup game before taking the long, inclined ramp to the upper-level pedestrian walkway. It was a good thing he'd worn sneakers.

The salty ocean air breeze was a solid breath of comfort and restored his sense of purpose. A pleasant stroll after a successful Saturday of good clean fun. He lifted his face to the muted sun to feel its gentle warm caress. He enjoyed the perambulation because it made him feel like he was John Wick walking across the bridge in the film *John Wick Chapter 2*. And since he identified with the killer anyway, and in fact been told he resembled the man, it wasn't that much of a stretch.

He crossed the bridge leisurely, enjoying the stroll on the warped wooden boards that seemed out of place in the concrete and steel of New York in the twenty-first century. The howling of the north wind gusts drowning out the noise of the city traffic. He was glad it was summer; the wolf of winter's wicked fangs would be sharp. Making the stroll over the bridge impossible. Especially dressed as he was now.

Upon reaching the Brooklyn side of the river to make his way through the nabes he slowed down; he knew it was nothing more than a self-defense mechanism kicking in, trying to keep him from getting to the shitty excuse for a house in the weary impecunious neighborhood that he called…anything but home. Even though it wouldn't seem so to anyone who was judgmental, but he had too much self respect to call it home. The nabe too old and rundown for anyone to even have an interest in gentrifying it. But at least he wasn't living at the YMCA. Surprisingly, not uncommon for the somewhat less than well-to-do in the city.

Chapter Seven

He no more than abided where he lived at the moment. It was more than a garret but not by much. A typical garret being not much larger than Harry Potter's cupboard under the stairs. Assuming the worst, he guessed it wouldn't be long before his permanent residence would be a six-by-eight foot cell at Sing Sing Correctional Facility up the river, literally, up the mighty Hudson, where the term up-the-river was coined, which would make a garret seem luxurious, after a short stay in the notorious Otis Bantum Correctional Center on Rikers Island where the night noise and steel bars clanged in your subconscious, a guest of the employees of The Department of Corrections, less commonly known as New York City's Boldest, along with their fifteen thousand other daily guests in one of the most historic and infamous slammers in the country at least until he was sent to The Clinton Correctional Facility in Dannemora, New York or literally up the river to Sing Sing State Prison in Ossining, New York.

Unless or until he was shrunk by some two-bit jailhouse psychologist and thus decreed crazier than a chest-beating gorilla in which case he knew he would live out his years among the real crazies in the nearest asylum complete with the expected wails of mania and desperation. Not that he believed he'd be that fortunate because he judged himself to be as normal as anybody else.

In fact, much like a few of his deadly brethren he preferred the label 'multiple slayer' to serial killer, believing it classier or even sexier. He thought he might even try to work it into a convo with a hot chick; without giving himself away, of course. Of course, as a last resort, as opposed to life in prison or an asylum, he could always decide to commit suicide by cop, or once in prison it might be a staged suicide by correction officer; more common than one might think in those situations. Think of Jeffrey Epstein. He knew he would be unable to expect professional mutual courtesy. No honor at all among law enforcement or thugs. Of course, disappearing into the ether seemed a more palatable option than the other two.

With much reluctance Brody finally willed himself to return to the once proud Victorian house that was now well past only showing its age. Mrs. Goodman was sweeping around the Icebox on the front porch when he turned up the sidewalk. He'd never seen an icebox before that one. Of course he knew of refrigerators and freezers, but an icebox? They were of a different generation. Only old people knew about them. Even though the temperature was in the high eighties she wore an ancient green cardigan sweater over her house dress. Doubtless because she was old.

"Good afternoon, Mr. Brody."

"Mrs. Goodman."

Something about her just annoyed the hell out of him. It may have been only because she was old, but all old people didn't irritate him that way. Maybe it was because she smelled old. The smell of mothballs, ancient clothes imbued with the aging smell of fried foods, and dentures that needed cleaning. And he knew that The Swordsman would have already paid her a lethal visit if he weren't just as sure that he would be the prime suspect.

"I cooked a nice pot roast if you'd care to join me. With carrots, potatoes and fresh white onions." It was her sainted mother's recipe. Indeed the house was redolent with the unwelcome smell of pot roast.

"Sounds delicious, but I had a rough week at work. I'm gonna turn in early." *I'd rather spend Saturday night alone than spend it eating pot roast with her. I never did like that shit anyway. It reminds me of my mother and she couldn't cook worth a damn. I just hope I won't smell that nasty shit in my room.*

"Well, if you change your mind. Or I'll have leftovers tomorrow. A lot of people think it's even better the next day, you know."

He raised his hand as an acknowledgement and signal that he'd heard her as he turned to go to his room.

Brody opened the door to the stairs that led to the pathetic old room where he did nothing more than sleep, and after entering hesitantly, eased it to, hoping against hope, hopelessly, that the old crone wouldn't hear and might even forget he was there. And forget about her offer of pot roast.

In his room, he took a whore bath— applied a damp worn out dingy wash rag to his underarms and face, but even he was smart enough not to do it in that order. Then got out of his clothes, and pulled on fresh boxer shorts and an undershirt.

The somber charmless room he rented wasn't small, but it wasn't large. Some would call it cozy. But not him. With little money came little need, or want. It was probably twelve feet by fifteen. He'd have to step it off sometime and find out. But who really gave a flying fuck? It was what was in a different era known as a housekeeping room; where the hired help would have stayed.

In addition to the bed with its rusted iron peeking out through chipped enamel, the brown turning to ugly aged yellow bureau, the table, and the chairs, there were, huddled in one corner, a sink, a two-burner gas stove, and some shelves of pans and dishes. He had to go downstairs to use his landlady's washer and dryer when it wasn't in use because it wasn't like he could take his dirty clothes, if they were blood-stained from one of his horridly felonious encounters, to a dry cleaners. And talk about a waste of time. In his mind he was a busy man.

Knotty pine paneling on the walls and enough space for a double bed with a sagging and grossly stained mattress sitting on a dirty tan patterned oriental rug that did little to disguise an aged wood floor. It wasn't solely that it was old; it was cheap when it was purchased. Now it was cheap and old, and worn. A window air conditioning unit was noisy but at least it worked to keep the room relatively cool. And served to mask the sounds of the loud-mouthed couple next door when they got into a screaming match that could be heard all the way to the Battery. An ancient mismatched scarred dresser and chest of drawers. Brody turned on the mid-century small black and white tube tv resting on the dresser doing double duty as a tv stand. It sat next to a toaster-oven he seldom-used because of fear of fire. Not that he cared if he burned the house down, but he wouldn't want to perish in a conflagration. The dresser surface underneath it charred from heat as it was. He then took four steps to the dorm-sized fridge that sat in a corner, and retrieved two bottles of one of the city's best ales, from Five Boroughs Brewing Company, right there in Brooklyn, and crashed on a sad brown wide wale corduroy sofa that came with the furnished room. And he had most of a fifth of Tito's Austin, Texas made vodka left, too.

He wished he could still find Olympia beer, his all-time favorite but they had announced they were going out of business and he couldn't even find cases at Walmart anymore. Probably the only good thing about living in the shitty room was that his landlady was at least half-deaf and couldn't hear him if he was loud. And only God knew what he had to be loud about, though.

He punched the matching corduroy pillow with enough starch behind it as if he were angry at it and scrunched it under his head. Finished the beers before passing out from his tiring day; drinking and not eating was one of the easiest tricks for staying lean. That and being jumpy in his movement. A satisfying killing and a healthy stroll in the sunshine and fresh air had tired him out.

He was awakened by the familiar dramatic theme music for the eleven o'clock news' beginning. The latest slaying by The Swordsman was the lead story. Upshot was nobody saw anything or knew, anything. Good news for Brody. Then a news conference. At the massive Manhattan city jail, where they typically held these things. There were all sorts of gendarmes—armed policemen—and high ranking mostly Caucasian, rusty, bland hair, flinty-eyed but flaccid-faced each; either a job requirement or caused by the job, NYPD brass decked out in their natty dress blue regalia standing at attention unsmilingly in the heat on the broad sidewalk in front of One Police Plaza, an insular institution commonly known as One PP, where above the entry are inscribed at a recent count, the names of seven hundred, thirteen law enforcement officers who have fallen in the line of duty, and many decades removed from when headquarters was in a nondescript small white building with green shutters in Mulberry St., the main artery in Little Italy. One PP also adjacent to what cops referred to as The Tombs-one section of which was also known as the Men's House of Detention, or derisively known by men that had been there not by their own choosing, as the slam. Flat-faced men all, the fleeting thought crossed Brody's mind to wonder if they had ever smiled. The ability or willingness to smile most definitely was not a job requirement.

The look the officials were going for was redoubtable or choleric; but the closest they got was petulantly acrimonious. And they hoped for fealty, but although fealty was born by virtue of rank, it was somewhat less than earned by performance. No mere members of the rank and file, these were the highest members of the upper hierarchy of the department. Thinking they had established hegemony due to being Irish alone, but without the symbols of rank there would be none.

Of course the Italians felt the same. None of the senior officers looked particularly canny. They sought a dour stalwart look, but Brody thought their uniforms, even in spite of the gold badges shining in the bright sunlight almost made them look like they could have worked as ushers in the Radio City Music Hall theatre. Some more unctuous than others. None better than lackeys. Tura-lura-lura sons of bitches,

All they needed was the conical-shaped little red fez with a gold tassel hanging off it to complete the comical look in order to work at the theatre or look at home in Morocco. And that fleeting thought caused Brody to smile as he recalled the great song, *The Fez*, by Steely Dan. Undoubtedly one of their very best efforts. He liked to vibe out to it every chance he got.

And since the big shots didn't give the appearance of being long on uncommon common sense, Brody felt decidedly good about his chances of remaining unapprehended. He thought they looked like little more than mere gandy dancers, but not by much. Without the comical dress uniforms, they almost, almost mind you, looked to Brady like they could be members of the former Irish organized crime organization, the Westies. Most looked like they could have recently disembarked a ship from County Cork Ireland; appeared to be in their late fifties or early sixties, with Irish red hair running to aged gray, simply trying to hold out until retirement, to collect their pension, that and for their own glory, not for the glory of the department or even its benefit, but still with an ineffectively officious look about them. The main reason most of them were still working, if one could call what they did work. That and their love of obeisance. Their collective wish was presumably to appear omnipotently grim, but the worst they could muster was heavy-handedness.

Get up every day, shower, shave, except for their heavy Irish mustaches below their broad noses, get dressed in an ancient and fraying but nevertheless crisp uniform, to go put in an appearance at headquarters, and watch the clock, taking care of their fingernails while counting the laggard minutes inching by until the senior officers could go back to their homes in their safe comfortable city suburbs of Syossett, Jericho, Manhasset Hills and others like them to wait to do it all over again the next day. Brody thought most of them looked like goddamn micks, and none looked particularly robust or vigorous, and in fact looked like they'd be smoking cigars if it wouldn't reflect badly on the department, even though they thought they looked right smart, with their ginger hair and the camber of their barrel chests complete with protruding stomachs, making them look like good members of the United Brotherhood of Carpenters, not from long-suffering workouts with repetitions with iron, but genetically passed down as a legacy from generations past of hard working farmers, who knew of hard work of the type the present generation had never or would never do—but who were no doubt envious of the detective doing the job they wished they were still doing, or even worse, had never done, instead, the closest they'd come, their dogs barking from walking a beat while twirling the black batons they hoped they'd get a chance to use; to crack a skull or two.

All the while thinking they look their sharpest while standing in the background getting prime camera face-time trying their best to look clement at the impromptu press conference. In reality, if they knew Rossi they were jealous of him, or they knew of his contumacy and didn't much care for him because of it, something they'd invented in their own minds, and he didn't particularly like them, so they were brought to what was once known as a Mexican standoff. If they did actually know Rossi they would know he's a good guy, or in the vernacular of a past era of cop speak, 'good people'. To Brody, in their heavy dark uniforms they didn't look cool; just hot, and no pun intended even though he laughed at his funny observation, like the uncoolest men he'd ever seen. If he noticed anything about them he thought he imagined them watching the detective with cool disdain in their collective eyes. Or jealousy; or both.

If they weren't cops they would mayhap be Irish or spiritually Irish gangsters. They probably still listened to archaic Irish folk music by the old-world Clancy Brothers. What they likely enjoyed most about being in law enforcement was that they themselves didn't have to obey all of the the laws that applied to the common man. Laws like speeding since no brother policeman would dare give them a citation, for visiting a woman of dubious repute, Lord knows there were plenty of those on the avenue corners dressed with hauteur—the way Broadwayite hookers should-with the usual heavy face paint, where their main man, their beknighted pimp, dressed like he was from Puerto Rico even if he was born and raised in the Bronx, skulking in a darkened doorway, could keep an eye on them, to even more serious laws.

And Brody could almost smell their cheap-ass aftershave through the tv screen. Funny thing was, if it weren't for the uniforms he'd be unable to tell if they were cops or dirtbags.

But their mouthpiece, a Lieutenant Sharp—with an insincere viscid smile on his face, was well-groomed, but Brody cleverly thought that he didn't look like a particularly sharp lieutenant or especially acute—in fact, quite the opposite-dim in appearance and quite unremarkable looking, responsible for overseeing the investigation, spoke, his words rustling on the wind and getting lost in the sounds of traffic, without saying anything of import before introducing the lead detective on the case. The real policeman; six-foot one inch, a little too heavy even for his taller-than-average height with a body like a tank. His perfectly oiled, almost too abundant for a policeman, black hair etched with rising silver, soon to be more silver than black, his brow beginning to develop deep horizontal furrows. He'd joked with his wife that he was going to get Botox and she got his goat by telling him not until after she did.

The man trod not fast or slowly, but deliberately to the microphone, putting a finger in his too-tight shirt collar and stretching his neck from side-to-side, a man on a mission, as usual wearing a cynical look on his always irascible face, but like it took every ounce of effort he could muster to get there, while also wearing a fixed pained look, a look of distress no matter the expression that served to disguise his rectitude, on what not that many years ago had been thought of as a handsome face.

An unkind person might call him hatchet-faced, but then they'd never seen the way his grandchildren gazed lovingly up at him, or he at them, or how he spoiled them beyond rotten. And with that they all lived well; and always would or at least as long as the good Lord allowed them.

Chapter Eight

Brody perked up at the sight of this man. It was said that tv cameras add ten pounds; Rossi's once longshoreman-like defiant jawline had just a suggestion of the beginning of droopy jowls at the collar. That and the hint of a pair of parenthetical lines at the corners of his determined mouth were the only obvious signs of age, at least for the time being. He had the physique of a hard linebacker losing the battle with age. An avowed verity, time cures youth. His face still had the solid look of primordial granite but it was beginning the aged turn to doughy. The starch in the collar of his white shirt as well was losing a battle with the more than slightly humid warmth.

He had the look of a bourbon drinker—someone perhaps deep in his cups, but not without nuance—most likely Woodford Reserve, Double Oaked. Brody had never had a taste of it himself; for it was far too pricey for his pocketbook, but he'd heard it was pretty damn good. In truth, Rossi would on occasion have a tumbler with two fingers of bourbon or fine rye seasoned with three cubes of ice, but never more than that because he was afraid that the hard liquor might cause him to be dain bramaged as he referred to the unwanted condition, thinking it made him sound at least a wee bit clever. And he certainly didn't want to become tartled. Indeed, dain bramage was a worry he didn't have with the lower alcohol content of red wine.

And in truth Rossi very nearly drank red wine only, because he felt it wasn't possible for one to be civilized if one didn't. And even though most people thought Italians were bigger drinkers he knew he couldn't hold a candle to most of those goddamn micks. In reality he wished he could. In truth it made him jealous if he thought about it. A fucking mick out drinking a Wop. There was something positively unnatural about it.

But he wouldn't have looked out of place as a character in an outdated Charles Bukowski novel even without the affinity for stronger spirits. Not an altogether sinister view by anyone.

Being this near to the Battery meant there was always a cacophony, so after pausing a moment for the noise over his shoulder from first a ferry loaded with tourists, then a nearby lumbering barge to diminish up the East River, taking a shortcut to ports up the Hudson by using the big river as far as its small but determined little brother, the Harlem River, just past Hell Gate, that separates Astoria, Queens from Randalls Island and Wards Island, before traversing northwest as far as it would take him to the mighty Hudson; at least there were no fireboats adding to the noise this morning, so, Detective Rossi began to speak, less heartily than was typical for him. In the manner of reading from a script, or an outline, which in fact was what he was doing. The sneer on his face proof of the contempt he felt for the media horde.

The only one in the crowd Brody couldn't get a grasp on was a fresh-faced young Asian man wearing a benign expression of reverence standing at one remove, watching the proceedings, and listening attentively, unlike some of the others. Maybe a trainee from Southeast Asia, taking back what he learns; how to handle the bad guys, maybe a new detective. An acolyte, or at least a committed follower. Hard to tell. But he beheld the man being presented, with unfaltering admiration in his gaze. Thralled by the senior detective's manner, his words, his countenance. Deferentially, as if he were observing something historic.

Of course Detective Rossi was known to have a flair for the dramatic, the theatrical. He was Italiano, after all. In this city where the very air one breathed seemed to be infused with, unsurprisingly, redolent with, the warm aroma of garlic and olive oil. Indeed, Rossi believed love and garlic were two sides of the same coin. It was impossible to have one without the other.

Detective Rossi had the aloof and somewhat more than a trifle patronizing look of a veteran cop, not a callow LEO, but not exactly a gumshoe to use an archaic term for a police detective, but even he knew he was a throwback, if not anachronistic. He walked like a cop-easy but with a purpose; presumably from walking a midtown beat, faster even than a horse drawn calash, past

lumbering busses and the most common vehicle in the city—
faltering yellow taxis. Faster than the brutal New York traffic-
jammed cars moved, part of the heart and pulse of the capitol of the
world, when he was a young patrolman, if he'd only been Irish,
otherwise known as a peeler, wearing out shoe leather. He was glad
he had invested in the best shoes he could afford to keep from
wearing out his feet from all the walking. Of course all that walking
kept him leaner when he was young. He hoped it would payoff by
helping him live longer as well. Instead of just helping to make him
so damn good looking.

At least his beautiful new wife thought he was. Couldn't keep
her hands off him. That's what he teased her of, anyway. In reality
it had taken him quite a bit of time and copious amounts of good
wine to tear down the mighty walled castle she had built around her
heart. They took the subway for dates but he always walked Ella
home from the station. At the same time they had been cautious.
They didn't consume wine recklessly; typical-size bottles only,
never jeroboams. And it hadn't been only the wine. But it had been
worth it for them both that he had torn down that castle.

It had been unfailingly easy for them to fall in love, and stay in
love. She told her mama she fell in love with him because of his
eyes; when she looked into them she could tell there wasn't a mean
bone in his body-which wasn't bad either she had to admit-and
knew he'd never mistreat her or the children they would welcome
or if they were so blessed, grandchildren. Of course in the
beginning they hadn't been married long. He hoped the newness
would never wear off; although he was pretty sure it would. Didn't
it always? He knew, as the old adage says, 'nothing ever lasts
forever.' Although Sal still liked her fulsome boobs. And that alone
was enough to keep him off porn sites. And he intended to disprove
the old adage "What do they say about husbands — ninety percent
cheat and ten percent lie."

Smaller buildings, most fin-de-siecles no more than three
stories in height, unchanged since the nineteenth century, defined
the packed crumbling scabrous streets of midtown west; the worst

you might see were tagged with the graffiti 'art' from the gang artists making their presence, and their art, known. None thinking they would be a present century Vermeer or Klimt, even if they were aware of those greats, but each having hopes that they might be, but trying without much success to become the next former grafitti artists turned commercial successes, Keith Haring or Jean-Michel Basquiat. Nevertheless, the area not as bad as the Bronx where you might find a burned-out shell of a car sitting upside down in the middle of a street less-traveled, but not nearly as nice as downtown and the better parts of midtown with their shiny new skyscrapers.

A mature section of the city, anachronistic, but somewhat current; not as tired as some; not as fresh as others. Proud and ashamed. That's not unusual. None of the luxurious brownstones that staked claim to both the upper east side and the west. Even though he'd been young he'd never been callow. His family history of law enforcement assured that.

The progenitor, three generations previous, a member of the Carabinieri in the old country. What most people didn't know was that the Carabinieri was almost as bad as La Cosa Nostra. The two subsequent generations had worn NYPD blue. The result was Officer Rossi had been young, but never inexperienced. With that familial history on the job he was born experienced. And his father and his nonno indeed taught him the ways of a cop.

Some neighborhood kids would say they were going to be firemen, or work on the docks; but not young Salvatoré. He was always destined to be a cop. So when the kids in the nabe played cops and robbers, he wasn't playing. He was serious about that shit. Even with that the somewhat more than a little unpleasant disposition hadn't yet taken root. He would walk, the sidewalk jammed with people any hour of the day, the back of his light blue uniform shirt dark with sweat and sticking to his back, taking measure of his surroundings; his keen ears aware, listening for anything out of place, his stony eyes ever alert, watching for a surprised movement. Passed a hand-lettered cardboard sign someone had tacked to an ancient telephone pole as a public service announcement reading, DON'T BE A FOOL. STAY IN SCHOOL, which sounded like something the former bouncer turned tough guy character actor of questionable talent, Mr. T, might say. Officer Rossi thought that was a particularly good admonition. Especially in this neighborhood. Good for you in more ways than one. Give kids an education and keep them off the streets. Helped the nabe at the same time.

Here on the westside one could easily hear the loneliest sound in the world; the sound of a foghorn on the cold Hudson River. Which was even lonelier at night.

Chapter Nine

Steel shutters were being rolled up from their task of covering store windows and early delivery trucks were double-parking, beeping warnings as they backed up. The air smelled fresh under the blighted morning sun as it cast its dreary rays on all as he mechanically but adroitly ducked, bobbed, weaved in and out, jostled, shouldered, and elbowed his way on the sad cracked and tired sidewalk like the native New Yorker he was, past an old man-looked like a WWII vet-rattling a tin cup for wont of an infusion of change, perhaps annoying to some passersby, but otherwise benign, until he passed the slatternly gaggle of hunched over and frowzy but happily smiling gray haired mappy vein-faced blowzy old women with an overpowering smell of sweat and dirt, both clothes and skin, probably carrying little half pints of gin in their worn out handbags who were feeding pigeons.

If there had been a lake nearby they would have been feeding ducks, and talking to them. Like an eight-hour shift at a job they did; fed the pigeons, then walked home. One Latina, probably Puerto Rican, maybe Dominican; one African American; the others, three or four, Caucasian. White, yellow and black, although it didn't matter their skin color. They, hollow-cheeked and each of them the color of spackled gray. Indisputably, dirty, gray and ragged. Even if they hadn't been the same sallow shade they didn't notice skin color. If they did notice they didn't care.

When Rossi grew up the Latinas were known as Hispanics, but he tried to do what they wished and refer to them as Latinas. Although he still didn't like the Italian pejorative, wop. From appearances, some eating well, or at least a lot; others, attenuated. He also now referred to blacks as African Americans, especially his friends or ones he worked with. There was no way to know if the frumpy old pigeon ladies lived alone or in a group home of some kind. Either way, it was where they waited to die then waited to be buried by city jail prisoners, skells from Rikers Island who would place them with as much dignity of which they were capable in one of the many huge anonymous unmarked graves that typically held forty-eight coffins in one of Hart Island's one hundred acres in the still waters of Long Island Sound, in the shadows of New York City's tall buildings fighting each other for air and ground space where for over a century and a half, more than a million indigents, the unclaimed, homeless, or the other marginalized ones-many from epidemics like tuberculosis, the flu of 1918, and AIDS, unknown or without family even to report them missing or possessed of even a single copper penny to pay for a proper funeral and burial had been interred on land which formerly held a mental hospital, a tuberculosis sanatorium, and a boys reformatory among other institutions, since the civil war.

Of course, if the pigeon ladies lived in assisted living homes they'd likely be cleaned up a bit better. And if any of them lived alone it was most likely in no more than a shabbily and sparsely furnished low-ceilinged roomlet with way past worn out passed down furniture, faded and peeling distempered paint and most likely without even one window, in one of the minuscule rooms repurposed as what are misleadingly and dishonestly called studio apartments in one of the many ancient small hotels that pepper the city that had been reborn as boarding houses for the indigent and commonly referred to as flophouses; but with only one bathroom per floor instead of one in each rented room like in traditional studios. Where it was considered an amenity if one's room was near the fire escape or a bathroom, God forbid.

Nothing on the familiar cracked walls except in the old Latina's room, where even before she took up residence, she hung a faded eight by ten picture of the Pietà to cover a crack in the plaster that resembled the jagged scar on Harry Potter's forehead, the smell of a neighbor cooking cabbage on an ancient hot plate even through the closed door, essential but old furniture; a tired sagging bed, a tatty brocade sofa, the color unidentifiable from age, cheap well worn almost dresser-like dresser and an almost bureau-like bureau combination, not even a matching plate and saucer or two drinking glasses that matched, unless they were a pair of cheap giveaway jelly glasses, which didn't even matter since they usually took their meals at a church's free soup kitchen for the down and out, dispossessed or indigent. They all over town. Of course having but one picture on the walls sped up packing when moving or sped up one's family having to move everything out after their beloved family member died. And if one were fortunate, they'd have a ratty green crushed velvet-covered chair with dingy white lace doilies pinned to the arms, each likely hiding a cigarette burn or a stain of some sort, the rent commonly paid weekly because even the elderly tenants themselves weren't sure if they'd live to see the end of the month. And if they died before the new month dawned then they'd have a few more dollars to leave much to the surprise of the family members that never came for a visit.

They muttered aimless conversations to themselves, even though you couldn't hear them above a Department of Public Works employee, his huge stomach jiggling under his dirt and sweat stained formerly white tee shirt, pounding the concrete trying to repair a pothole with a pneumatic jackhammer in the next block it competing with the backfiring of a truck, a burst water main shooting a jet tower of water sixty feet in the air, a noisy hydraulic Sanitation Department water wagon standing by, its engine roaring loudly waiting to repair the rent, while typically of this part of the city, traffic was inching along and a nearby street preacher was shouting in a phlegmy voice at anyone who made the mistake of glancing his way, and soon regretting it, who was as crazy as the old women feeding pigeons. He from time to time competing with street singers, dancers and poets.

Lost souls in a lost world, each. Perhaps it was because of the pigeons or mayhap in spite of the pigeons, the old women might be described as dispirited. Every part of the city had them; all looked the same. A grim scene in whichever shabby nabe it might be. To the neighborhood they all had the same name; first name-pigeon, last name-lady. Whether referring to them or speaking to them. If it weren't for that they wouldn't have names at all. Faceless, identity-less. They didn't think of themselves in that way or refer to themselves in that manner. But like many New Yorkers they had allowed others to label them.

If they were only younger they might be called waifs. Each anonymous. Most wore worn out bedroom slippers on their flat shuffling bunioned feet; no matter the rest of their dress, whether ancient faded house dress with support hose; aged faded flowered bathrobe over who knew what, and nobody wanted to; or faded purple crushed velvet warmups they'd never worn for a workout in for even an hour of their lives.

Smelly yellowed dentures, unless they were lacking of teeth; natural or manmade. If they weren't feeding the pigeons they'd probably be mad as hatters instead of only ninety percent of the way daft. Assuredly, they weren't firmly grounded in reality. But as long as they stayed out of the path of an Eighth Avenue bus....

He passed three sailors in their summer white uniforms, feeling no pain, taking his thoughts away from the pigeon ladies for a brief moment. Looking sharp in their best-looking starched unis probably hoping to pick up some young hotties after months at sea. Or with pockets full of cash working girls were always a viable option. If it had been Fleet Week there would have been a lot more of them, their ships docked at the west side piers, alongside the great World War II aircraft carrier ship, The Intrepid, now a popular wartime museum, parked in its permanent berth.

Nevertheless, as commonplace as the sorrowful scene was, It made the sensitive Rossi sad to think about it because he knew that anyone who could spend their entire day feeding pigeons had to be a tad askew mentally, even if they thought it perfectly normal. Although when they were young they were sure to have had dreams and hopes like everyone and certainly didn't think they'd be feeding pigeons in their years of gold. Anything but dour they were, however, happily feeding the pigeons, none appearing to be bothered by stress or anxiety.

On second thought, maybe there was something to be said for feeding pigeons all day. Any of them would have loved to be described as plain. Undoubtedly, it would be a kindness. But even that would be dishonest in the extreme. The one with the noticeable dark mustache being particularly unattractive. Except for mouthing a silent Hail Mary and making The Sign Of The Cross as he passed, Rossi ignored them like everyone did, even though what they were doing was against the law. One of those things most beat cops did because most of them really were okay guys. Something they learned on their own-being compassionate and unenforcing laws that shouldn't be a law in any event. Not for nothing, like leaving the working women, referred to in a different era as strumpets, alone; because when it came down to it, who were they hurting, really?

Although this was a noble endeavor, it was no zen koan. It hadn't been difficult for Rossi to learn. All he had to do was remember—there but for the grace of God go I. Contrary to, if not diametrically opposed to the atheistic zen koan. More like a temporal activity. Moreover, the guileless old women didn't know the act was against the law. You could believe them when they said it, incapable of guile as they were, indeed not even knowing what the word meant.

The sadly dressed elderly pigeon feeders were in sharp contrast in both age and dress to a group of small children in their crisp Catholic school uniforms. All of them over the top cute. Rossi couldn't help but smile. Very little blonde-haired-blue-eyed boys and girls, olive-skinned ones with dark hair-probably Italian, or little Latinos, maybe both—but who the hell could tell what ethnic background they were?

Just cute. Runny-nosed boys in pressed dark blue pants and white shirts with matching dark blue ties, and the girls in wool red and blue plaid skirts with white cotton blouses to match the boys. Holding hands happily, they were, all of them. They weren't exactly dancing or skipping down the street but walking enthusiastically; happy in their reverie, one could see their bright shining eyes reflecting each other's happiness, full of life and boundless energy, excited that the school year was almost at an end.

Gently, respectfully nudging the dismal indigents, sleeping

unsheltered in doorways—most of them met incidental to his job but in fact not because of something they'd done; some looking as vulnerable as small injured birds—not with the cold wooden nightstick, but rousing them with his hand, even though his goal was not in any way to win a congeniality contest. They, almost like family, sleeping in the somewhat less than adequate cover of unassuming buildings' entries, Rossi getting phlegmy throat-clearing morning coughs in return. He knew the regulars. Without even money enough to ride the subway these were not straphangers; to join the many others who sleep in the fetid subway at night to keep warm. These were people of the street, whether awake or asleep, moving about or at home on the cardboard box pieces they'd spread on the cold hard concrete for comfort and insulation, usually with an empty bottle that formerly contained cheap wine lying nearby. Next to their head, a plastic bag filled with empty beer and soda cans they would sell later after the sun got warm. The older ones' flesh covered in liver spots from too much time spent in the sun's harmful rays.

Chapter Ten

Truth was he'd enjoyed walking a beat wending the narrow downtown streets and hadn't looked forward to getting a promotion to a patrol car because he wouldn't have as much freedom and fresh air, or a relationship with the citizens, with his people, and that's what he'd enjoyed most. And he was sure walking a beat had strengthened his spine mentally if not physiologically. And helped him to keep his weight down, besides.

The only part of walking a beat he hadn't liked was when it rained. Covered in rain gear and still he got wet. Just unpleasant as shit. In hot weather or cold, it didn't matter. New York weather tended toward the extremes. But at least walking kept his back from killing him and kept him from getting hemorrhoids like all the cops that were in patrol cars for entire eight-hour shifts. And after being in a car all day for years half of them were so stiff they couldn't even climb in or out of it.

Having been led to believe the old police adage, "There's plenty of law at the end of a nightstick, then occasionally having to go upside somebody's head with the hard black billy club in the event someone, desperation taking over, came running out of a long narrow shotgun bar, shady jewelry store, seedy pawnshop, OTB operation, Chinese restaurant, no name corner coffee shop or souvenir store, the proprietor hot on his heels shouting, "stop, thief, please, somebody help." The only difference was the accent with which the chaser used to yell at the chasee.

Rossi didn't enjoy it when he'd had to do it, but somehow administering a beatdown felt both primal and normal. Like something men had been doing for multiple millennia and so it was okay, and it worried him that it felt natural if not altogether pleasant. Then he'd make the sign of the cross and ask the Holy Father for forgiveness-at least for the way he felt while giving the beating. Isn't that what the worst sins are. How one feels about them? Or even worse, how one doesn't?

And even though he had to deal with the stray mug or bad guy at least he needn't concern himself with bears or wolves or other nocturnal beasts. As a native New Yorker and city dweller he thought those were unacceptable on many levels. But the city's occasional overly large rat was the only four-legged creature ever to be encountered.

Saying good morning to the merchants—the market/dry goods store owner with warty eyelids and a Tourette's Syndrome-like twitch wearing a short sleeve white shirt with a fraying collar and necktie-probably a clip-on, no effete him, using a long hose and a large push broom to clean the sidewalk in front of his emporium, his accomplishment, his life's work; spitting around a Lucky Strike drooping from the corner of his sagging mouth, onto the concrete after each whisk of the broom probably since before the sun rose; the barbershop owner, a portly old-timer who wore pince nez eyeglasses, and said that with them perched on the end of his nose it helped him to see better to cut hair, who himself was always in need of a trim, them returning the wish, pleasantly; tipping his cheap fedora to the ladies and them smiling shyly back; and saying hiya, kid, to the children.

The small sign on the pole pointed west and read 'Lincoln Tunnel,' the midtown tunnel to Weehawken, New Jersey, the only vehicle for going to New Jersey in midtown—most assuredly the busiest and most famous of Manhattan's tunnels—gave him comfort because he knew he was where he was supposed to be. Of course on the upper west side one could take the George Washington Bridge, or further downtown there was always the Holland Tunnel. But For Rossi, the area not unkindly referred to as Hell's Kitchen was his home away from home.

His work home. The Midtown North Precinct in West 54th Street between 8th and 9th covered Hell's Kitchen-not a place that most would want to call home, but those who did wouldn't live anywhere else. Even Rossi, when first stationed there, wasn't thrilled with the place, preferring to have been stationed at a downtown precinct, but it had grown on him and eventually he wouldn't have wanted to be elsewhere. The ones he spoke to, like him, were native New Yorkers, kvelling New Yorkers. Proud of their heritage, their native homeland, their city of their immigration, the way they were raised, the way they raised their kids and grandkids. He spoke to workers, husbands, students, to tattered panhandlers-begging for spare change. They were the only ones he felt sorry for. He felt compassion for them all, but sorry only for the panhandlers; the homeless, especially during the hard winter's brittle chill.

These people of the neighborhood, from the neighborhood, were the only reason the neighborhood didn't get worse. Those who spoke English, Español, Italiano, Yiddish, a sprinkling of intonated Jamaican-accented English and street.They at least tried to keep the neighborhood in line. The ones that called it home; they felt a sense of duty. Of course helping the neighborhood to get better instead of just not getting worse would be a full-time job for somebody—maybe a lot of somebodys. A nabe with no highbrows; lowbrow or middle, all. Not upper west side, but not squalid.

Then he'd slip into a bodega in Eighth Avenue, a crowded luncheonette—they always were in the city— or maybe even a drugstore soda fountain to sit at their cheap Formica-topped lunch counter for a pleasant noontime meal—good places to eat were figuratively speaking a dime a dozen in Hell's Kitchen, no matter what you desired, American, or ethnic food from any country in the world. Even if—God forbid—one wanted sauerkraut.

Rossi thought that was one of the great things about living in New York, the food, even though he still believed Italiano from Mama Leone's, famous because of the 70's pop song by Italian native New Yorker, Billy Joel, and the celebrities who went there for the food, swimming in red gravy, to be the best; alas, it was long gone, but wherever you went, them all smelling of stale coffee no matter the time of day.

And you had to be careful where you chose to get a cuppa because whether you took it black or regular, it didn't matter, because invariably, some of it was some vile shit. But Rossi had learned over time and from personal experience which ones to avoid. And the buildings all still looking like they did a half a century before. At least. Most were from the late-nineteenth, early-twentieth century. Some of them had been through a trifle updating. Most had not. Little to no gentrification to be found in this part of the city. Take it as it comes. This was Rossi's New York. Old school. Reminiscent of the potter's field that was now Bryant Park before it was decided to move tens of thousands of bodies to be reinterred in one of the mass graves of their permanent resting place on Wards Island in Long Island Sound.

He wasn't a fan of the new modern Central Park Tower. The tallest residential building in the world at ninety-eight floors and over fifteen hundred feet high; the apartments selling for many millions of dollars.

Occasionally he'd sit at a drugstore's white speckled Formica-topped lunch counter on a red vinyl-covered high-backed stool to people watch in order to gain a different perspective and to pursue private thoughts. But by their very nature, weren't all thoughts private? He'd sometimes have lunch while looking over a copy of the tabloid-style Daily News. He'd never dream of reading an e-copy. He wanted the paper to rustle as he turned pages and his fingers to be stained and smell of newsprint when he'd finished. Rossi had been born and raised in the city but the people still amazed him. The genders, the types, the colors, friends and foes, the shapes and sizes, the attitude, most of all the attitude. All proof that solipsism is merely a theory to be pondered but not existent.

And undoubtedly too diverse to be the cast in a Woody Allen movie, the nabe looked like a west side branch of the iconic east side headquartered United Nations Building. Not exactly a Pax Romana, Rossi believed, but for the most part, all living in harmony. Except for the occasional hot blooded Italian cop giving them shit; or at least that's what they thought. And who was he to dispute it? It gave him something to live down…or live up to. And the differences weren't like in the sixties. They weren't what you would call evolutionary or even societal.

No one in this neighborhood even knew anyone who was a part of high society or a member of the corporate boardroom, much less they themselves a part of it or even aspiring to it; and they wouldn't dream of bidding farewell by saying ta-ta with a finger waggle. And even though everyone looked different, they were alike, right down to their blue collars, even if they wouldn't admit it, even to themselves, maybe especially to themselves. On the street New Yorkers have their guards up. Sitting at a lunch counter, or in a bar, or in a comfortable store, they were more relaxed. Eating his lunch at a counter aided Rossi in relaxing as well and sometimes helped him to learn more about people.

At a disparate counter in a disparate or desperate neighborhood of the type where haves and have-nots not only coexisted but from time-to-time even rubbed shoulders or other less familiar parts. Rossi thought that caffeine to raise you up and a relaxing atmosphere to calm you were healthier than the seconals and dexedrines that some cops popped like candy. And if he required a trifle more relaxing, then two glasses of red wine after the end of a shift were commonly all he required.

Not often, but sometime one of the unprepossessing neighborhood gin-mills of the week that all look the same, except for one of the most popular pubs in all of New York along with P.J. Clarke's—the White Horse Tavern in Great Jones Street, the street unchanged since the day people were driving horse drawn carriages and dray wagons and the day after, motorcars and trucks—it famous for artists like Warhol, his friend and fellow artist, Keith Haring, who died of AIDS at the age of thirty-one, and even Haring's friend and fellow artist, Jean Michel Basquiat, until he perished at age twenty-seven from a heroin overdose, living near there, and as a notorious hangout for junkies still, and where the verb, jonesing, originally used when someone went to Great Jones in need of a drug fix, was created, but now used for any craving, even pizza, the street's character off the chart—for no more than two glasses of red wine and the New York staple-meatloaf and mashed potatoes, but in truth, only because Salvatoré sometimes wanted to give Ella a break from cooking.

In actuality, a Jones Street pub, especially, could give him the same prayerful comfort as mass, except, if he were to be over-the-top honest, he really didn't enjoy drinking with a bunch of strangers at a no-name bar. Assholes, mostly. And invariably Rossi ended up making sure at least one of the assholes knew he was an asshole. Fortunately Rossi was a fairly big man and most of them knew he was a cop and carrying, so it did not trouble him too much to remind them that they were assholes. He was sure that most of them were the type assholes who would put a cigarette out in a glass of fine rye, quickly being diluted by formerly large cubes of melting ice. A disgusting thing to do if there ever were one. He thought most bar drunks with their shots and beers, day drinking, were disgusting, anyways. If they had any sense of self pride they'd stay home and get drunk. Behind closed doors: do it in private. And all they ever wanted to talk about was the Yankees or the Giants, depending on the season; didn't even matter if they sucked. In fact they probably talked about them even more when they sucked. Less frequently the Jets and Mets. Or boxing.

But all the old drunks thought Marciano was the greatest. All they wanted to talk about was Marciano and Robinson. And don't get them started on Dempsey-Firpo. You want to start an argument, tell one of them that pound for pound Sugar Ray Leonard was the greatest of all time, then you'd see a fight up close and personal.

Most of the time Rossi didn't mind any of those subjects but the drunks never knew what the fuck they were talking about. Or when to shut the fuck up. It was the same thing over and over and over, and it truly bored the shit out of him. He still didn't like drinking with strangers even if the Yankees or boxing was on the big screen tvs. He'd rather watch them at home if Ella were asleep.

In addition, he didn't particularly care for bartenders. If they did not start drinking early in the morning-considering it part of their job training, then they tended to look at the world disapprovingly.

Probably started tending bar when they were young men and

were now late middle-aged. Over thirty years most likely. Didn't matter if they were Italiano or mick or Filipino. Different skin colors, different backgrounds, different languages, but aboriginals all, humankind members. And that was the kindest thing he could find to say about them even if he tried hard. He was not being racist; he thought all bartenders talked too goddamn much. Just talked their asses off.

And they had that bass-ackwards, because plenty of people thought of the neighborhood bartender as a therapist slash counselor; an amateur psychologist who would listen to their problems, offer advice if wanted, but if they never shut the hell up…and in addition to that, they never gave ample pours of wine, or made their mixed drinks strong enough. They wanted you to think they were being noble; trying to save the bar owner money, then after closing they'd steal bottles of booze so they could drink for free at home.

They just annoyed the shit out of him. He was sure they would annoy the shit out of shit. But by going to a bar Rossi got brownie points for being a good husband. And he found it ironic that by going to a bar, which most husbands would want to do, he was making his wife happy.

But he didn't care for the pubs because they were too dark and too loud. And the bartenders too verbose. No thanks. Unless it was the White Horse Tavern on Great Jones, but only because of its historical significance. But, even it didn't have the panache of the Kicking Mule, the make believe New York bar in the lesser known Elton John song, *Ticking*, about the murder of fourteen people in a pub in Brooklyn. And hopefully that would not happen at the White Horse; not on his watch, anyway.

Rossi liked the look of the bar, and the altogether pleasant smell of the place and even the pleasant sound of occasional Celtic music, favoring the old world sounds of The Pogues, especially when it was the nostalgic, at least for drunk Irishmen, *Fairytale of New York* at Christmas, or the Clancy Brothers or even the current popular bands-Dropkick Murphy, or Mumford and Sons, and their huge hit, *I Will Wait*. Invariably, someone, maybe more than one someone would start singing along with the upbeat song with the killer banjo rhythm. And some of the authors didn't have terrible voices. Once again proof that if an artist were creative in one endeavor he probably would be in others as well. Irish pub food cooking infused with the smell of aged wood floors, nicotine smoke-stained ceilings and brick walls. And not that much smell of nicotine smoke even though some folks smoked in the establishment. Could you imagine asking the great Welsh poet, Dylan Thomas to put out his cigarette? A rhetorical question; but hardly. And furthermore, any of the current crop of nicotine-addicted writers might be the next Dylan Thomas. And oh the stories, those bricks and wood and ceiling tiles had heard, but keeping them all to themselves. Each of them known to be closed mouthed and not given to gossip. Popular in the 50s and 60s for its bohemian culture, The White Horse Tavern remained a place for writers and artists to gather on Great Jones in Greenwich Village.

In one of the less proud moments in its checkered past as a popular hangout, for one of its most famous patrons, the world-famous Dylan Thomas, before he drank eighteen shots of whisky in one setting, a personal record as he exclaimed, stumbled out its now infamous door and died a few days later in his room at the Chelsea Hotel where he'd been staying during a book signing tour. And others renowned, Hunter S. Thompson, Norman Mailer, Allen Ginsburg and even Jim Morrison, the belated great singer-poet of The Doors.

Although Rossi would like The Dead Rabbit Pub better if it weren't for so many goddamn Mick assholes in it every night, he liked The White Horse's familiar comfortable smell as he entered. And although he was neither a writer nor artist, he could picture them in their ateliers, their writer's retreats, with an aging writer's desk covered with sheaves of manuscripts, and thought it must be a cool existence; doing research, creating, writing, admired by many.

Yeah, he thought that would really be cool, but as much the

character as any of them, drawn in as he was by their brilliant minds and radical thoughts, he enjoyed rubbing shoulders with those creatives who did so much research for writing and had so much arcane and esoteric knowledge that made for interesting conversations, both with him as a participant or of tidbits he eavesdropped, at the heavily scarred honest dark wood historic bar where he could watch their reflections in the dark huge gilt and etched oxidized mirror behind the bar, the colorful bottles of pricy liquors in front of it, or maybe it was just an old dark wood bar with the varnish worn thin from decades of elbows resting in those very spots; each pair close to the next where real men stood close to watch the Jets or the Giants on the tv and drink their whiskey neat with two fingers of lament, which was a better world, and the black scarred floor from cigarettes cast down and stubbed out underfoot.

The only way it could be more real were if jazz was still en vogue with the masses, instead of just popular with some enthusiasts; making seniors smile nostalgically and young people palm the sides of their heads and scream. Rossi liked the place way more than the usual cop bars in the area. Hanging out with cops after working with them all day just bored the hell out of him or worse; they annoyed the shit out of him. Even if he did only drink coffee, unless of course he splashed, as the Irish say, a wee bit of their whisky in it.

And he would only arrest any of the drug dealers lingering among the colorful umbrella shaded tables on the broad sidewalk patio that was enclosed in the frigid months of New York's winter when he left, if, thinking he were a potential customer, they aggressively approached him; otherwise, if they left him alone he left them alone. He thoughtfully considered that they were in enough pain already; because in order to support their own need he knew they could not help what they do. Selling drugs in order to do drugs they required. Not because they wanted to, but because they had to.

Rossi was undoubtedly pretty sympathetic for a cop. He definitely was not sure if this was a good thing or a bad one. Tough but sympathetic. But he knew himself. They had only approached him a couple of times, but a formidable appearing man in size already, he looked even more so when he flipped open the leather case revealing his stern gold shield. And it tickled the shit out of him to see the shocked look in their eyes when he flashed the recognizable totem of law enforcement. In truth, if he were honest with himself, times like those were when he most loved his job.

Rossi was sure a couple of authors he'd spoken with, including Shane Etter, had used him as the inspiration for a crusty old veteran police detective in one of their novels, causing him to wonder who would play him in a movie. His personal hope was for the great character actor, Oliver Platt, since he'd been told on more than one occasion that he held at least a passing resemblance to the man.

Chapter Eleven

Rossi knew which Greek diner had the best reuben on rye, generous with the Russian dressing, which one had the best pastrami on rye, served in a small plain white sack with a styrofoam cup of coffee regular, a New York City term everyone knew meant with cream and sugar, but not a large one, because that late in the day it would keep him up at night—for lunch and most days would take it to go and eat while he walked, even though it was against department regs; the same as smoking was.

Sometimes, for a change he'd have what was commonly known as a New York schmear; a jumbo bagel with cream cheese, smoked salmon, chives, a slice of red onion, capers, tomato and lettuce—any other way was criminal, but he liked his toasted. New Yorkers probably thought the original breakfast sandwich was an acquired taste here in the land of the bagel's Genesis.

Not too strong of a word, Genesis, as many people considered that a bagel with a shmear was one of God's greatest gifts. Back then Rossi drank his coffee regular. Now, he most often took it black, unless he pleasured it with a shot of Jameson's. He rarely did that however. Dammit, at least those fucking Irish finally got something right; even if it was only their whisky.

Nobody would rat him out for eating while he walked, though, because he was more than kith alone; he was family, one of them, an Italian beat cop, of their street, of their nabe. Even though they had never been to the others' houses they were still family.

It was an undeniable truth you would find no transplants in the neighborhood; no one that had moved from Atlanta, Chicago or Dallas. Transients none. Everyone knew that transients were somewhat less than desirable. No diaspora, all born, raised and moored right where they lived. Unless they were of the bohemian life. Either way, it gave the neighborhood a sense of home, of permanence. a phenomenon like no other in the world.

Rossi'd always felt he was safe from detection as long as he didn't drip any of the rich dressing on his tie. He knew that at least one half-alert cop would noodle it out if he did.

He especially enjoyed the routine in early autumn when summer's high temperatures had broken and the nascent cooler temps made it more pleasant especially that close to the river.

He'd really liked that, and although he loved being a homicide dick, on some elementary child-like level, down deep, he missed walking a beat. It wasn't possible to stay a patrolmen for a career however. In a department full of wops—rarely called that anymore from its disrespectful beginning meaning 'without papers'—and micks, also known as harps—one of the requirements for getting promoted-membership in the Catholic church, was a given, and therefore that obstacle was hurdled before it could even become an issue. So the rest; show up on time, come dressed to play, and keep your nose clean, was up to you.

The only thing he hadn't liked about walking a beat was when it was raining. The rain could be real aggressive in New York, and last all day; but it would clean the dirty city. And under leather soled shoes the sidewalks, particularly the lightly pebbled ones, would get slippery.

The only other thing he didn't like was wearing the black leather gun belt, holster, weapon, ring of keys, spare cartridges for the blue steel revolver, cuffs, baton and flashlight weighing him down. Must've added up to at least twenty pounds or more. God help him if he ever got into a foot chase wearing all that shit.

Rossi thought the nightstick was overkill anyway. He'd hoped back in those days he'd never have to use it. It wasn't that he was a pacifist or cowardly, and it wasn't that he kept it in abeyance; it was ready if he required it, it was just that he knew he would hate the shit out of the sound, and especially the feel, of cracking somebody's skull. He really wished he could have been an equine officer; riding one of those beautiful steeds; now that would have been cool, but alas, no such luck. But as a detective he didn't mind not wearing that heavy-ass gun belt. An inside the waistband clip-on holster with the small frame 9mm semiautomatic was far lighter and much more comfortable; even if he didn't but walk a beat any longer. The biggest difference was that the people that lived and worked on his blocks didn't belong to him anymore; the ones of whom he knew their families, their failures, their successes, their hopes and their dreams. Those the biggest changes—the people and all the phone booths that used to be on the sidewalks back then. At least one on each side in every block. Probably more. Especially in the longer east-west blocks.

Now unworking, aging objects of art; unappreciated pop culture sculpture, at least by young people. If the unnecessary items even still were there. Not all of them were. And if they were, they were mostly being used as emergency toilets. Unless one had an empty Snapple bottle. Alas, the city that never sleeps, never ceases to have need of restrooms. Some things never change.

He had been introduced as a multiple times decorated recipient of the NYPD's Medal of Honor, the department's highest prize, meritorious service citations and other encomiums. Rossi had been awarded the highest honor when a suspect fired on his former partner, and Rossi returned fire and killed the man stone cold deader than shit without breaking a sweat. Surely saving both of their lives. His sterling reputation already incapable of being lauded further, was burnished even more by the award.

In truth it had troubled Rossi. He'd never killed anyone before and hadn't since. No matter how emotionally tough someone is it's catastrophic to kill a man. Actually it had been the only time Rossi'd ever fired his weapon except at the department shooting range far out on Long Island. And the only time in anger. And even though he'd only done it the one time, it made him know that shooting at flesh and bones was something he hoped he'd never have to do again.

Of course, Rossi knew he'd do it again in a New York minute if The Swordsman were in his sights and it would stop the son of a bitch from killing anyone else. Then he wouldn't have to worry about some goddamn Jew or dago-wop lawyer getting his sorry ass off. And then he'd probably kill him again if it were possible. Because he knew serial murderers would kill again, and again, and again, until they were caught or killed. They never stopped. And most weren't haunted by what they did; If anything, they were proud. Always competing to be the most prolific of their damnable closed world.

Chapter Twelve

Brody had to know everything he could about the man charged with catching him. Salvatoré Rossi. That was the only thing he needed, he thought sarcastically; a goddamn Italian on his ass. Definitely not one to be trifled with. But at least he wasn't a Chechen. Nobody liked those sons of bitches. Probably a Sicilian-the worst sort of Italian. Even Italians considered Sicilians a different stroke from a broad brush, living in the same country, but different language, different ancestry.

Even Rossi found it ironic that Sicilians made up the dominant percentage of La Cosa Nostra, as well as the NYPD. Fortunately for Rossi, his beautiful wife, his Ella bella, whose parents bestowed her with that lovely name because of their affection for the great jazz age songstress, although she impishly liked to tell people her parents dropped the D from the indomitable Della Street's name, the secretary of Perry Mason renown; had not been even remotely taken aback by him being Sicilian even though she hailed from the lovely Toscana, and his somewhat more than a little questionable heritage that being Sicilian brought with it. And his faith in her, her loyalty, commitment, belief and love would stand the test of time and cement his faith in the Holy God. Her and their beloved children and their even more beloved grandchildren were the result of their blessed union.

But either way it still meant to Brody that he was a goddamn Catholic. Not that he had more of a problem with Catholics than with Jews or even Baptists. Alla those arrogant bastards thought theirs' was the only way to get through the pearly gates.

Of course Brody already knew his eternal destination; after what would most likely be an abbreviated stay in the Rikers Island Correctional Facility during a trial, followed by a somewhat longer interment at the infamous Sing Sing New York State prison literally up the river, the mighty Hudson, at Ossining where the famous phrase had been invented. Of course he would probably kill himself in one of those shitholes. At least that would be the

NYPD's official statement after his body was found in his cell. As most people believed, the same thing that happened to Jeffrey Epstein.

But if he were found to be afflicted with diminished capacity; not as severe as being declared insane and commonly resulting in a sentence of life without parole where he would be placed on suicide watch. Yeah, like that would keep anything bad from happening. He was was fully aware that there were plenty of people in law enforcement who wanted him dead, whether by a judge's order or by taking it into their or the DOC's nefariously proficient hands. They most likely had a lot of experience with *suicides*.

He knew there would be no earthly redemption awaiting him the same way he knew there would be no heavenly clemency awaiting him, just as he was positive his next stop would be the fiery depths of hell. All libertine reprobates went there. Where else could they expect to go? And he was well familiar with the old saying, karma knows your address, and he knew that sometime; either in this life or the next, he would be paid a visit by the unholy haint.

He recalled every detail of what he was taught about hell from those mortally boring as shit summer catechism classes from when he was a kid; worse even, hell apparently knew all about him and so its demons could use his weaknesses against him. Every goddamn morning, wearing uniforms to catechism class; exactly like school. When he should have been outside playing like his non-Roman Catholic friends. Not that he liked those sons of bitches either.

The detective cleared his throat in an attempt to impersonate a redoubtable newscaster's resonate basso. An impossible task since his ungrandiose voice sounded like glass being crunched underfoot on concrete, certainly not a soporific one. And not what one would expect from such a considerable chest. His swarthy face was blanketed by a coarse blue-black Italian stubble, even though he was most likely recently shaved. On anybody else it would be a five o'clock shadow. Brody thought the detective looked like a no-

nonsense self-righteous son of a bitch. A scary goddamn WOP. Even though the pejorative, within the restrictive confines of its original meaning, without papers, wouldn't, in its strictest sense, apply to him; the intent of the pejorative would. Brooding but dogged. Worse, he most likely felt a profound sense of moral obligation to the citizens of his ancestors' adoptive home of New York. Which would naturally give rise to proudly making him feel morally superior. He looked like he could have been a made man in la Cosa Nostra, la familia,—if he hadn't been so self-righteous and chosen the dark side, instead. Brody's humorous aside made him chuckle. The NYPD, the dark side. Brody was struck by the thought that he resembled the great, but in his opinion, under-appreciated actor, Oliver Platt, famous for the movie, *Don't Say A Word* filmed, and and set, in New York.

Rossi wished that he looked more New York, like the characters in the musical, and movie, *Rent*. 'Now, they looked like New Yorkers,' he'd told his wife, his angel come down, somewhat more than a few times.

Of course if he were honest with himself he wished he could sing as well as the *Rent* actors could. But he didn't have the pipes for it, and if the word of his wish got out among his brothers in blue he'd never be able to live it down. Alas, his huge gruff resolute Italian voice was not meant for singing.

As a homicide dick Rossi worked out of any of the city's precincts. Whichever one was nearest a crime scene, but they generally held this Circus Maximus, or dog and pony show, whatever you preferred to call this shit, on the corner of White and the broad Centre Street on a large concrete apron in front of One Police Plaza, also lovingly referred to as 1PP.

Rossi didn't like going there since he felt like no real police work ever got done there. Unless one could define chicanery as work. He was quite sure that virtually nobody who worked at HQs ever used the muscle between their ears. Literally not exercising it at all, except for the aforementioned chicanery. And he liked to believe that even though they would outrank a senior sergeant of thirty or more years' service, that one of those enlisted veterans still might have sufficiently big *cojonés* to give them a good lacing just for kicks from time-to-time. Although, probably the most he could hope for was one would have no truck with them.

He looked like central casting's idea of an NYPD detective. His countenance, the cop's displeasure, was easily inferred or deduced even by a non-detective, by the scowl on his face; it appearing that the detective was somewhat less than happy about being there. And it was obvious from the look on his face and being Italian that he had little experience or practice at concealing his feelings. And it wasn't that it was his first barbecue; but you could tell he didn't like these things.

At the same time, he, like everybody in law enforcement, knew that the overwhelming majority of serious crimes were solved not because of brilliant investigative work, but because some fine citizen came forward with vital information. So in his mind the pressers were a necessary but unwelcome evil to encourage someone who might have knowledge of the killings to present him or herself.

And Rossi felt the need to do all he could do, including the pressers, in an attempt to keep the state police from sticking their noses into his business. Admittedly it was a matter of pride with him, but he would never bend to the pressers.

On that he was unequivocal. But he would do them because he took murder personal. But in doing them he still had to maintain some sense of dignity, even if it didn't appear to others that he did. And with that in mind he had even broken himself of the centuries old Italian habit of talking with his hands. He'd found out the hard way that it didn't look professional on tv. And he had been called out by his supervisor about it.

Flint in his eyes, he squinted into the bright television camera lights, his nascent crows feet deeper with the act, in turn drawing his pronounced laugh lines into the expression as he stared at the satellite trucks with the recognizable Fox and CNN logos on the side that looked out of place next to the One PP sidewalk, then looked askance, seemingly as if he smelled something bad. The lights illuminated liberated dust motes that looked like snowflakes suspended languidly on the leaden unmoving air. His squint was close to becoming permanent however, betokened of staying pissed off at criminals. His dark skin bright but at the same time dull yellow, from the glare of the beams. His face remained sanguine. His left eyebrow was slightly interrupted by a barely noticeable small scar. A gift from a noxious drunk who'd tried to brain him with a wine bottle. He hadn't been paying sufficient attention at the time of the action. It was the last time he'd let that happen.

The only part of him that didn't look like a cop were his eyes. Heavily hooded dark Italian eyes, they still exuded uncomfortable warmth. They weren't yet soulless from everything he'd seen. That showed he hadn't been gutted by the visions. And they didn't look like what some referred to as "cop eyes;" even though they missed nothing they weren't suspicious of everything and everybody except when prudent; when they needed to be.

He wore the cuffs of his long white sleeves turned up and the skin of his right forearm, the color of the bark of an olive tree or an Italian cypress from his native land, showed a tattoo that appeared to be solemn writing. Unlike those that were totems of hipsters male and female in all areas, large and small. Brody couldn't make out what it said.

Of course he wouldn't have understood the Virtus et Honos—Latin for "Strength and Honor", that the man, confident of himself, wore as a tribute to his Italian heritage and its roots in the Roman Empire. A different world in a different lifetime. But real to him. And he was so old school he pronounced his homeland's name in the way of his ancestors—Italia. Or the other forearm that read Memento Mori—"remember that you will die" a Latin tribute to his brothers and sisters in blue that regrettably, had, in the line of duty.

He glanced at the new wristwatch he wore, a Raymond Weil, trying to will this charade to be over. Alas, his watch was unconcerned with the time and wouldn't allow that the wearer should be.

It had cost more than he cared to spend for a watch, but it still was less than the Breitling he really wanted, and though he wasn't given to being prodigal, it was nevertheless a fine timepiece and he hoped it would last long enough for him to bequeath it to his young grandson, his namesake, Salvatoré, who had recently started calling him grandman, at the time of his eventual but nonetheless inevitable passing. But hopefully not too soon. Since, although he had been shot at before he didn't know how to be dead. That watch and a gold wedding band, less than a quarter of an inch wide, were the only pieces of jewelry he wore. Not a typical Italian in that respect; no gold chains, no diamonds, no bracelets. Class all the way. Nothing showy. Certainly not like the Italian mobsters. His worst character flaw-swearing like an Irish Catholic priest.

Brody thought he might like to get another tattoo; this time maybe one of a dagger dripping blood. Thinking about it, he was actually surprised that he hadn't gotten a second one already. The one he had, of a grinning skull, was so old it was already changing; the faded blue the color of a dead person's skin. He'd have to put that on his to-do list, for when he had the extra cash. Like that was ever going to happen, living hand to mouth, as he did.

Detective Rossi's face glistened with perspiration but one couldn't know if it was from New York's lovely nascent summer warmth, the television lights, or the pressure he felt from needing to apprehend The Swordsman.

In truth, television cameras made him claustrophobic. Only a few short blocks away, the bells of historic Trinity Church where the great American statesman, Alexander Hamilton, was buried in the small churchyard, chimed. Detective Rossi appeared comforted by the sound.

He pulled a dingy white handkerchief from a rear pocket and took a swipe at the sweat beading on his swarthy brow, wet not from the pleasant afternoon, the temperature not fierce but bearable, but from the cameras and newspeople. Then puffed on both lenses of his black-framed reading eyeglasses that made him look even more like Oliver Platt, before giving them each a swipe with the cloth; the way he did it almost reverential, like making the sign of the cross, before returning it to its place.

After gazing at the lenses and deciding they were the way he wanted, he reached into his right trousers pocket, apparently adjusting something then pulled his hand out empty. He was probably silencing his cellphone since most people could do that without looking, from touch alone. Even dumbshit dago cops. His face appeared scarred, but scars from living a full life, not from hardness; heavy-lidded dark eyes, his brow beginning to furrow, a still rugged jaw, but with that his primordial Roman nose unbroken, looking the way it should for someone from Italy; bent like an elbow joint, but at least it was natural, though it appeared to be uninterested in the least in the proceedings.

The protuberance itself an unwished-for genetic handicap for Mediterranean noses. Anything but a stately patrician. Then tucked his still-gallant well-boned chin in a vain attempt to hide the wattle above his too-tight collar; before he ran a black comb through his slick backed Vitalis-soaked Mediterranean Sea black hair with its healthy sprinkle of silver mixed in, even though his last name meant red-haired or red-faced in Italian, and he was neither.

He'd always run a comb through his hair when he got nervous, and the only time he got nervous was when he was talking to reporters; and on tv at the same time. He fished out his glasses again and re-examined them before deciding they were clean enough and against giving them another swipe and returned them to their usual place on his scrunched nose sniffing the noisome diesel fuel mixed with salt air that was always present this close to the East River that wasn't a river.

And he would make damn sure he wasn't in front of the tv when the local news came on at 6 or 11pm. He certainly didn't want to watch, or even listen, to himself

Rossi took advantage of the moment to let the atypically comforting familiar roar of a jet airliner that sounded like a big 747 cutting back on its engines on final approach into Kennedy

International to pass, and not drown him out. God only knew where it was arriving from; could have been anywhere, Paris, Tel Aviv, Budapest.

He could picture a wagon train of carriers backed up on the taxiways—what he knew most people wrongly call the tarmac, but doesn't exist on any significant U.S. airport grounds since tarmac is an acronym combination of tar and macadam, more commonly known as asphalt, which would never hold up to the pounding of the massive airliners which require runways and taxiways to be made of concrete—of one of the world's busiest international airports waiting for it to land and for their moment of glory and liftoff. Of course even being in that airway backup wasn't anywhere near as frightening as landing at LaGuardia on Long Island's bay shore on the runway that extends hundreds of yards out into the water of the East River mouth of Long Island Sound within yards of Rikers Island and its ten thousand daily prisoners of the city of New York.

Even after the airliner passed there was still the incessant sound of New York City traffic. Always the evocative inescapable sounds of traffic. Engines and horns that never cease in the city that never sleeps.

Truth was he was attempting to delay the inevitable since he'd rather face down a heavily armed and pissed off contingent of La Cosa Nostra made men who'd made their bones many times over than that media horde. Diffidence was not the cause of his hesitation. The God's honest truth was he just disliked the shit out of anything that took him away from his job; from doing real police work; pressers because he knew the newspeople would parse his words into something akin to what they wanted to hear and what's more he thought them a waste of time, necessary though they were occasionally.

Fortunately he wasn't called on to do pressers often since the angst he felt because of them made him question whether the job was worth it. And because delaying appeared an obviously desperate tactic; fleeing, fleeing like a stampeding herd of wildebeests eluding hunters on the Serengeti seemed an altogether better, and somewhat less embarrassing option.

So, after delaying as long as he thought he could, he finally began. In his only somewhat less than sonorous voice he started to read from a précis of his notes. His tone as dark as his hair was before the silver began to take up residence.

After finishing, he somewhat evasively refused to answer questions with a raised eyebrow while looking at them soberly if he thought the answer might give away too much info to the suspect—if he happened to be watching—the detective answered a handful of questions from local news reporters, plus a couple from Telemundo, Fox News and CNN but made damn sure he sounded and looked equally putout by them all. Just because he was pissed off by the whole goddamn affair he made the conscious decision to use as much cop-speak as he possibly could instead of everyday vernacular, and pretend not to hear if anyone asked what some esoteric term meant. Indeed, he'd learned from experience to vouchsafe the information he held. And anyone watching would be unable to tell how he felt about them.

One particular middle-aged male reporter that he recognized, but wasn't sure from which network, sporting the prototypical reporter's perfect coiffure, asked, "is there anything you can tell us about a suspect?"

Rossi, without using copspeak but with more than a little attitude showing, said brusquely, "no." He was pretty sure he'd made his point. Anytime he'd had to do pressers it was obvious that he and the press had a strained relationship at best; at worst, a heated feud with each other.

Brody thought every goddamn Italian he'd ever known was given to meaningless prattle. The exact opposite of laconic. Just talked their asses off. So this Rossi must have really hated doing this shit.

It was obvious to anyone that the taciturn Rossi wasn't happy by the way his thick jaw worked while worrying the inside of his mouth. The cords in his neck tight, the opposite side of his mouth

from the eye that had suddenly developed a tic that would cease as
soon as he ended this circus act. He really did try to smile—Ella,
the wife he'd done nothing to deserve, but cherished nonetheless,
always told him he should—but it always seemed to turn out to be
a grimace, instead.

He wasn't really a disaffected detective; or a timorous one and
even though he sounded like it it wasn't like he intended to be
recalcitrant. He just hated the shit out of this. And he always
thought he looked daft on camera—he'd have to remember that
word, daft, to use for Bookworm's sake. Rossi knew his friend
would like it—before appearing to start a vendetta, when the news
people lost decorum and started shouting their questions the
detective made a big show out of looking at his watch, then choked
the dingy white handkerchief again and began, with a weary hand,
to shine his reading glasses—which had more effect on his serious
face when he wore them—before flashing them a vexed glare,
showing more than impertinence, indeed, revealing exasperation,
bordering on hostility, and instead of his usual sturdy, harsh deep
baritone, said stridently, "sorry folks, I'm going to have to cut this
short. Got to keep New York City safe. We got a bad guy to catch.
No time to dilly-dally. Please and thank you." Detective Rossi had
really liked the *John Wick Chapter Three* movie when someone
told Wick no time to dilly-dally and he thought the presser could
use some levity. He really would have liked to have sounded
sincere, but he was tired and just didn't have it in him when dealing
with these press assholes. Indeed, it took more energy than he was
able to muster and he came across as only somewhat a little less
than arrogant.

And with that he gave Park a surreptitious manly wink, and the
totally unpleasant but apparently—in some people's minds—
necessary task completed, left with more energy in his step than
when he arrived. Unlike most men who immediately lost a couple
of masculinity percentage points as soon as the winking eye
opened. Rossi hoped Park would learn to do as he says, not as he
does. But what he really wanted to do was to get to St. Malachy

Holy Roman Catholic Church in midtown for the daily six o'clock mass.

Chapter Thirteen

The aroma of incense and candles from masses previous lingered as he entered. The huge sanctuary old amongst the new. New lean and sinewy glittering glass and steel towers that look like futuristic powerful missiles that were being erected in all sections of the borough.

New York was changing always but always stayed the same. That could be counted on; that its history, architecture and unquestionably, its very soul, would remain. Rossi hoped so, anyway. He was old school and in his view the city should never modernize. He guessed it was okay for Lincoln Center since the American Ballet theatre was there. It was modern; but it had been that way for so long that the modern had become old.

Rossi was old school Italian. The parish was home for him. In all ways and manner. Courtesy, and respect were given and expected in the parish. The center of his metaphorical… and real, universe. Not that Rossi was that devout; he wasn't, but he clearly enjoyed the peace he felt here in this place of stained-glass Saints, early Roman paintings and sculpture, although his favorite work was a medium-sized portrait of Pope Francis, the first pope from the Americas.

Rossi was a traditionalist and preferred the sodality of mass and the church the way they are. He would prefer that there were no changes whatsoever. He enjoyed the peace he felt there, and he hoped, too, that his soul would rest in peace as well. But wasn't that what everyone wanted?

The five o'clock mass wouldn't be as crowded, mostly retirees not having a clock to punch, but the six o'clock would be packed with all the folks getting off work, plus the wiseguys ending their somewhat less than proper, or at least legal days…before their nascent but nefarious nights began. One could tell when they were there by the number of huge black limousines in the church parking lot.

At least the senior wise guys didn't bring their crews with them to holy mass. Mass was not an appropriate setting for a la Cosa

Nostra conclave. At most each would be accompanied by a single burly young man, a Luca Brasi wannabe, wearing a dark suit and a beaver skin fedora, who was their bodyguard-slash-attendant-slash-driver, and Detective Rossi would take note of the faces for future reference. He enjoyed the six, as it was colloquially called by the parishioners. He had long thought it amusing; Italian cops and Italian la Cosa Nostra, penitents partaking in the body and blood of Christ, side-by-side, familiar strangers eyeing each other a little more than somewhat cautiously.

It seems that's all goddamn wops were good for anyways. Being cops or criminals. And neither profession was all that respectful. But at least the mugs weren't Russians or Croatians awash in too much cheap aftershave.

And the fact that they never missed mass or communion was proof that they weren't as bad as the Yakuza, an even deadlier brand of Japanese gangster. Although the two groups had been known to cooperate with each other, to the benefit of each.

And if they were able to keep those sons of bitches contained to the Japanese section of Chinatown they could keep them somewhat under control. Everyone knew that compared to any of those miscreants the Italian wise guys and made men were choirboys. And la Cosa Nostra thugs and NYPD detectives have one thing in common, even if they don't want to admit it; only the clever ones grow old.

Rossi always wondered somewhat morbidly if any of them had a body in their oversized black limo trunks that they needed to dump in New Jersey's dismal pine barrens or bury under the end zone in the Meadowlands Stadium after holy communion while listening to an Italian opera composition on the drive to Jersey, on the limo's stereo that probably cost as much as most people's cars before nobody could stand the smell because it got too rank. Everybody knew it was next to impossible to get the disgusting primal smell of a dead body outta the car once it sets in. Then maybe a quick trip to Six Flags before they headed back to the city. And everybody knew the barrens were where the bodies were literally buried. Bodies have been found buried in the area west of The Garden State Parkway, but only because someone with knowledge of them came forward while trying to curry favor with a DA. Which was rare because most of the wiseguys still believed in the code of omertà. The code of silence. Except maybe for the younger ones. Everybody knew they didn't have any heart. The barrens had bodies coming outta it's ass with alla them; the flotsam of wiseguys, their scent overpowering even the strong smell of creosote and organic aromatic fragrance of the many varieties of disinterested conifers. Going all the way back to the days of the Lord High Executioner, Albert Anastasia; Al Capone; Lucky Luciano; alla the great ones.

It had long been the mob's preferred dumping grounds. While it was possible the wiseguys would be going to bury bodies after mass, Rossi was going to the dry cleaners to pick up his shirts and a suit for Sunday mass. Heavy starch. When he got heavy starch he could get two wearings out of a shirt as long as he didn't get too agitated at work and sweat too much. Fat chance of that happening. Then to the package store to pick up wine for Sunday afternoon and evening. Save him a special trip after Sunday morning mass.

Neither cops nor criminals knew the names of those in the other group. But Rossi assumed somebody was named Tony, To-NY, that there was an uncle Junior in the bunch, maybe somebody with the nickname big pussy, and who the hell knew what else. Probably took their names from watching reruns of *The Sopranos*. No imagination, these guys. But you could be assured the good Reverend Monsignor knew their names.

But the cops and the bad guys, they just knew each other as that guy at mass.

And they'd never dream of shaking hands or speaking to one another. Even if they could. Many of the Sicilian wiseguys never bothered to learn English. Sicilian to their very core as they were; although some would partake of Latin, if it served them. And the revered Monsignor looked no less on one than the other. Probably at least partly because the wiseguys put larger bills in the collection plate than the cops did. But they had more money because organized crime paid substantially better than the NYPD did and they were attempting, with their generous donations to the church, to buy their way into Heaven. But the right reverend needed police to watch over the church. Hence, cops were equally important, even if their donations weren't as largehearted.

From experience Rossi was positive that in addition to being huge, that the assistant was packing heavy heat and it was highly likely that it was a larger caliber than the weapons he or any other cops attending the mass were probably carrying. And he would know from a ton of real-world experience, how to use it.

Indeed, the old parish was thriving; now bigger than ever. Although the frosty temps of deepest winter could cause attendance to drop off a bit; especially if it made the sidewalks slippery and dangerous for the elderly. The time of year when the rock salt crunched with every step. Rossi really enjoyed the Right Reverend Monsignor Aquino's homilies, and always found a tidbit he could apply to his daily life.

And with that Rossi always put a twenty dollar bill in the offering box before leaving—and calculated that if he went to mass several times a week, if not daily, and put a twenty in each time, that God and the Monsignor would be pleased with him—and lighted a few candles for long since gone family members relations and cops of the same misfortune, all faces, snapshots in his mind, and always made sure to tell the good Father how much he'd enjoyed the homily as he made his exit. Much like some people make sure to tell an airline pilot it was a nice flight before deplaning in a rush. Always figuring it couldn't hurt. With God or a pilot. Thinking of that caused Rossi to recall the old joke; what's the difference between God and an airline pilot? God doesn't think he's an airline pilot. That one always gave him a chuckle. But he didn't like it as well as the one; 'A tourist visiting New York stops a man on the street and asks for directions, how do you get to Carnegie Hall. The helpful man replied, practice, man, practice.' That still killed Rossi. He was sure it always would.

Chapter Fourteen

He anticipated opening a bottle of Chianti Classico with a gentle sensuous pop, to sip with dinner, but before that he'd start with communion wine served at holy mass and using an old Italian trick he'd be last in line so he could finish the off the wine in the chalice. He'd get more that way. which was definitely not to be confused with the morbid purple grape juice Baptists sip at their services and have the unequivocal chutzpah to call the blood of Christ.

And recalling that Christ changed water into wine they'd better pray that that unholy habit doesn't piss off the Good Lord. That in itself a reason for confession.

Rossi was old school and still liked the term confession more than the newer word for it; reconciliation. Of course catching a whiff of a wee bit of single malt on the priest's breath made him feel like all was right with the world. As much as when the priest gave the benediction, 'the mass has ended. Go in peace now to love and serve the Lord.'

He thought affectionately of his wife as he took measured strides down the long hall. Marrying her was the best thing he'd ever done. Rossi and Ella lived in a fairly nice building, at least by New York standards. The muffled industrial-carpeted corridors weren't what one would call well lit, but they weren't depressingly gloomy, just dim.

The address certainly wasn't what one might think of as tony, but it wasn't redolent of the sour smell of cabbage cooking like so many buildings he tended to have to enter on the job as a cop. But those were mostly buildings where Irish lived, though. And that was almost always explanation enough for the cabbage smell.

Of course these days there were only a trifle more than half as many Irish as there were Italians in the city. But red gravy cooking didn't come close to having nearly as oppressive a smell as cabbage. Rossi couldn't wait to get home. Getting home before the cloak of darkness arrived, to the delicious dinner loaded with red sauce his wife had told him she was cooking, and to open a genteel bottle of Italian red. Not expensive, but not execrable. A good mid-price Chianti. Decent but he wasn't infatuated with it. Quality notwithstanding, he hoped he'd find one with a screw top for ease of opening. Made from Sangiovese grapes alone. No blend. Or maybe start with a pony of brandy. Or after the nonsense of the presser he might crack the seal on a bottle of bourbon; he thought three fingers of bourbon, neat, might be just what the doctor ordered, or just to be different; rye whiskey, while he put his feet up and enjoyed the delicious aroma of Ella's Italian feast cooking. True enough, life was full of choices.

Most of the time Rossi stayed away from spirits, but occasionally he liked a finger or two of rye for a change. A drink of providence. Or at the very least, steadying his nerves. A drink for guidance and care, and to preserve his good nature. That made him chuckle since not many people thought him good natured. Except for Ella and the grands.

He liked the serious whiskey's warmth. Not that it was cold out; it wasn't. But its psychological and emotional warmth.

It could be counted on to do what it was supposed to do. Finish the job of relaxing him that attending mass had begun. Help him come down from the nastiness of the presser. Come down from the circling wolves and readying for the attack under the guise of doing it only for the public good.

And reporters have the unmitigated gall to actually say they believe that shit. Like anybody believed it. Have three fingers, which would last him all night, while reading and waiting for dinner and then after dinner. Rossi was rereading *Alas Babylon*, one of the first apocalyptic novels about the start of a nuclear war, by the infamous author, Pat Frank.

From half a lifetime together he'd learned most of Ella's little tricks; if she didn't tell him what she was cooking, because she wanted to surprise him, then it was almost guaranteed they were having sausage and peppers. He loved it the way she made it; Italian sausage, orange, green and yellow bell peppers, with only the occasional red thrown in; heavy on his favorite, the yellow, medium on the orange, and light on his least preferred, the green, all covered in her to-die-for marinara sauce, heavy with garlic. Once he started eating, though he'd have to remember to save room for one of Ella's hand-rolled cannolis; maybe two.

And it sure beat the hell out of a delivery pizza pie. And along with the Chianti, so good it would make you want to slap your mother. Even if you were a cop. And your mother a sainted Italian mother, grandmother and great grandmother.

Rossi didn't take his meals anywhere but at home if he could help it. Especially since Beefsteak Charlie's and Mickey Mantle's Restaurant had permanently shut their doors. He had loved Charlie's steak sandwiches; alas, they were no more. And steaks and televised sporting events that always turned into a party at The Mick's place.

That passing thought caused him to recall the old New York saying—you can order lobster at a steakhouse but never, under any circumstances, order steak at a lobster house. And even though Mick's was old school even it didn't have cigarette girls, the scantily clad young women of a different era who walked around clubs with a tray of cigs for sell, hanging from a cord around their necks. They would have been more prevalent at 21 or Toot's place decades previously.

Rossi was recalled of an evening seeing traffic blocked on Central Park South where the popular restaurant was located, by a huge crowd of so many excited colorful drunks on the sidewalk outside that spilled into the street, peering through its large uncovered window to watch a Mike Tyson boxing match on the restaurant's flatscreen TVs suspended over the long mahogany bar, where the bartenders wore Yankees pinstripe no. 7 jerseys as a tribute to the restaurant's owner and their favorite baseball player of all, even if he had retired three decades ago…and died at the fairly young age of sixty-three of liver cancer.

Rossi thought good restaurants like those were almost, almost, mind you, the city's apology for the plethora of crappy national fast-food chains that occupied every block. Including the ones like TCBY, Sbarro and even Taco Bell that were less common than the big three in flyover America.

Alas, Beefsteak Charlie's and Mickey Mantle's had gone the way of the dinosaur. And before it moved to a basement in Times Square, he even liked Hard Rock Café, but only at the original location on 57th Street, where one night he sat a few stools down the bar from Bruce Hornsby where he sat alone, when he was at the height of his popularity in the late eighties.

Not wishing to annoy him, Rossi resisted the urge to ask him to sing Jacob's Ladder at the piano that was a permanent fixture on the stage for live music, and left him be except for saying hello. But he thought he was tall and real cool. But now, after two-thirds of a lifetime of Ella's cooking he'd prefer it if he never had to eat elsewhere. And as long as she was willing to cook for him they had an amenable working arrangement.

And if he closed his eyes and imagined real hard he could smell the fragrant warm aroma of olive oil and garlic cooking. But maybe he'd take his shoes off first and put his feet up for a few before the dinner he could imagine was coming.

He knew as soon as he'd made the last remarks that he shouldn't have. He'd spoken rashly without thinking of the consequences. He hadn't meant for the statement to be evocative. But at the same time insubordination fit him as comfortably as a classic James Taylor song.

And he wore it proudly, like an old glove. The absolute last thing he wanted was to be accused of spreading a furphy, or worse, being mendacious. And for good measure, he knew he'd be called into a parley—otherwise known in the department as an ass-chewing—to be excoriated by the higher ups, and that his superiors at every level would gladly take their turns giving him hell about it; and the news folks would be quoting it back to him at the next press conference about the case, if, God forbid, they hadn't caught The Swordsman by then.

***

Out of habit, and drawn in by its bright blue and red neon Pabst Blue Ribbon sign in the window that's illuminated day and night, on the way home Rossi pulled his unmarked cruiser to the curb in a no parking zone being sure to place his laminated NYPD placard in the dash before stepping onto the sidewalk and past an old homeless gentleman before wending around an ancient shoeshine stand where if you imagined it you could hear the buff cloth pop, now used by the neighborhood bookmaker as his office while chain-smoking and taking the action; most often for Giants, Jets, Mets or Yankees games, to look at the specials handwritten in colorful feminine script on white paper signs hanging in the large windows of Mozingo's, the neighborhood Italian market sandwiched between a barbershop and a butcher-shop; across the broad avenue from a White Castle with a 'now hiring' sign in the window and a small neighborhood firehouse.

Mozingo probably got a discount on his insurance because of its proximity and ate White Castle burgers for lunch every day. If a Latino of any nationality owned the market it would be a bodega—that smelled of aged wood floors, of many years and a few oriental herbs, but mostly of fresh fruit and vegetables—which had never had a crime committed against it-not even petty thievery because no one would dare try anything nefarious against an Italian-named market, for fear of what violent strongarmed wiseguys—hooligans with names like Guido and Rocky, men with severe square faces like clenched fists and hooded eyes who, as if that weren't enough, look pissed off all the time—with whom he might be acquainted. People who took care of those kinds of abstract insults.

Old man Mozingo was a Neapolitan and had only one good eye. His wife was Sicilian. She didn't care that he only had one eye.

The story going around was he had been a local welterweight boxer of some renown fighting under the name of Kid Vittorio, even though with good Italian food and the passing of years he was now more the size of a super middleweight if not a light heavyweight; but suffered a detached retina and had to give up the fight game. But he would keep his one good eye on you from the moment you entered his store until he heard the bell over the door ding your departure. God only knew, with but a sole good eye with which to keep watch what he did if more than one customer was in the store at a time.

Rossi was glad the man chose to open an Italian market nearby instead of a bar like many prizefighters, following in the giant footsteps of arguably the greatest heavyweight of all time, Jack Dempsey, and his eponymously named midtown bar on Broadway, famous for its owner and for being a setting for scenes from the first and best Godfather movie.

He entered the stridently squeaky ancient door to a tiny ancient Asian woman holding it for him and bowing obsequiously while saying something indecipherable. He nodded his gratitude while smiling; would have tipped a fedora in a different era or if he wore one. She bowed deeper.

He guessed that somewhere among the assortment of Italian pastas the proprietor must have some egg noodles for his Asian clientele. Rossi didn't know if the woman or the intonated language she spoke were Thai or Filipino, other than knowing the two groups resemble each other in appearance more than other discrete Asian peoples. Of course, he wasn't an expert on Asian people or their languages.

One of the old derelicts had tried to follow him in, but all it took was for Mozingo to clear his throat loudly and give him a stern glare for the bum to reverse his course and exit hastily.

After Rossi entered, the old Asian lady left and pulled the door closed, shutting out the loud din of the city from the quiet calm inside the store; quiet enough to hear his own percussive footfalls on the ancient and scarred wood floor. And sealing in the miasma of succulent Italian smells. The store was somewhat, although not a lot cooler than the warm late June summer eve.

The man was most likely trying to keep his energy costs under control. Sitting behind the ancient cash register, reading the Daily News. He was near the back of the paper, probably the sports section. Checking the race results from Belmont out on Long Island. The News always had them first. Keeping his eye on Rossi at the same time. The man knew he was a cop, but it was a years old habit; he couldn't help but keep an eye on everybody.

The thought occurred to Rossi that New York's extreme weather changes from hardest winter's ill-tempered cold, so cold that it burned, and sometime traffic snarling maelstroms of snow-to summer's unexpected heat and humidity surprises many visitors. And the unmistakable smell of stables, unexpected in the city, where the NYPD housed the equine officers' mounts.

Rossi never did the actual necessary shopping; Ella, of course, was responsible for that, for him it was more of an entertaining impulse whenever the mood struck him and he would stop in the neighborhood market, look over the specials and pick up something. He'd have to remember for them to take a trip to Long Island soon to go to one of the large supermarkets to stock up on basics since there were none of the large stores in Manhattan.

The vermicelli and linguini didn't interest him; he knew Ella would have all the pasta she needed. Today, he was going to pick up a panettone—the small Italian bread-like cake with small pieces of candied fruits, raisins and almonds they both loved buttered and toasted, and a bouquet of orchids. Even if the fresh fruits and vegetables looked perfect.

Then, once home, he would walk in the door and become Salvatoré, no longer Detective or Rossi until he went back to work Monday morning. After over half a lifetime together their love probably wasn't as fervent, but it was deeper. He knew the little gifts would make Ella happy. Both were faves of hers. Now, thinking about it, he wasn't sure which would make her happier—the panettone or the orchids. That would be a tough call for almost anyone.

The smell of fresh coffee brewing almost enticed him to pick up a small white styrofoam cup with something illegible printed on the side, from the worn and wobbly folding card table set up as a comfortable small coffee station with all the ingredients needed to make it as all New Yorkers call it coffee-regular, and have some, but he decided he'd rather not delay getting home to the fine Italian dinner Ella was preparing. It wasn't a sense of urgency directing him, but an urge to start the weekend of good food, wine and relaxation that would cure him of his lassitude caused by the stressful week. Besides, he needed to stop by the dry cleaners to pick up his suit for Sunday mass. He didn't know what tricks the Chinese knew about dry cleaning but he was glad they did. Not only would his suit be clean; it would smell clean. And they put enough starch in his white shirts to suit him, and it built up over time, from cleaning to cleaning, making it even heavier. And Mr. Wu was always happy to see him. Grinning and bowing respectfully.

Chapter Fifteen

There was little to distinguish their grave-faced pre-WWII ziggurat building with a stab at an art-deco lobby that just missed the mark, and three painfully slow elevators—the self-appointed casbah appearing to command most of the block, wide, husky, fourteen stories, with a frieze above the entry, battlements for appearance more than their rich historic functionality and a proudly castellated and mansarded roof, with tall decorative pilasters that gave the appearance of sentinels on guard, ochre, or perhaps light brown turning to the very color now of the city's bedrock, from decades of the city's dust dirt and ash.

Narrow enrubbled alleys flanked each side of the building benignly. Nothing in each except dumpsters, rats the size of house cats and views of clanging rusting iron fire escapes attached to walls above. Rossi exited the elevator that sounded tired from age onto their floor.

Their typical for New York City four room apartment was the last one on the right. The neglected undecorated corridor was tunnel-like and narrow; dark in winter, dim in summer. The foreshortened uncovered window at the hall's end not bountiful enough to enlighten the always dark grayness.

One would never know Ella had been cooking by the innocuously stuffy stale smell of the nondescript featureless walkway like hundreds of others in New York, with the fading beige carpet at least where there weren't parquet floors, beige walls, beige ceiling; even if it hadn't been that boring shade when new, anything that had once been white had turned an innocuous beige from use and age years before.

The building wasn't terrible by New York standards, but not upper end either. It from the first half of the twentieth century; the neighbors on their floor, more than acquaintances; but not quite friends. Even the old Jewish couple down the hall told them they thought their Christmas tree was lovely the previous December. The longer they lived in close proximity the nearer they came to friend rather than mere acquaintance.

Tired from a long day at work, his verve waning if not replaced with lethargy, Rossi shambled slowly to the end of the forlorn stale hall, but home now, he looked forward to an early vespertine feast that he knew Ella would be finishing putting together. It was around 6:15 when he cracked the door gently and heard Ella singing softly, but joyfully, an Italian song of *amoré* that blended with the red gravy she cooked that poured out from the warm Italian kitchen and her warm heart. The sweet sound of her voice and the aroma of the Italian feast he knew she was preparing perked him up from his arrival in lethargy and his typically melancholy or pissed-off face, relaxed.

Rossi's trained detective's Italian nose impressive in size if nothing overly special in its ability, detected the warm scents of homemade red sauce, garlic and freshly baked bread that greeted him the moment he opened the door. And the wait from the long day was worth it.

Even though they didn't particularly need it, out of habit he wiped his shoes on the small doormat. Then handed Ella the panettone and bouquet of orchids he'd bought at the market. He followed that by hugging his wife lovingly then asked immodestly, "How was that for an abrazo?" He always said Moorish España and Italiano were practically one and the same. Unquestionably, two sides of the same peso…or lira.

"Orchids, you know how I love them, and the panettone, both of them. You're incorrigible. You must be up to something," she said, throwing her hands up suspecting he did something wrong he was trying to atone for.

"When did you get so cynical? You wouldn't love me if I weren't," Salvatoré said drolly, then, even more incorrigibly, said, "What? I can't bring my wife flowers and a panettone?"

"I think you were thinking of yourself getting a panettone."

"Alright, now," he said, feigning attitude.

Forgetting about where the questioning was going, she routinely asked him about his day. She could tell it had been a fairly good day. He hadn't been shot dead and she hadn't gotten a call telling her to race to the hospital. Those were always the best days in her mind. After all these long years she still worried about him and had told him countless times to be careful when he left each morning. In some ways she'd never gotten accustomed to being the wife of a cop.

He gave her a 'meh' answer. He knew that it was and the thought made him wonder why since he wasn't Jewish.

"Are you hungry?"

"What do you think?"

"I think you probably are."

"Good guess."

"I know my man."

He chuckled at that.

He took off his suitcoat, shook it and then draped it haphazardly across the arm of an unused scroll-armed clear plastic-upholstered red brocaded chair with a padded seat at the glass dining room table. He was glad the chair was padded so he could eat comfortably for as long as he wanted. New Yorkers in general and Italians in particularly covered their fabric furniture in clear plastic to protect it from stains.

A tradition passed down for generations. He then went straight to the fridge to retrieve a bottle of red, how all people who know their wines, keep reds chilled before opening it to breathe, being sure not to touch the old hob's cooktop where red sauce was coming to a boil in a medium-size sauce pan and careful to duck under the copper cookware she was so proud of that he'd bought her for an anniversary gift that hung from a metal frame that he'd installed in the ceiling of the typical for the city small but adequate kitchen.

Then to the living room, the carpet burnished with strips the width of the vacuum from where Ella had cleaned earlier in the day before getting serious about cooking, where sagging from his bulk, the cushion exhaled a huge fart of warm air as he dropped heavily down in his once-plush but near-antediluvian burly brown leather Barcalounger as old and squishy as overripe fruit, that sat waiting expectantly for him a tabouret next to it on which to place his glass of wine, across from Ella's fancy bergères upholstered in a fabric of red and gold, then pulled on the long wooden handle on the side to raise the recliner's tired leg support that groaned in unison with Sal before he loosened his tie and unbuttoned his shirt collar, before loosening the laces of his brogans and unbuckling the cincture around his waist in anticipation of the huge repast being prepared. The living room was overcrowded with furniture, framed pictures of children and grands and bric-a-brac. A double stack of novels, read and unread, sat on a hardback upholstered chair in a corner of the room next to a wall with built-in floor-to ceiling bookshelves that were original to the apartment.

The antique grandfather clock from Italy chimed, insistent in its purpose of everyone knowing it was seven o'clock. It was 6:15 when he walked in. And Sal thought about how happy they were there in their little home. The apartment was comfortable and well lived-in. Well-cared for framed keepsake photos of children and grandchildren covered nearly all surfaces and walls.

Relaxed and breathing deeply, he gazed meaninglessly at the dingy white wood molding between the wall that possessed the decorative iron heat register that was happy to be getting a much-needed summer break, and the ceiling. He left the tv off. The news would be on for a while. He certainly didn't want to hear about war in eastern Europe or the newest conflicts in the Middle East or any of that other shit. He didn't want it to be even a backdrop of white noise to their pleasant dinner and wine.

He could turn on the eleven o'clock news later if he were still awake and he felt a sudden urge to torture himself. Doubtful, after two fingers of rye and a couple of glasses of red. Then he turned on the Tiffany-style floor-standing lamp next to his chair. It gave off a warm yellow glow through the plastic trapezoid shaped shade in the slowly dimming room.

Slit the foil on the gentle yet bold bottle of red with the penknife that he always carried, and pried the cork loose using the waiter's corkscrew he picked up from the coffee table he referred to as a wine table, which he thought was way more accurate, where he'd mindlessly set it after putting it to use a few nights before. Reaching for his seldom visited but nevertheless familiar old friend, the cut crystal decanter of Basil Hayden's rye whiskey from a shelf behind him, while inhaling the wonderful aroma of red gravy, garlic and ground beef browning, he thought, life is pretty damn good. The beautiful decanter, and the fine rye it contained, warranted and deserved his admiration, The decanter didn't get a lot of use because he didn't drink rye that often, but it was a special eve when he did. Without a doubt there weren't many things better than a fine rye whiskey.

He retrieved a short highball glass from the freezer where one was always chilling and two glasses of their delicate fine stemware from where they were stored in the antique glass doored wooden hutch that had been bequeathed to Ella from her *nona* on her father's side.

Recalled by all who knew her as a mean, but generous, old woman. The glasses a purchase of their own when newly married. He gave them each a generous pour of the Chianti Classico; Ella's less generous than his own, of course, same as always.

Then, as an afterthought he went to the bathroom to brush his teeth in the event Ella was feeling frisky, and to take a Losartan for his high cholesterol since it was a given he'd be eating a lot of the offending foods. But fortunately it was the only prescription med he took, along with a daily 300 milligram aspirin on his internist's advice. He popped a couple of the aspirin preemptively as well; on the chance he might overindulge a little in red wine. A good idea since he knew himself. Nothing worse than a red wine headache.

Then pressed the switch on his Sonicare toothbrush and nothing happened, jabbed it harder, still nothing—so he used it manually like a typical manual toothbrush, trying in vain to hum Wagner's Ride of The Valkyries as he did. The expensive dental appliance had worked as advertised that morning, but now was deader than a doornail. He hoped it was the battery. A new Sonicare wouldn't be cheap. And he'd rather spend those precious dollars on a good bottle of Cabernet Sauvignon.

Propping up with one hand on the sink and brushing with the other, he stared at himself in the mirror dulled and clouded with age as he brushed, and thought he didn't look bad for his age and thought if Hollywood ever made a movie about him, who would play him. He hoped for Johnny Depp. He mistakenly thought there was a physical similarity. And that in mind, wondered to himself that if he got undressed and went to dinner unclothed if Ella would take the hint or if that would be too much.

After a moment of clarity and some clear headedness he decided that yeah, it would probably be too much and shook his head at his image in the mirror fixed to the wall, disbelieving he'd even had such a thought. But in the event it were to happen he patted some Old Spice after shave on his cheeks and put a dab on each wrist. The old school original scent, not the newer one for young men.

He knew he should take a shower but he didn't want to delay getting to the fabulous dinner that would be waiting. In the confines of the closed bathroom, he passed gas, hopefully not loud enough for Ella to hear because that would certainly be a mood killer. Must have been the Philly cheesesteak he'd had for lunch; but the act would serve to make him more comfortable for eating, and help just in case she was in the mood. Then put on his fleece-lined slippers. Might as well be comfortable on a Saturday night.

Ella had set a proper table using their fine china on their best linen, making it a special occasion and it wasn't long before she called out in a mirthful treacly voice, "dinner's ready," as he returned, while dimming the lights to enhance the mood. He loved her voice as much as the message it delivered.

It wasn't necessary for her to importune him. Ella was glad her Salvatoré was home. She felt as safe with him now as she did with her father when she was but a wee girl. She knew that nothing bad could happen to her when her man was around. And she was right because if anybody even attempted to do something to Ella it would be that person's last desperate act on earth.

Chapter Sixteen

The sultry temperature and the heavy dark clouds that hung over the city and resembled dirty cotton balls portended a summer thunderstorm and soon after the first intimation of aeolian rain advancing relentlessly began to lash the terrace in angled sheets from New Jersey, so heavy it must end presently, eliminating the necessity of watering the potted plants and flower boxes for a few days before it did, however.

Heavy rivulets of water like the legs of red wine in a large globe glass already sluiced down the sliding glass doors that provided a beautiful view of all of Manhattan to the north and gave out to the small north-facing patio even though by city standards it was quite large, an exterior addendum to the apartment to contribute to its total of just over two thousand square feet of usable indoor and outdoor living space-at least in clement weather. The lights of the city pulsed through the heavy gray Manhattan rain.

Discrete small puddles formed before coalescing into one patio-sized, and the sky changing from jaundiced to ethereal black, as the living room followed suit turning from curbstone gray to dark as charcoal as the temperature dropped a few degrees and the room dimmed, which seemed not only normal, but perfectly proper, after the front from the west, crossed the greenness like it always is of Jersey, provided primarily by a generous backdrop of deciduous trees and somewhat fewer bluish-green conifers, and except for the lights of Newark, before it hopped the Hudson leaving dark pregnant but diaphanous clouds on the surface and was now hammering Manhattan.

So heavy you could taste the rain's smell. Sal thought that even inside it smelled fresh, a faint rumor of the pine barrens in Jersey that had left its aromatic scent on the downfall as it blew through. As a happy byproduct at least it would chase the mosquitoes away. And besides it was still much better than ten inches of snow out there like the previous winter. The late afternoon losing the battle with nighttime's dark. Ella liked how the lights of the city reflected in wet streets during a heavy rain. Torrential rain and thunder though, made their four-year-old grandson and Sal's namesake nervous. She wished he were with them now. Sal didn't belittle his feelings, but he thought their grandson was much like many native New Yorkers who became depressed when the city was dark and wet.

Ella always seemed younger and happier when she was doing something she enjoyed for her beloved husband. Her paragon of a man; good provider, husband, father, nonno and respected NYPD detective. Indeed, they had learned to wear each other well and they carried their love for the other everywhere they went.

Ella wore no jewelry except for her wedding ring. A conservative slim gold band. Sal had offered many times to buy her a huge gaudy diamond to wear with it, now that he could afford it, but she would have none of that. "Nonsense," she would say, "I love my ring."

She was cute in a commemorative navy-blue tee shirt with "Broadway" in sparkling silver script splashed across the front. Her hair pulled back in a band for the cleaning she'd been doing earlier. She had bought the shirt at the production of *"Rent"* she'd attended with her oldest friend from parochial school days before matriculating at the famous Jesuit school, Fordham University together. Since uni days they'd been virtually inseparable. They'd arrived early at the theatre so they could have two glasses of Chardonnay apiece purchased at the lobby bar before the production began. Not enough to get them drunk, just enough to put them in a delightful mood to enjoy the show. It must have been a wonderful girls' night out.

They still talked about it. And said they needed to do it again. They were thinking about *"The Phantom of The Opera,"* or even *"Pagliacci,"* at The Metropolitan Opera. They like the musicals best. Sal not as highbrow as Ella, he told her she owed him a Jets game now. She had responded by making a face that made it obvious how she felt about that. He told her that wide receivers were as graceful as ballet dancers. He didn't think he convinced her. At least the Jets had a modern new stadium with all the creature comforts for the fans now. It's not like they still played in the ancient polo grounds far up by the Harlem River like they did when they began their run as the New York Titans. Wearing blue and gold before their now iconic kelly green and white; back then you might have seen Jackie Gleason, Frank Sinatra and Toots Shor at a game...together.

Sal moaned while rising from the recliner, and said "Thank you, Lord," dramatically, as he stood with the two glasses of Chianti and gave credit to whom it was due for providing what his wife had cooked, as he made the sign of the cross. A challenge with the wine glasses in each hand; but the effort nonetheless given up to the Holy Father.

Sal thought he was not concerned about eating too much on this night while he eyed the table laden with the delicious Italian delights and inhaled the wonderful aroma, and in fact, said, "I think I look good with a few extra pounds." In truth, he was like most Italianos who liked indulging in their native dishes and he would never be thought of as being an ascetic.

But at least his Kevlar second chance vest still fitted him; if and when he needed it, and he hoped he never did. But he'd tried it on recently just to make sure. Truth was he'd put on about ten pounds over the last year, but as long as he didn't do that every year he'd be okay. And if he'd just cut back on the cheddar cheese everything bagels he felt sure he'd be fine. Or easier for him, just give up the cream in his morning coffee and have it black.

"Of course you do," Ella said appeasingly, or so it seemed. It was easier to agree with him than to hurt his feelings since as a typical Italian he was sensitive.

Sal practically snorted some of the last swallow of the fine rye through his nose, surprised by Ella's good-natured agreement. Always concerned about his health, typically she would have taken that opportunity to lovingly chastise him.

Before sitting Sal asked, "would you like some music, my dear? I can turn on the radio. You know the public station plays

Mahler-my favorite; the great Italiano composer Verdi, Debussy, and occasionally even some by the euphonically exquisite Chopin and Liszt on Saturday evening. And don't forget to send them a donation, by the by." He pronounced it "rahdio" like it was done in his home country of Italia, where indeed the device had been invented by the brilliant Guglielmo Giovanni Maria Marconi.

"I won't forget; and no thank you, but I might enjoy some nice light jazz." It the music of the city or at least of 1950's black and white noir New York City crime films on old tv.

Sal found the best station for jazz on the old school tabletop stereo console, then moving on, sat at the dining table and lifted the large globe wine glass to his lips and resisting the urge to gulp it, gave the Chianti Classico a cultured sip then held it aloft toward the ceiling light, and tilted it from side to side to examine the color from every angle. While Sal wished for the music of Satie, the smooth-voiced nighttime deejay announced that the selection beginning to play was from Ramsey Lewis' album "Tequila Mockingbird, and of the same name.

Ella said, "You should get an iPad for playing music. That stereo is so out of date it's embarrassing."

"Look at that beautiful purple hue," Sal said tilting his glass to the light and ignoring her comment, at the same time, knowing she was right, before casting a quick sideways glance her way before taking a flirtatious sip while looking forward to a glass or three with dinner, then maybe a vodka martini or a snifter of brandy after.

"You're such a wine snob," said Ella. In truth she wasn't as enamored of the bottle as was he.

"I know. And I wear it proudly," he said unabashedly. "Since it's part of my heritage. You know, being Italiano." Although, in truth he preferred the term epicure better than snob.

"Yeah, that's what you always say," she said gently and with all the sweetness of which she was capable. "I'm Italian too, remember?

"One of my more likable qualities if I do say so myself. And of course, I remember, dear."

She ignored his first comment.

Ramsey Lewis stopped playing and a cut from the great pianist, Bob James' album Heads, took his place.

For the most part they ate with little conversation. Nothing like if the kids and grandkids were there. Then it would be an Italiano crazy house. A whirlwind of tornadic madness. More often than not, he relished their time alone together. At other times it was too quiet to suit him. After thirty plus years together he knew they didn't have that much longer and he didn't want elegies sung for him and that's when the somber quiet would begin to get to him. At the same time he didn't resent the youth of others.

He'd spent the greater portion of his life with his love and he was good with getting old; but that was one of the reasons he thought he might like a dog. Probably a sweet mixed-breed female and call her Pearl like the private detective, Spenser's, in the late great Robert B. Parker's novels. One Sal could scratch behind its ears when he needed comforting. Ella frowned on him scratching her behind her ears, even when he needed comforting. He was quiet with his thoughts. Of course what did he know from dogs? What do they eat? When do they nap? How do you house-train them? He knew Ella would never put up with dogshit all over the house.

He thought about retirement; not that far off, and how he'd like to buy Ella a house; nothing grand, just a small house with an above ground chlorine-scented turquoise-colored swimming pool with a screened in gazebo next to it out on Long Island. Maybe encircled with privets; make it especially homey. She'd like that.

Above ground pools were about the only kind people installed in New York and New Jersey. If one were on final approach into any of the area's four international airports—most people forgot about Stewart International, or didn't know of it forty miles up the mighty Hudson from the city's center and its better known three brethren that surrounded the metro area, or even into Teterboro on a corporate Jet—the bright clean turquoise ponds could be seen in backyards all over the two states. The more he thought about it, he was fairly sure that with the way New York real estate prices were constantly on the rise that they could sell their apartment for a healthy profit and be on their way.

And maybe he could open a bar; he always thought he'd like to tend bar. At least it would keep him out of Ella's hair and give him something to do in retirement; as long as he didn't drink up all the profits. He was of a mind that if retired boxers could open a bar then certainly a retired NYPD Detective could. He wasn't sure what the logic was in that but he thought it sounded good. And if he bought a house with a fenced yard he could get a dog. He thought he'd like to have one. Not a pure bred; just a mutt; but one with a good temperament. Happy to be part of a family.

Ella could plant rose bushes. Her favorites-yellow ones. Tend to them while she sipped her morning coffee. She'd like that. She said the yellow ones were more fragrant than other colors and she always said she liked the way the morning dew collected on the gentle petals. And the grands would love using the pool when they came for a visit. And he could teach them to swim and dive from the attached wooden platform at the side. If only he still knew how.

He probably could only do belly flops at this point. He unfortunately had the thick waistline required for it now. It had been a long time since he was a kid and went swimming in Bronx public pools filled with all of the other joyous loud summer children. Summer felt and smelled like stoopball then, between school years, before they had to grow up, and get jobs. Get serious and make their families proud.

They enjoyed their dinner and quiet evening at home together and turned in early to sleep since Salvatoré's long week of work had finally gotten the best of him.

***

Late in the eve, Bookworm kept one eye on the news report also, while the other eye scanned the talent around him. Parked on a stool at the bar in a crowded upper west side watering hole only a short block from Tom's Diner, the real-life Monk's from the great *Seinfeld* tv show. A little further away, south down Broadway, stood The Dakota at the corner of Central Park West and 72nd St; sadly infamous for being where the former leader of the Beatles, John Lennon, lived and perished in the breezeway of the building, after he was shot and killed by Mark David Chapman who had waited a few days for his target's appearance and just the right moment.

The saloon would never be mistaken for a prohibition era speakeasy since a bright neon sign that read 'BAR', illuminated its doorway brightly and made it too easy to find; he watched a typical police drama without sound on free tv on a small flatscreen hung high in a corner over the bar, easy for inebriated eyes, while he sipped a Cuba Libre made with Coke Zero Sugar, unknowing that that was a new product name, changed from the original Coke Zero, while others at the bar tippled the latest and greatest trendy alcoholic concoction.

Bookworm even knew the most interesting story of how the Cuba Libre was invented; a part of his self-acquired education while at Princeton. The part acquired in taverns and beery pubs. Bookworm still wished his bar tabs had been included as part of the tuition that had been covered by his scholarship since he learned much in those charitable and amenable places of knowledge.

The story of the Cuba Libre had been told many times over by drink aficionados for over a hundred years. 'When a U.S. soldier stationed in Cuba who, while in a bar, poured some rum into a glass of Coca-Cola and ice with lime and toasted his Cuban comrades at the bar by saying, "por Cuba libre," to a free Cuba, and with those few words a legend was born.' And at the very least it's a better toast than the infamous line that's not nearly as clever as the inventor thinks, 'Champagne for my real friends and real pain for my sham friends.'

The ice in the drink Bookworm unconsciously spun on the bar top was mostly melted, and watered down. He didn't much mind though, since it kept the glass fuller longer, kept him from drinking as much, and wasn't as strong. Furthermore, drinking was something he had to do to pay rent on a stool at the bar. And it gave him something to do to keep his hands and mouth busy. Except with the ice melting he could no longer crunch it.

It was a different crowd late at night than the thank-God-it's-happy-hour crowd. Mostly dates late. Mostly people looking for dates early. And it would be busy until the city's legal three a.m. closing time on a Saturday night, an hour earlier than other nights.

Bookworm was thinking about his future professionally and likewise, Reefer's while he gazed at the tv not really paying attention until he recognized his friend, Detective Rossi's, scowling mug. "Turn it up. Turn it up," he all but shouted, without thinking, at the bartender. Before that he'd just about made up his mind that he and Reefer should open a private detective agency instead of continuing to work as lowly informants. He was pretty sure Reefer would go along with the idea. It looked to Bookworm like Rossi'd cut himself shaving that morning.

Seeing him on the tv screen, gave Bookworm the passing thought that he'd never thought before, that Rossi resembled the great but in Book's opinion, under-appreciated character actor, Oliver Platt, one of the stars of the frightening movie, *Don't Say A Word*, based on the critically acclaimed novel of the same name by the brilliant author, Andrew Klavan. Bookworm had loved the book. In fact, thought it the author's finest work.

The bartender, exhibited a healthy dose of Gotham City attitude, that he hoped was similar to Batman's and acted as if he felt like he had more important things to do than cater to a customer's tv watching desires, when he practically threw the remote at Bookworm, and said, "turn it up your own damn self."

Bookworm didn't even notice the bartender's attitude. Instead, noticing the dour look on Rossi's face that he'd seen before, he thought, damn, he doesn't look happy. It was definitely not a look that one could mistake for affable. And he wondered if Reefer was watching it. Eleven o'clock on Saturday night. Not damn likely. Unless like Bookworm he was watching it on a tv over a bar. If he knew Reefer, and he did; he was partying the night away. Bookworm would call him in the morning; didn't want to interrupt him now if he was doing anything…or anybody…interesting.

Chapter Seventeen

Before long Brody returned to the sleep of the dead, or at least the dying, literally, and dreamed of blood, severed heads and gutted eviscerated bodies, the norm for him, until Saturday Night Live came on.

He was excited to hear the opening chords of the song *Murder Incorporated*, by the iconic show's musical guest of the week, the Boss, from right across the mighty Hudson, from where he'd probably taken a stretch limo—New Jersey's own Bruce Springsteen, when he was awakened again. Brody found the grim song refreshingly inspiring.

He left the tv on for the white noise, sound, to sleep by. And as his tortured mind began to drift, wondered why they constantly repeated the same commercials over and over again ad nauseam, for months, or even years.

After the two beers, he got up once about three a.m. to take a piss, and returned to the couch instead of going to the sad bed. The couch had conformed to his body and was cushy in all the right places. And sleeping on the couch instead of the sofa helped him to think it was a temporary situation.

Chapter Eighteen

Well-rested after a sound night of deep sleep, Salvatoré rose not exactly energetically, but with nonetheless more enthusiasm than he had anticipated, with the first gray light of the peaceful new day. He liked walking to mass on days like this. It reminded him of walking to mass with his parents when he was but a small boy. The previous night's pelting rain that had helped him sleep had ended, but an early morning antisocial gray murk remained.

The pregnant full moon in all its buttery yellow glory. The aroma of garlic and red sauce from the previous evening had dissipated and he could smell the delicate fragrance of the orchid now. At least he could until the aroma of fresh hot coffee began to fill the apartment.

Being careful not to wake Ella he started it brewing, then, still dressed in his usual sleepwear of Yankees pinstripe athletic shorts and a dark blue NY Giants logo tee, went to the patio French doors and gazed north over the Manhattan skyline he loved.

She would be happy to wake up to the fresh hot smell of caffeine that she didn't have to brew, especially without the klaxon-like sound of her cellphone alarm going off. Although she liked her spot of hot sweet tea—usually two cups—on special occasions-like Christmas morning. And making Ella happy always worked in his favor.

He regarded the northern view, quietly contemplating the brightly lighted Empire State Building, its slightly shorter but nevertheless just as impressive Chrysler Building, its polished silver façade fashioned from the hubcaps of old sedans and coupés, the early morning sward of the green meadow of Central Park, the vast gloomy dark reaches north of those, the bright lights of the Bronx piercing the dark, still further north.

He absorbed them all. He never tired of the view. In the early morning dark and quiet he thought the city turned from a busy fast teeming city of energy to a peaceful idyllic place of peace. Except for the ever-present red taillights from the cars that never stopped.

Stars sparkled above in the still early morning. A perfect Sunday morn dawning to shape the ones to come. In the early morning quiet Sal thought about the citywide blackout of '77 when he was just a kid. He was too young to remember the first one in '65; he was barely a newborn, although he remembered his parents talking about it. Talking about how hot it was with no air conditioning; his mom worried about looters and other thugs on the prowl because of the lights being out. He recalled that in '77, the only brightness was the pinpoints of light from the stars above. The city as dark as a tomb.

Ella rose and started cooking oatmeal for breakfast—and not that single serving instant packaged shit, either; real honest-to-God cooked oatmeal. With real butter and sugar and cinnamon; the only time she let him have butter or sugar. And after two cups of coffee each and enjoying the quiet time together they took showers to ready for mass. Not together because Ella knew if Sal got worked up in the shower they'd never make it to mass on time. She had to put her foot down occasionally.

They loved walking to mass together on the pleasantly gray Sunday morning although Ella had to take two steps for every one of Sal's because of her short legs. And he would take her hand like when they were young. He wore his freshly laundered Sunday suit, a pocket square adding a hint of levity.

Going to mass was as connate as breathing to Sal and Ella and was as spiritually satisfying as it typically was to the pair; soul nourishing.

The homily was what they had needed to hear. The message that life is wonderful but brief. The even better life that followed in Heaven indescribably more wonderful. Rossi had to admit in his moments of deep contemplation he looked forward to the next life, the better life. One with no mugs, or killers. He loved his career in law enforcement but he looked forward to the afterlife without all the shit.

Then they partook of the body and blood of Christ. The best part of the celebration for them both.

Chapter Nineteen

Returning home after mass, Rossi retrieved his gun-cleaning kit from the upper shelf in the hall closet. He always cleaned and oiled his department-issued weapon, a dark menacing-looking 9mm Glock model 19 with two magazines, on Sundays after attending mass.

He was unable to see any irony in attending mass and then cleaning his weapon after. It was an hour-long chore and habit that was years in the making. He made sure to perform the necessary task even if it hadn't been fired, which was usually the case, unless he'd been to Rodman's Neck Firing Range in the Bronx, which he typically did once a month.

Even if he hadn't it couldn't hurt to break it down, clean it and make sure it was in fine working order. Unless it did hurt if his hand got bitten at some point by the slide slamming home. It was unfortunately an occasional hazard of being conscientious. But a pinched thumb was far less painful than getting killed by some two-bit mug and that could be the difference. A thorough cleaning could literally mean the difference in life and death. And it always seemed like it was a new weapon after the necessary chore was done.

Once completed there was nothing left to do on a Sunday afternoon especially if there was a Mets game on tv. Except they sucked this year and so that might be the worst thing to do to screw up an otherwise pleasant Sunday afternoon unless you had fortitude plus a really good attitude.

Of course, according to his father baseball was forever changed when the sainted Dodgers left the cathedral that was Brooklyn's Ebbets Field and decamped for Los Angeles, lousing up the Bronx forever as his father had put it. The end of the Bronx as it was known. He hadn't even known what the word *louse* meant even though he could tell it wasn't good. How in hell could they have done that? Indeed, he knew it was a rhetorical interrogative. And the New York baseball Giants left for San Francisco the same year adding salt to the wound. Both teams cited the inability to turn a profit as the reason for the moves. Claims that were hard to swallow in the huge New York market. Of course he was way too young to have ever been to any of the games at Ebbets Field or even to the original Luna Park at Coney Island, or to have ever drunk any Fleischmann's vodka while chasing it with a beer. Even though he remembered seeing young men drinking it from the bottle while sitting on their stoops, showing how grown up they were. And even the Saturday Review of Literature had passed. Never to be missed or even considered since. And he was way too young to have been to the Saturday afternoon movies when newsreels showed black and white news updates from the war in Korea.

Chapter Twenty

Brody didn't have a headache when he rose Sunday morning. Two beers were no big deal for someone with as much experience with alcohol as he. In all truth, he considered himself to be a competitive drinker.

He awoke with the intention of visiting a local gin joint he knew, Punchy's, in the afternoon. Punchy's real name was Angelo, and he had been a pugilist, a prizefighter in another age. His nose had been broken more times than he could remember, and it looked like it. Fancied himself another in a long line of great Italian boxers like Marciano, and though not as hearty, actually bore a similar physical resemblance to the former young heavyweight contender, Gerry Cooney, except for his prominent chin.

The resemblance ended there as it turned out, since although large, Punchy's appeared to be made of crystal rather than the iron like that of former heavyweight contender Randall "Tex" Cobb whose chin was considered to be the strongest of all time, and was considered a requirement to be a contender. But all he could do was flail away at other down and out early undercard palookas in nearly empty venues and drink, so when he got too old to fight anymore, he turned to what he was still able to do and did best, anyway-drink, and what better place to imbibe, than in your own gin mill?

Punchy himself became famous, at least in his small Brooklyn nabe, for the clever saying he came up with on a particularly busy Saturday night when feeling frustrated and pissed off by the crowd, he asserted in reply to an impatient customer, "I can only serve one asshole at a time."

As it was, the bar was as sad as his wretchedly failed boxing career; dark, disturbing on many levels, dirty, drunk, a place of muted lost dreams, and no soul. It wasn't often a place to see patrons passed out drunk on the floor but to see someone with his head at rest on his folded arms on the bar did, on occasion, happen. But stay out of the filthy facilities if you could manage. It was better to go in the parking lot and run the risk of getting arrested for indecent exposure than to step in the shit—sometimes literally, on that floor. 'Course most of the cops were cool and would look the other way if one happened to see you unzip and drop trou. The dingy beige walls adorned with mostly black and white cheaply framed boxing photos. Of Punchy and the fighters he fought. At least half of them pugilists that kicked his ass and helped him to earn his nick and lend it to the eponymously named bar. And invariably a drunk would start to pose like one of the fighters in a photo, or start throwing jabs and hooks in the air, hoping to show everybody in the bar what a badass he was. And hopefully for him he wasn't challenged to prove it.

Unusual for a classic New York bar, the on-duty workers kept country music lamenting and coffee brewing in a classic Bunn coffeemaker from before the pub opened until after it closed.

Even if no one ever requested a mug, the reverent aroma of caffeine helped to disguise the smell of dirty carpet soaked with sour whisky and God only knew what else; the typical sick smell of blue-collar workers' bodily odors redolent in the joint, as well.

Then occasionally, mostly during winter's numbingly frigid months, someone would ask for a mug of steaming coffee flavored with bourbon, or if they thought they were hotshots, rye. Fortunately they didn't have too many of those assholes. The capricious pungent fragrance of grass contributed to the same masking affect as the caffeine.

An antiquated eight track stereo with inadequate speakers provided a horrible but nevertheless loud din that some had the audacity to call music even though it was of somewhat less than questionable quality and none of which would qualify for the Great American Songbook. Punchy's was an establishment of the kind which made you want to drown your sorrows, or worse, yourself.

Before opening the eponymously-named bar Angelo had thought about taking up cage fighting or Mixed Martial Arts, but decided that would be akin to jumping from the frying pan into the fire, so a gin mill had been the next and probably smarter, or at least healthier, choice. Brody liked the place because it made him feel better about himself. He thought the bar itself and its usual clientele were even more troubled than he. On this day the crumbling remains of a white-frosted birthday cake most likely purchased at the small bodega down the block, graced the top of the bar. What was left of someone's celebration with their bar family.

Brody always thought himself a self-aware man and sufficiently cognizant to know that his clothes wouldn't allow him to fit in at one of the multitude of high end yuppie pubs or fern bars in Manhattan, but for a dive bar in the more than a little blue collar Brooklyn he knew he'd be okay. Its usual clientele was typically bikers who wore all black and leather with long beards and covered in ink, but they accepted him more readily than the usual habitués of Manhattan fern bars and taverns. Probably because they sensed that he, like them, was an outcast.

And they comforted themselves with domestic beer and shooting pool on one of the two green felt-topped tables in the back or playing chess on a black and white marble board and ivory pieces that seemed conspicuously out of place sitting atop a whiskey barrel in the front window of such a blue-collar establishment. But only to people who were judgmental. As it was one could watch two of those blue-collar patrons staring at the chessmen crafted from ivory aggressively matching a knight with a knight. As committed to it as if it were the Jets vs the Giants.

Brody dressed in non-designer loose fit Wrangler jeans, although brought up old school in Brooklyn he still referred to them as dungarees; a white short sleeve polo-style shirt, but one without a logo, neither crocodile nor pony, since he couldn't afford logoed brands. He was so old school, or maybe that was too cool; maybe old-fashioned was a more accurate description, that he would still shop at Filene's Basement if it were still in business.

He would never have been accused of shopping at the upper crust Bonwit Teller. The polo-style shirt came from either Wal-Mart or Sears; he couldn't remember which. And cheap no-name imitation leather boat shoes without socks. He wouldn't be accused of cutting a dashing figure; certainly not like an honored CBE-

Commander of the British Empire. More accurately he looked like a blue-collar member of the International Brotherhood Of Electrical Workers, which was accurate, because he was. Try as he might, he couldn't recall the last time he wore a necktie. Probably when he got married going on fourteen years before. He thought not wearing socks made him look cool. What he didn't realize was that while that might have been true twenty years before, or thirty even, now it just looked out of date.

It was good, he thought, though, because she had bare legs under the brightly-colored, flowery cotton sundress she wore, held up by thin shoulder straps, and aided in their task by her ample chest. The thought crossed his mind that his bare ankles went with her bare legs which were longer than the longest day at work.

He had one pierced ear, his right—he'd done it himself with a sewing needle, and it had hurt like a motherfucker; no matter what you heard. He didn't know that no self-respecting man would wear only one earring. NFL players had been wearing diamond studs in both ears since the early nineties. But one was cheaper than two, and besides his was a cubic zirconia, because it was a helluva lot cheaper than a diamond and virtually nobody could tell the difference. And even if he could have afforded the diamond he would have bought the cz because it would make him proudly think that he was putting one over on people who thought they were so smart and better than him.

And he thought that was funny as shit because he was cheap and lacked class. But he was a self-aware man. At least he had that much going for him. Which, even he admitted wasn't much, although better than nothing. At least he knew what he was.

He knew he didn't overtly look like a killer, not hinky in the least. But he knew he looked blue collar. But New York blue collar which was different from southern blue collar. And he knew that most killers looked like killers. And one could substitute the word losers for killers. Except for Ted Bundy. One of the most prolific killers in U.S. history, who was over the top handsome and intelligent and used that to his advantage to lure unsuspecting smitten young women into his deadly clutches. Clever, soft spoken and articulate, Bundy was anything but the stereotypical serial killer. But he was literally the only one that bucked that trend. Think John Wayne Gacy Jeffery Dahmer Albert Fish Richard Ramirez. Each psychotic pieces of shit (and looked it); the main character trait they had in common.

So Brody's somewhat attractive but nevertheless average looks worked in his favor to help him to disarm people, most of all women, when a vicious monster with the basest of intentions inhabited the inside. He was a self-aware man, and he knew that his anything but serial killer looks helped him to do what he did. Of course he didn't want to be known as but a killer of women. It would serve to make him too predictable and even more importantly, cause skeptics to believe he wasn't badass enough to kill men.

Couldn't have anyone think that. It was important that everyone knew how badass he was.

Chapter Twenty-One

By the time he was ready to leave in the late afternoon however, he had changed his mind about Punchy's and decided that some Mexican food and a couple of Margs would be just what the doctor ordered.

One had to be choosy about Mexican food in New York. Particularly for the well-being of one's stomach. It was not like it was as good as the TexMex one would enjoy in the southwest. And wasn't something the city was known for like the ubiquitous slice or bagels and lox.

Sited conveniently for him. not far away, on the white beach just inside the western limit of Coney Island, discovered by the great explorer Giovanni da Verrazzano, and only six miles from the massive bridge named for the man, where nothing was far away since the famous resort island that was no longer an actual island since the silting of Coney Island Creek in the 20s and 30s and is only four miles long and a half mile wide, he would go to one of his occasional spots. The Taco Shack. It appropriately named. The owners hadn't intended for it to be a dive bar when they'd envisioned it, but it was slowly evolving into one. Transforming before their very eyes.

It had probably been more than a year since Brody'd been there, so if an opportunity arose it was unlikely that anyone would recall seeing him. A special treat for him, Brody only liked Mexican food occasionally, not like those damn Texans who ate it every goddamn day; unless they ate barbecue.

The 40's era white-shingled small composed bungalow that had been remade into a restaurant and was in need of a fresh coat of paint and a few gray wooden roof tiles replaced sat on the edge of the omnipresent arid sandy soil, was anything but fecund. There were a dozen cars in the white seashell parking lot with grass that sprouted sporadically like an old man's sparse hair through the porous surface. Mostly newish imported small SUVs and sedans. Except for one shiny fire engine red Porsche 911. It truly pissed

Brody off. He deserved one. But he wasn't going to hold his breath waiting until he got one. That would be an exercise in futility on an HVAC repairman's meager wages.

He made his heavy entry and the apron of broken oyster and scallop shells with the occasional crushed soda can crunched loudly under the car's tires. Brightly illuminated neon signs that read Tecate, Modelo and the ubiquitous and as American as apple pie, Miller Lite and Bud Light, illuminated the restaurant's windows dark in the brilliant late June sunshine.

The worn front door looked like it was original to the cottage but had been carelessly painted a heavily-lacquered cheerful vermilion. There was no other door like it in all of New York City proper. Attesting to its age, the door squeaked stridently in protest when it was opened. Competing with the the pounding of the surf and the nautical sound of buoys dinging off the shore.

Inside, even though it was in New York, it smelled like a Mexican restaurant should smell; the aroma of chili, tacos, jalapeño peppers and beef and bean burritos was welcoming. But, sited on the beach as it was, all of the delicious Mexican aromas were seasoned with a hint of the cheerless salty sea.

A grinning, slightly pudgy—probably from eating somewhat more than a little too much good Mexican food—Hispanic man with shiny straying black hair and an almost nonexistent receding chin in his mid-forties, possibly the owner, maybe the manager, greeted him at the entrance with "*hola, mi amigo*; good to see you again," and after Brody asked him for a seat at the bar, that had formerly been the rear wall of the cottage sitting on the flagstone patio, his back to the soulless charcoal Atlantic Ocean he was led to the rear and opted for the second stool he came to at his occasional place. It wasn't that the personable man really remembered Brody. He greeted all customers in that welcoming but sincerely sounding manner in an attempt to make them feel like they really were south of the border. Even in New York.

In addition to being a pleasant place to enjoy his afternoon, sitting in the sunshine allowed Brody to leave on the sunglasses he wore along with a New York Yankees traditional dark blue ball cap with the iconic white NY logo as his sole disguise so that people wouldn't think it curious that he would wear them indoors and pay him unwanted heed. The opposite effect of what he wanted to accomplish. He'd gotten the cap as a free giveaway on baseball cap promotion night at Yankee Stadium a couple of summers before. Funny because Yankees caps were standard headwear for serial killers. Even those in Kansas or Tennessee. The team must get a kickback of some kind.

The giveaway had been the only reason he'd gone to the game to see them play those goddamn Baltimore Orioles on a hot August night. That and the cheap right field bleacher tickets his boss had given him for having the fewest complaints of any technician for a month. Which in itself was unusual, since he typically had the highest number. So it really had been a celebration of sorts. Especially considering the copious amount of beer he drank.

The walls of the darkened dining room that he was able to see from his position in the bright sunlight were adorned with framed pictures of seagoing fishing vessels. Appropriate for a seashore restaurant, even if it served Mexican food solely. Besides, they had fish tacos and it's possible someone, even an employee, might have caught the seafood fresh with a pole.

The water of Long Island Sound, on the bay side of Long Island, would be fairly peaceful. But not the ocean side. The sky was the color of dishwater. Same as the jaundiced sea. Hard to distinguish between the two where they congealed at the horizon. The marine world, sea and sky, blurred. Like a hundred summers before. True enough, like the first summer, at the edge of the world.

The crashing and salty fresh ocean waves brought as they were on the levanter, undulated as they came off the North Atlantic after making their way from their genesis where the tilting sea said farewell to the shores of France, Portugal and Spain; as loud as they were strong was good for the soul and renewed him spiritually— hard as it is to believe, even serial killers need their souls to be renewed every once in a while, and it felt pleasanter than the eighty-eight degrees the thermometer on the wall conscientiously reported.

Sixties and seventies rock and roll from expensive weatherproof outdoor Bose speakers provided the contrapuntal sound and the bass line to the gusty north wind and the boom and roll of the surf. Not Brody's preferred music, not by a long shot, but he knew most people with little imagination liked it. Except for *Caravan* by Van Morrison, and anything by Steely Dan. He thought they really killed it. Especially on *Your Gold Teeth II*. And *Rose Darling*. Classic bangers that still slapped if there ever were any.

But then, he thought the songs were about him. And even though they weren't they would have been had the band known him. And he knew Steely Dan required a nuanced ear of which most people weren't possessed. The infusion of pop, jazz, and rock and roll an interesting mix.

And Brooklyn's own Simon and Garfunkel-especially on *The Boxer*. Nothing else had to be said. And Queen, but only…every song they did at Live Aid, but then they had Freddy Mercury. So how could they not be great? A rhetorical question if ever there were one. It wasn't possible for them not to be. Of course when he thought of the great Brit bands; The Beatles, the Stones, Queen and the Police, all among the greatest of all time, Brody had to wonder if it was something in England's water.

The restaurant wasn't full but had a decent enough Sunday afternoon crowd with most in groups of three or four clustered around slightly dusty textured tempered glass-topped tables on the large patio and two couples sat at the other end of the bar. Most of the customers anglos or African Americans.

Young, successful, beautiful New Yorkers enjoying the rewards of their success on a beautiful early summer Sunday afternoon; the pleasant warmth and fresh clean scent of the season making itself welcome on the patio. The small terrace had a brick fireplace for those cool early summer evenings dining, and drinking, al fresco. A derelict brown dog of indistinguishable heritage was stretched out on his back on the temperate stone surface hoping for a benevolent handout or at the very least an accidentally dropped tidbit, or worst case, a belly rub. His presence was so commonplace people thought he belonged. Brody felt sorry for the wretched animal. His proximity to them, warily accepted by the crowd, but not a part of the crowd.

Two men, both fortyish and dressed blue collar with fresh sunburns were nearest the dog. One wearing a dark skinny necktie that looked out of place around the collar of a short sleeve shirt. Neither really fit in with the rest of the crowd. One said with more than a little minor selfpride showing,"and don't forget; I have a CDL and a clean driving record." It sounded like a job interview and he was trying to persuade the other man to hire him.

The smell of the freshly mown swords of grass, on each side of the patio—where there wasn't heavy sand—was pleasingly fragrant. The only organic scent since the sandy soil wasn't conducive to growing flowers. The shell, sun-bleached gray driftwood, and mollusk-covered sands of the white beach appeared hopeful, hopeful that summer was here to stay and it would never feel the cold again.

Seagulls danced playfully overhead squawking and barking like dogs, while hoping for scraps. All tables had nearly empty red plastic baskets of chips and small bowls with varying amounts of salsa remaining in the centers of their flowered Mexican tile-topped tables and mugs with differing levels of Margaritas. Probably mixed with Herradura tequila for those New Yorkers blessed with deep pockets. Most with rims encrusted with salt, or for those less urbane tipplers, but who how-so-be-it, nevertheless thought they were, sugar.

The Margarita, indeed the ubiquitous drink of all Mexican restaurants. Comical to Brody, because he worked with some of the ethnic variety as he considered them, who he knew that if they drank alcohol, most Mexicans drank cervesas and that Margaritas had been a creation to satisfy the tastes of predominantly Caucasian Americans. Most of whom would finish them greedily. Half empty or half full depending on one's level of hopefulness, or hopelessness. But in the end weren't they the same? In a philosophical or a psychic distance sense? Or more than philosophical; transcendent. Whatever the sense, nevertheless cynical. Although, when pondering depths of tequila, it was without even a hint of profundity. But, in a way, similar to the dreaded great abstruse final exam question all college students of the Philosophy 101 course faced: "Why?" The answer: "Because." Never to answer "Why not," as that was not an answer, but a contradiction. And the professor vainglorious shan't, under any circumstances, be contradicted.

Large screen tvs hung over each end of the bar. Tuned to ESPN showing Major League Baseball. Proof again that sports are the lowest common denominator among your typical bar patrons.

Sitting a couple of stools down the open-air bar from Brody was a comely but not overly attractive woman of around his age— the perfect type for his needs. Drinking a beer in an icy heavy glass mug; cold perspiration running down its tall glass sides. Probably an authentic Mexican cerveza; a Modelo or Dos Equis.

Her best feature were pale azure eyes the same color as the briny unhesitatingly warm Atlantic behind where they sat. New Jersey's favorite son, The Boss' *Born To Run* blew up the stereo. That was more like it. And he was practically a New Yorker, him being from right across the Hudson as he was.

"How you doin'?" Brody said, reminiscent of one of the comedically unhip guys in the early nineties Bud Light commercials. He sat one leg crossed over the other, ankle on thigh, so she could see he wasn't wearing socks and hopefully to him, think he was cool. He never had been known for being particularly good with women. But nonetheless, she tilted her head down at her lap and picked at a piece of lint before blushing appropriately.

Then he ordered a Margarita on the rocks. He preferred frozen but he was almost sure they wouldn't have a machine to make the icy concoction due to the exorbitant cost for a small local resto.

The youngish middle-aged African American male bartender

was six feet tall, long limbed attenuated frame and he wore a do-rag in New York Knicks blue and orange with the NBA team's famed logo. And keeping with the whole coastal summer moderately warm weather vibe he wore faded frayed denim cutoffs, a green tank-top with Taco Shack silk screened in white over the chest, a shiny gold ankh on a matching bright gold chain hanging around his neck and centering the shack, and yellow rubber flip flops.

His right upper arm was decorated with an Omega Psi Phi raised tattoo. It looked like it had been painful when it was done. Brody was a fan of the Knicks dreaded enemies to the north; the Celtics, even if he did mispronounce Celtics with a soft "c" instead of the hard "k" sound like was done in the old country. He didn't really know why he was a Celtics fan, but had been since he was a kid. But he wouldn't give the man any nevertheless good-natured shit about his Knicks do rag since it might not be conducive to getting as substantial a pour.

The bartender was congenial, like all good bartenders and would have looked right at home in Florida or the Caribbean Islands. Ice cubes fell loudly down the chute of an industrial strength ice maker into a metal tumbler and obviously not his first rodeo, he used a long-handled shiny silver spoon, to quickly mixed the drink; then gave it a quick but thorough theatrical shake and poured it into the iced glass mug. Then slid the heavy salt-rimmed clear bowl glass with green petals across the unblemished shiny aluminum-topped bar.

It was still early, only a wee bit after five, but Brody suspected that even on a Sunday, that it would get busier in the next hour.

After he delivered Brody the most important thing a thirsty customer wants—a drink, the bartender returned with an aged menu of stiff white paper given to yellow from use with both cursive and block red print depending on the item described and someone's idea of marketing, and bright white paper-sleeved silverware and an aged menu of cracking and stained stiff white paper given to yellow from use with both cursive and block red print depending on the item described and someone's idea of marketing

Almost without thinking, Brody plucked a thin tart lime wedge from the heavy glass rim, and squeezed it over the huge mug before coolly dropping it into the icy concoction. Used his straw to give it a perfectly insouciant swirl, then lifted the heavy glass, tilted it in his cohabiter at the bar's direction, and said, "cheers," and after waiting gentlemanly for her to return the greeting, took a healthy swallow and said, "that's gas," before setting the now not as heavy glass back on the bar. She watched his Adam's apple bob up and back down. He knew from a couple of the overly cool brothers he worked with that "gas" was the same as "good," and thought that using the word would make him as cool as they. As if a word could make one cool. But he wouldn't know that.

Brody wouldn't require the silverware since he ordered a bowl of queso with ground beef. He didn't know how some people could eat the melted cheesy dish with jalapeños. He calculated it had to be cultural. Maybe if one was from Texas you craved the heat. Otherwise, he couldn't understand it. He actually didn't mind their taste but the heat from the damn things made his sinuses drain like crazy. Probably because he's a native New Yorker.

The bartender returned in moments with the popular dish that was obviously prepared in anticipation of the requirement.

Brody dug in eagerly. The young woman cast a sideways glance at the bowl of queso, making him feel guilty, or at least he was sufficiently aware to make out that it did, but it gave him the opening he'd wished for.

"You're welcome to have some," he offered, between poor mannered mouthfuls.

"No thank you. I really can't."

"You really can. In fact, you really must. I insist." he avowed in a way he hoped was charmingly cute, or at the least engaging. While she was making up her mind, he took a large chip from the basket, dipped it in the invitingly warm cheesy dip and without moving his barstool across the rough concrete, leaned close to put it in her mouth. He was confident enough in himself to be sure that she would have to find it a delightful, or at the very least, a sweet gesture. She was surprised by the intimate move, but it apparently worked, nonetheless.

"Alright, then. But only because you insisted." And some might consider that offer acceptance proof that the butterfly effect changed...and shortened, her life dramatically. And it would be possible they would be right.

"It's settled, then," he said wiping his mouth with the paper napkin instead of his usual sleeve, before he slid the bowl of queso and a red plastic basket of chips down the counter and scraped his barstool's metal legs loudly over the concrete and flagstone patio annoying everyone around them, to join her.

I guess she hasn't heard the song Heathens, by twenty-one pilots from The movie Suicide Squad*'s soundtrack, and it's seriously frightening line "you'll never know the murderer sitting next to you, you'll never know the psychopath sitting next to you" or she'd be more cautious about talking to strangers, but in her defense, nobody is. Thankfully for my sake.*

"This would be good with jalapeños," she said, unaware of the internal debate he'd had with himself only moments before.

Without comment on the observation, he said, "I'm Gage. Gage Brody." It didn't concern him to give her his real name since he was pretty sure she wouldn't survive the afternoon.

"Pleased to meet you, Gage. I'm Alice."

"On," he said surprisedly, "and is this Alice's Restaurant?" he asked, with a dumbass grin, giving himself more credit than it warranted for his attempt at being clever.

"Good one. Corny, but still pretty good. And nobody's ever tried that one on me before, so you get points for originality."

"Thanks. I have a lot of practice at being corny. But truth be told I never much liked the song."

"Yeah, me neither. Although I do like Dylan. I just never thought it was one of his better efforts."

She thought Gage came across as kind of cute without trying

too hard. In a harmless goofball sort of way. In fact, Brody had practiced his nuanced manner to put others at ease, which most serial killers did. It was an acquired skill. Much like that of developing one's personality, which he did as well, to enhance his ability to procure victims; male and female. And if the serial killer gig didn't work out he could always become a Baptist preacher. That canting thought was always good for giving himself a laugh. An altogether chuckle without mirth, however.

They spent the next hour sharing queso and chips and enjoying their different but nevertheless traditional Mexican drinks while making pleasant conversation. Serious talk, then light-hearted. Politics then movies. Something and nothing. Brody didn't have to say much. He knew that the only thing most women wanted was to be listened to. To think that someone thought what they had to say was important.

An unmuffled 70s muscle car on the beach road made conversation difficult for a moment, but only for a moment. As they talked and ate and drank and talked some more the patio and the beach became less crowded by the moment from people unenthusiastically departing on a late Sunday afternoon to ready themselves for the coming work week. The lonely beach becoming lonelier without its temporary guests. They going back to the city for the week of work ahead of them.

They polished off the queso and as she took the last delicious swallow of her golden cerveza, Brody said, "It's not as crowded now. How about we take a nice stroll on the beach?" Who knew? Maybe he'd find enough privacy to make it a double kill weekend.

Or even stumble across some buried treasure; it left behind by the pirates of a different era and guarded by the skeletons of those created by the infamous pirate, Captain Kidd, who wouldn't trust their formerly living counterparts to know where it had been buried. Everyone had heard the rumors of the treasures. Only the exact location was a mystery. True though it might have been, alas, wasn't that always the case?

"I have an even better idea. I took an Airbnb summer rental not far down the shore. We could go there and walk on the beach. Or stay inside," said Alice with a gleam of naughtiness in her eyes.

"That is a much better idea," Brody agreed. He thought to skylark on the beach sounded delightful. He could imagine only one thing else that sounded better.

Chapter Twenty-Two

"I'm in the white Miata. Follow me," she said, while pointing toward the little convertible she thought mistakenly was cool, with its cloth top lowered for the comfortably clement weather, in the parking lot. New Yorkers do like their convertibles. To New Yorkers convertibles were a make of car, no matter the manufacturer.

After laying cash enough to cover both tabs under the edge of his now empty mug, Brody followed her at a distance to the little Japanese-made two-seater. Didn't want to call undue attention to them leaving together.

He gentlemanly opened the small car's tiny door and kissed her, not passionately, but real. She did the same.

I'm getting the idea this might turn out pretty well, Brody thought.

He returned to his crappy car where he'd stored his hori hori knife. He was beginning to feel good about it being a two-kill weekend. Although he was still somewhat more than circumspect about doing the deed in his own borough, indeed so close to the house where he lived. Alice waited before pulling out onto the busy afternoon road for him to follow.

She had been right. It was less than a mile down the beach road in need of repair, in little traffic; a couple of family cars and small SUVs, past a 60s era convenience store—swear to God, Brody thought he could smell the stale dirty water hot dogs turning on the steel rollers as they passed by, and an iconic green and white Hess gas station; he, Leon Hess, the now deceased, much-respected former owner of the NFL's New York Jets, indeed he even decided the team's uniforms should be of the same green color as the great man's service stations—before they made a left turn into a small neighborhood of rather cute, but uninspired fifties era beach bungalows. Well-kept, not moldering.

Fortunately for Brody, late on a Sunday afternoon, most of the houses appeared empty. The majority of the summer residents, or vacationers, already making their way back to the city. The cottages waiting for their next impermanent resident.

Third cottage on the left into the driveway of an extremely haimish well-kept rental. Brody thought it would serve him well as an abattoir, and a temporary house of slaughter. It would only have to serve the purpose once. The skills Brody had learned since becoming The Swordsman had served him well. Served to keep him from getting caught thus far.

Of those acquired skills, choosing the right victims and the right places in which to do the deeds aided him in keeping from being nabbed. And ironically, the nabe that would become his next killing ground was not that far from the Howard Beach home of the late mob boss, John Gotti, he, the murderous head of the Gambino crime family. Not far in distance, perhaps, but miles apart in status. It was somewhat more than a little unlikely that he and any of these homeowners in the modest neighborhood had run in the same circles.

Brody watched from his car while she dug in her purse for a key to unlock the door. Success—she stepped inside and the stoop light came on even though the subdued summer sun was still visible in the low sky over the tall buildings of Manhattan and the barrens of New Jersey beyond. He snaked out his deadly blade from its place of safekeeping in the pocket of the passenger seat back and slipped it carefully in the waist of his jeans at the small of his back.

The door closed behind her as she entered, but by the time he got there she was opening it, then locked it behind him. The home wasn't a mess but it wasn't tidy. Like it didn't belong to her so she really didn't care. It looked like what it was; a temporary vacation rental and she wasn't expecting a guest.

"Welcome, Gage," she said, formally.

"Thank you, Alice. I'm happy to be in your home and not your restaurant," he said.

"Groan," she replied, then, "but a man has to be funny for me to be physically attracted to him."

"Is it working?"

"Let's just say you're getting there."

Brody grinned sheepishly with the acknowledgment that he was getting there.

"Would you like a glass of wine? A nice persuasive Chardonnay?"

Then, without waiting for his answer, she said, "Alexa, play some soft jazz."

The music started. Brody didn't know where the Echo Dot was. He'd heard about them but he'd never seen one. The music sounded like it was from either the Taxi Driver soundtrack or a seventies porn movie. It was a tossup.

"I'd love one," he lied in response to the question of Chardonnay. The truth was he hated the effeminate shit. He hoped the look on his face didn't betray him. Moreover, if it weren't for light beer or Margaritas he'd have to seriously consider giving up drinking. He knew however, that wine would probably work to make her more compliant, and if it helped him to get in her pants then he'd find a way to get the disgusting shit down.

As it turned out it it wasn't as gut-wrenching as he'd thought it would be. But he was just as sure it would never become a habit.

They finished their large glasses and Alice said, "How about that walk on the beach? The sun is setting and it's a beautiful sight." The beach not far from where Kramer, on the uber-popular Seinfeld comedy, while practicing his golf drives over the ocean, hit one into a giant whale's blowhole.

"You read my mind," said Brody.

"Delightful."

True enough, it was delightful when she forewent the sliding glass door to the patio and the white sand beyond, and instead took him by the hand and led him to the bedroom. The room was comfortable but nothing special. A little old world for his tastes. A small flowered-fabric suitcase, obviously part of a feminine set, lay open on the floor, clothes draped over it where she'd been searching for the perfect outfit. Through a door to the bathroom stood an old-world tub with claw feet from an animal of undetermined origin. After jerking the tarnished brass chain to turn on the ceiling fan she slid open the double French doors beckoning one out to the small paver patio and Brighton Beach beyond and to allow the fresh smell of the salty summer ocean breeze to enter at will.

Alice's body was more attractive than her face and she was an intense and enthusiastic lover. He felt sure it was the first sex she'd had in some time. The soft jazz playing in the background gave the whole experience the feel of a 1970's era low quality porn film. And this was no sweet lovemaking.

They ripped each other's clothes off and tore at each other manically. He'd had to surreptitiously remove the knife and slide it into one of his shoes beneath the edge of the high bed where he'd haphazardly put them.

Neither thought it anything more than it was. A physical release. But he'd felt obligated to make it good for her even if she didn't know it was the last sex she'd ever have. If everybody thought that way when they had sex everyone involved would be happier.

"Wooh," she exhaled as she fell back on her back, sweaty and spent, and watched the ceiling fan above the bed spin and greet the ocean breeze from the open French doors to the patio. The fan hadn't done much to keep them cool. But at least with the pleasant sea breeze the air in the room wasn't stale like in a house that has been closed up between vacationers.

"I agree," breathed Brody as if it were his last. The truth was, it felt like a religious experience as they listened to the surf crash on the sand.

Brody leaned over the edge of the bed to gain his knife. Alice still on her back and mesmerized by the languid ceiling fan's ticking, the last thing she'd ever see. She didn't give heed to what he was doing. The Swordsman raised up in Brody's place and had to focus, focus on what he was about to do since the eerily ticking fan was distractive to the point of setting his nerves on edge and reminded him of the somewhat lesser known but nonetheless great

classic rock and roll song, *Ticking*, by Elton John, about fourteen
people murdered in a Queens watering hole named The Kicking
Mule. The song an inspiration to all killers, even though Brody was
sure that wasn't Sir Elton's original intent. And rather frightening
for local people when considering the song, since Queens was but
a short drive away from Coney Island's fairytale-like make believe
world. One that most people who had never been there, could never
imagine.

Even closer than Queens, stood the 24-hour Midnight Rose
Coffee Shop and Candy Store full of delights for children, and the
purported headquarters of Murder, Incorporated, the execution
squad for all of the mob's families which operated each afternoon
where they would wait for a call to come to hire their piano-wire
garrotes or deadly icepicks, with which they might stab a victim
more than fifty times.

From 1929 until 1941 they waited at a bank of pay phones on
the rear wall of the store situated beneath the Brooklyn El between
a hat shop and a hosiery store, above the store a Chinese restaurant;
Rose's run by an unassuming less than five foot tall spinster lady
with wispy white hair in her upper sixties called mademoiselle by
the gangsters as an unkind joke to her advanced age, Mlle. Rosie
Gold, even though it was probable that she wasn't even aware of
the fact that mademoiselle meant young girl, and of the joke they
made at her expense, and indeed, unknowing, thought the deadly
killers charming rogues.

Today, a bodega with refrigerated coolers filled with mostly
regional sodas of all flavors occupied the same wall. And unlike
the Bruce Springsteen song named for and inspired by the infamous
gang of killers, the Midnight Rose Candy Store wasn't fiction. Yet,
the bodega that had once been the candy store wasn't the only thing
different about New York's boroughs from that different era.

No Italian or Irish wiseguys nicknamed Jimmy Whiskers,
ironically bestowed the nick because even as a forty-year-old
grown ass man it wasn't necessary that he shave, since his face was
as smooth as a newborn baby's butt; Adonis The Greek, shortened

to Donny, although nobody would have dared to call him that to his face, and, so called and funny as shit to everyone except his sainted mother, since everybody knew he was a wop; or fat Joseph, Joey, Cannoli. No doo-wop singers under the fog-shrouded bleakly lit streetlamps or circling an oil drum fire on every corner around which huge icy flakes of snow swirled in the deepest of winter months, and heard when good folks were supposed to be in bed.

But that was another simpler time. Now, some would say the city had no personality anymore. But it was safer, even with the occasional maniacal serial killer haunting the 'hoods. Yet cold even in summer; though that was psychological.

Those not even as frightening as the real and true story of the haunted murder house from the movie, The Amityville Horror, only a few short miles east; based on the story of the Lutz family who moved into the house a mere 13 months after Ronald De Foe Jr shot and killed six members of his family in 1974 and left only a month later leaving all of their possessions and claiming that the house was haunted.

The fan's ticking was driving him crazy. And with every tick there was a flash of a blade shadow flicking around the room. Tickticktickticktick. No tock counterpoint like with a windup clock. Only ticking. How could it not drive one crazy? Even someone sane. Of course, to Brody, those were rhetorical interrogatives. He knew he couldn't be compos mentis. And he felt confident that that would be his defense if he were ever captured. Which seemed somewhat less than inevitable with each passing day and each horror committed.

When The Swordsman plunged the dagger into the hollow space in the center of Alice's ribcage and gutted her to her throat, blood and viscera erupting to cover all, her only reaction, not even a soft plaintive wail, but momentary shock in her wide open but unseeing dead eyes; focused on the ceiling fan still rotating slowly. Seeing nothing; or if she did she didn't let on. Not even the ticking of the ancient fan.

He spoke her name to the desecrated remains of the reposing

body, but there was no answer, no answer at all except for the inconsiderate and disrespectful ticking. The body already growing clammy. The veneration with which he'd performed the heinous act made it appear sacramental.

Except for him having to leap out of the way to avoid the messy raft of blood and bodily fluids and detritus for it to cover the pale purple flowered and green leafed summer sheets. There was nothing sacramental about that. Theatrical, perhaps in a twisted sense of worldview.

The sound the blade made when he buried it in her body turned him on. And the smell, the sanguine smell of the dead that erupts and then worsens to something else with the minutes passing. The smell that veteran homicide detectives say they never get used to, and don't want to, since doing so meant you were a step closer to losing your humanity. The Swordsman had grown accustomed to and even decided he liked it. It exciting him. Indeed, if she were still alive he'd be ready to go again.

But he would never do anything sexual with a dead body. He wasn't a necrophiliac. And since he murdered men as well, he absolutely wouldn't consider doing anything sexual with a male body. Not like that worthless piece of shit, Ted Bundy, who sometime returned hours or even days later to have sex with the bodies of the women where he had disposed of them, although he did admire how prolific Bundy was and the multiple movies he'd inspired.

The end goal of every killer to follow him, because he was the most successful U.S. killer and generally recognized second worldwide only to Andrei Romanovich Chikatilo, the infamous Soviet serial killer, The Butcher of Rostov, the killer and rapist of a known fifty-two innocent women. Even though it's difficult to know how accurate the numbers are from other countries.

Brody could only dream. Unless he stepped up his game his numbers were positively pedestrian compared to those two determinedly resolute men. And thinking about Bundy made him realize their names were similar; five letters, two syllables, starting with the letter "b," ending with letter "y." Maybe it was a sign; his destiny. Even worse, in his mind, than necrophilia; was cannibalizing parts of the body. And from his research and game planning his kills it was surprising to him to learn the number of killers that were into that. He might be a vicious killer but he was only a killer; he wasn't a totally sick son of a bitch. At least that's what he told himself. That he had limits. Of course he didn't know what those limits were, yet, and he didn't completely know himself; but he was aware of himself, and he was working on the other.

And for the moment at least, that would have to do. And like virtually all serial predators, he blamed someone else for his problems. For some, other kids were to blame; for bullying, teasing, abuse.

For some, many of whom were adopted, it was both adoptive parents. In fact, once arrested, many of those killers attempted to pursue a defense based on adoptive-child syndrome, claiming that adoption occasioned their mental illness. For most however, including Brody, since his father was often absent due to excessive drinking at whatever low rent watering hole was convenient, it was their mothers.

In Brody's case, his ex-wife also had to shoulder some of the blame. A thoroughly emasculating bitch if there ever was one. And though most of these psychopaths had certain childhood traits in common, including the big three; torturing and killing animals, enuresis and arson, also known in the psychiatric community as the MacDonald Triad, named for the man who popularized the idea; along with the addition of stuttering. Brody didn't want anyone to think he was afflicted with enuresis, commonly known as bed-wetting, not after age five at least, since that would be an embarrassment of which there could be none worse.

In fact he couldn't recall a single time he'd ever pissed his pants. He felt sure he must have when he was little, but he nevertheless couldn't remember it. Decades of research of serial killers by the FBI and in the halls of academia shows that virtually all serial killers had unhappy childhoods, with alcoholic fathers in common, and most suffered forms of abuse, whether sexual, violent physical, or emotional, or all three; if not the sole cause of their especial behavior, at least contributing to it. And a majority of whom were also childhood bedwetters, which sometimes lasted into adolescent or young adult years. True in fact, psychiatric studies of killers had determined that childhood problems are the biggest influencers of their psychopathic acts. And Brody was confident his childhood and familial problems would serve him well as a defense if and when he was arrested for his grisly crimes. If nothing else, even being sentenced to life in a mental institution sounded much more appealing than lethal injection.

It was too bad he hadn't thought to bring along a cheap raincoat to protect him from the deluge of blood and other somewhat less than pleasant bodily excretions that occur during or immediately after the act. But it would have been difficult to explain its purpose in the becoming sunny weather or when about to have sex.

She might have thought him a deviant. A sexual one, anyway. Mustn't have that. Might ruin his reputation. There was no doubt she was dead. The Swordsman withdrew the knife from whence he'd buried it to a macabre sucking sound. He liked the sound, too, but it didn't turn him on.

At least killing her in the manner he had and not attempting to take a trophy meant he needn't concern himself with carrying along a Hefty garbage bag to put her head in for carriage. Of course that took no imagination or creativity at all since virtually all serial killers use them for that purpose.

Besides he wasn't a sick son of a bitch, like that asshole, Ted Bundy, who would decapitate his victims and keep their heads in his refrigerator for a while. Although he could see himself taking something small, like a bracelet or earring as a token remembrance.

It would help him to recall all the lovely little details of the event warming him on frozen winter nights. But then, if the item were noticed as missing, ergo, some might think him no more than a petty, or even a grand thief for whom things went sideways. And he couldn't have that, since his image was more important to him than anything else. In fact, ultimately, once it all came to pass, he wanted people to understand that killing was his passion, nay, an ineffable higher calling. Kills were something to be done with verve when it's something you love.

In truth, killing was bigger than Brody. Something he had no choice in. It held him captive in its barbarically depraved grip. Although many used it as an excuse to elude incarceration or execution by claiming psychological problems; like many serial killers, Brody felt like a demon had inhabited him since he drew his first breath.

He'd been hardwired to be what he was. And when he considered that, he had to feel proud, special; that out of all the babies born in the world that day, that on that occasion, the smiling specter stood close to his crib and chose him to inhabit.

That had to mean he was special, unique, didn't it? A demon without soul, intelligence, measure, imagination, or order had chosen him. Likewise, a demon neither darkness nor light, neither error nor truth. Beast nor burden. Just being. Even so, killing didn't bother him in the least. In fact it was an event to be celebrated. Something that had been preordained when the demon entered him. What he didn't know was when or how it would manifest itself.

What he couldn't have known even if he had had the mental faculties of a man, was that the past dictates the future, so his future had been determined for him from the moment he was spanked on his bottom and screamed his first breath.

He'd lost his humanity almost before he was born. Indeed, by being born, with no choice in the matter, he'd made a pact, signed an unrelenting contract, with evil. A compulsion he could no more change than one could change the ineluctable seasons, or the tides.

Undeniably, such constancy was a good time for a beer.

A celebratory one at that. Unless he were to have a champagne cocktail. But he hated that shit. Most of all he hated the goddamn bubbles. They gave him gas. Unless it was the real thing, from France. He'd had it once, at a bachelor party, and he could actually force it down without gagging.

He needn't have to worry about her identifying him or describing him to investigators. He had no idea how long she would bleed. Stabbing someone rarely killed them immediately; it caused them to leak to death. Leaking blood. He never stuck around long enough after to find out. Since he always needed to get the hell out of Dodge. But he suspected she'd bleed for twenty minutes or so. It also depended on the position of the body in relation to the sanguinary abuse.

Brody was calm, surprisingly calm. Sometimes he frightened himself at how calm he was when he committed these little transgressions as he'd convinced himself to think of them. He wiped the frighteningly ugly and now gory dagger clean on the sheets, then jumped out of bed and hopped around alternating on one foot then the other while trying to pull up his snug slim fit jeans and buckle his belt at the same time, looking much like a man trying to pull on his britches and, hopping across the rear lawn, trying to escape from an irate husband.

Finally getting his jeans on accomplished uneventfully, he then tucked the knife in the waistband. The typically unflinchingly cold blade was surprisingly warm from the sanguinary mess that had covered it but moments before. He had to move fast.

Now for the most important part of the evening. The fun over, it was time for the work to begin. The part every serial killer likes the least about what they do. Wipe down every surface he touched or might have touched, the body unincluded among those only because he knew it was damn near impossible to get fingerprints off of skin—whether dead or alive—and slip out unnoticed by snoopy neighbors. It definitely was not his first barbecue.

He knew it could be easier said than done. There were always snoopy neighbors. Although they probably considered themselves dependable or reliable. People you could count on if needed. The Swordsman shook his head at that. And unless any of them noticed something untoward it would be at least the next morning before her absence was noted; when she didn't show up for work. So he was confident in his work and exit.

Finished with the cleaning job which included wiping down every surface he might have touched using a handful of paper towels and a bleach-based disinfectant spray cleaner he'd found in the cabinet under the kitchen sink, which he knew from experience was best for eliminating even a paucity of DNA or blood-type evidence that might be used to identify him. Even the minutest details overlooked were what could get you caught. That's why he never overlooked them. He then put the wad of damp paper towels in a pocket of his dungarees for safekeeping, then pulled the curtain back slightly and peeked out the living room window to take a survey of the 'hood. It not dark yet, but soon to be.

A kid was riding past on his aged and rusty faded but formerly red bicycle—probably a hand me down from his older brother or an older one than that—going deeper into the neighborhood. The innocent sight caused Brody to pause and ponder; ponder whether kids still clothes-pinned baseball cards to strike the spokes to make the pedal wheelers imaginatively sound like motor bikes. Probably not. He didn't think today's kids were that clever, or bought sports cards. Although they came free in bubble gum packs when he was a kid. Of course that probably wasn't done anymore, either. Besides, kids today only entertained themselves indoors with video games.

Across the street and one house further down, an octogenarian woman wearing a wide-brimmed straw hat with a wide colorfully-flowered ribbon encircling its crown was on her knees in the dusty brown dirt a trowel in her bony hand tending her flowers around the white painted mailbox post, doing her quotidian chore. Roses mostly; a variety of colors and hues. It would be hard to avoid her notice, if in fact she could see sufficiently well to remember him. And fortunately for him, that seemed doubtful at worst, impossible at best. And it was highly unlikely that she knew car makes, years and models. Especially twenty-five-year-old shitty Hyundais like the one he kept mostly because nobody would notice it. Or even colors. If it were full dark she certainly couldn't see him, but then it was unlikely she would be doing yard work if it were dark out. But one never knew.

Oh well, he thought. All in, he made the decision that there was no time like the present and to leave through a side door to the carport; shorter distance outside and he hoped, less conspicuous.

The last thing he did before opening the door was to slide the hori hori knife back into an ancient appearing baroque black and brass decorative metal scabbard, obviously a cheap copy, much like the dagger, itself, and then slip it into the waistband at the small of his back and make sure his shirt was pulled down to conceal it. The fancy sheath had been unnecessary since no one could ever see it but himself, but he had fallen in love with it and had to have it. And of course, like most of his purchases, a cheap replica and not the real thing, so he could justify it in his mind.

Brody moved as fast as he could scurrying in a crouch without running, figuring that should attract the least amount of attention. In the shitty old car, Brody fiercely exhaled an incarcerated breath. Then inhaled the sweet aroma of sex that clung to him still. He smiled at the pungent smell. He still wasn't safe though; he only allowed himself a moment's hesitation, in an attempt to slow his loudly percussive heart. The only sound he heard, the thump-thump of his own life source.

Now to drive away slowly, not attracting attention. Still, the sound of shutting the car door and turning the ignition caught the elderly blue-haired gardener's ear if not her eye as she paused long enough to smile and give him a neighborly wave. He guessed that that was a quaint habit from another era, however, and that she would never recall what he looked like or anything about him. At the very least that was his hope. A lonely dog making its presence known, barked in the distance.

A gloomy white and somewhat insubstantial scythe of a moon similar to the shape of a slim peeled banana and not far from its color, had already begun its rise in the pallor of the fieldstone gray of early evening gloaming; moody light summer clouds floating by heedlessly.

The bright lights of Coney Island, two miles away, where every night of the year looked like Times Square on New Year's Eve lighting up the nascent dark; to outshine the early evening stars, the tiny motes of brilliant light that were even brighter than the streetlamps. Even without the titanic lighted tower of Dreamland, since the world's largest amusement park burned to the ground in 1911. The people, burned red skin and smelling of sweat and suntan lotion after a day of strolling the enchanting boardwalks without a care among the creation from the previous century; taking a break from chasing the illusory American dream if only for a day, earnest in their leisureliness to forget, forget the rent, the power company bill, grocery bills —alas, without a parade of elephants making their way to their showplace as in days of old or even the one elephant, Topsy, electrocuted and killed by Thomas Edison to prove that his rival, Nicolai Tesla's, alternating current system of electricity was too dangerous for people to use.

Many of them not alive but not yet dead, like the black-cloaked mythical Count of old. A state merely between existence and not being. Plodding along in resigned recognition. Not that any of them appeared anhedonic lacking the ability to enjoy even the simplest of pleasures; moreover, quite the opposite; they were doing their best to experience pleasure in the face of the reality of life. All while recognizing their unavoidable lot in life. Lost people in a lost place.

A stoop-shouldered elderly couple holding hands for physical and emotional support shuffled along deliberately, cautiously, enjoying the day's last remnants of the warm June sun; while on the other end of the spectrum, and life; a young couple on a date sat on a rough concrete bench making out, oblivious to everything going on around them-even unhearing the screams of delight and fright from the world-famous Cyclone, the second steepest wooden rollercoaster in the world.

Like Brody, everyone doing what they must to survive. Though, hopefully unlike him in his particularly morbid gruesome manner.

And unless hit by the unexpected summer nor'easter, less common than its winter counterpart, a nor'easter snow bomb, it looked like Coney Island was set for a record-breaking summer attendance, even if some New Yorkers preferred Atlantic City, or the AC, as they referred to it. Famous for its magnificent casinos and Lucy the Elephant, the six-story tall hotel structure that had been drawing tourists to the Jersey shore since 1881.

Coney's hoped for record attendance would be aided in less than a month, by the annual Independence Day Nathan's Famous Inc., hotdog eating contest. The original restaurant still standing where it had for over a century, since 1916, from which you could smell the welcoming delicious aroma the minute you stepped off the fetid subway. Coney Island was not a place to be if you found a relaxed backwater comforting.

Chapter Twenty-Three

Alice's remains were found after she didn't show up for work on Monday and her mother tried to call her on her cell phone for a day and a half with no answer. She didn't want to seem like a hysterical mother, but Alice always showed up for work and always answered her phone and when she didn't her mom phoned the police who discovered the body while performing a welfare check.

Rossi coordinated a canvas of the neighborhood. And as was typical, nobody reported seeing anything out of the ordinary. It was not as if they weren't being honest in their efforts to be forthcoming, even though the cheerful reception they were given belied the results they were getting.

Not even that there should be scanty evidence, but Rossi well knew that most people do not pay heed to events outside their own circle.

Department experience told them that ninety-five percent of what wits tell you is inaccurate. A witness could have been drinking, or stressed over something, or old...or all three. That's why he tended to be circumspect when it came to trusting eyeball witnesses. And to question them gently, never sharply; especially the elderly ones. However, it was SOP and so had to be done even though he had learned from experience to disregard virtually everything he was told. Which made it little more than an academic exercise. And he used his iPad to take notes because he could easily delete them and waste not even a single valuable sheet of paper in his spiral bound notebook.

Except for an elderly woman in the house across the street who told them she had seen a nice-looking young man, not sinister appearing or menacing in the least, as she described him, leave the house on Sunday evening, get in his car and drive away.

But then again, it might have been this very day, she said wringing her hands.

And she was unable to describe him, or his car, anyway, she said, proud of her contribution, but at the same time, sounding disappointed with herself. Her recollections somewhat less than concrete. There was nothing spurious about her reveal. Just that it was somewhat limited by eyesight, memory and age. The crepey skin of her face stretched tight over the skeletal aged bones.

The tweedy elderly woman, Mabel, was probably in her eighties, and as thin as a perp's alibi, white-haired, and looking somewhat less than fetching even though she'd applied more rouge than usual for television, but still wearing her wide-brimmed straw gardening hat and a dirt-stained cotton house dress that fluttered in the steady ocean breeze that she smoothed with a bony hand shaky with age, while puffing on a cigarette hanging from her anguished mouth. Then hacked up a grating raspy cough and wiped her mouth with the back of the same worried hand.

The lonely old woman was now being interviewed on camera, an audible tremor of nervousness in her nicotine-affected voice, basking in the uncommon glory of her fifteen minutes of fame on the Tuesday evening news even though she had nothing to contribute to the investigation.

Though her words were elegiacal, her eyes were most likely more alive than they'd been in decades. That's not unusual. She had used her landline—she didn't even have a cell phone yet—and phoned everyone she knew to tell them to watch for her on the eleven o'clock news; that was only three people. She had told herself that if she lived another year she might break down and buy a cell phone.

Rossi squirmed with uncomfortable embarrassment for her given that she didn't have the wherewithal to be embarrassed for herself. The interview concluded, he dialed Bookworm. "Dude, we gots to do something," he said urgently into his cellphone. He couldn't help himself, but when he talked to Book it occasioned him to attempt to talk street. And Bookworm had to do street on occasion solely to make sure he hadn't forgotten how, lest people believe him preppie.

People would be totally aghast and their heads would almost certainly explode to hear a brother speaking perfect King's English as well as Bookworm. And he definitely didn't want to be responsible for people's heads exploding. That would get ugly…and messy. And even though he wore the coveted Princeton pedigree and the accompanying nous proudly he certainly could not abide anyone disrespecting him for it. It would tarnish his street cred, irreparably.

"I hear you. I've already talked to Reefer. We're in the street today."

"Sounds good. Don't be a stranger."

Book clicked off without either hearing anything else in reply from the other. It would have been unnecessary. And they both were aware of it.

Chapter Twenty-Four

After they had finished getting up to date on the latest murder Reefer told Bookworm he needed to talk with his boys. What he'd actually said was he needed to conversate with them, but after Bookworm kindly explained to him that conversate was not a word Reefer would be sure never to make that mistake again.

Reefer found his old crew in the ubiquitous lower east side Bowery. Known worldwide for its seedier side. They, up to their usual misdeeds.

He made sure they saw him and waited for them to approach him first. Just so he wouldn't screw up anything they were working on, even though he felt sorry for the targets of their larceny.

It didn't take them long. Spike, Insane, and Scout One and Scout Two. Spike's nick from the black leather studded collar encircling his neck. Insane's sobriquet from the song *Insane In The Membrane,* by the popular hip hop group Old School Players, and the two Scouts given their nicks by Reefer himself because that's what they were: the gang's scouts.

With a wry look on his face, Spike said, "I thought we'd be seein' you, Danté. I guess you're lookin' for some 411 on The Swordsman." Spike was about the only one who still called Reefer by his given name.

Reefer, said, "I guess you be right."

"Why don't we walk and talk," said Spike. "It's such a pleasant afternoon."

Although pleasant didn't sound like a word Spike would use, Reefer nodded in agreement, then glancing skyward, said, "Looks like rain, though, probably can't walk for long." Most assuredly, it was a pleasant afternoon, for the time being, at least. He hoped their walk and talk wouldn't ruin it… for either of them.

As they began to walk Insane and Scout One and Two fell in behind acting as if they were bodyguards. "What do you know about him?"

"The Swordsman?"

"Yeah, The Swordsman."

"He's a bad man."

"Everybody knows that. Tell me something we don't know."

"Word's out on the street. He's not like The Unholy Ghost. That guy was killing when he was in a fugue state. This guy makes the Ghost look like a parish priest. This asshole doesn't have multiple personality disorder; doesn't seem to be in a fugue. He knows what he wants and what he's doing. And why he's doing it. He just likes the fuck out of killing."

"I hope he's not that bad," Reefer opined.

"All right then, as bad as Patrick Bateman. You remember; in American Psycho? "

"I remember. 'Course I thought the book was better. You know, the one by Brett Easton Ellis?"

"You read, Reefer? I didn't even know you could read. Yeah, he was one bad dude. He really was a psycho."

Reefer gave Spike a dirty look about the 'I didn't know you could read' comment.

"Whenever I get the chance I do. Bookworm is the one who has really got me interested in reading," Reefer continued, "There's a reason for his nickname, you know. Now I dig it. In particular I like New York crime stories. But I don't want you to show up in any of those stories."

"I hear ya. So, who was really the psycho, Patrick Bateman or the author?"

"Nature or nurture? That's the never-ending question. But Brett Easton Ellis created Bateman, so I think you can take your pick." Reefer continued, "I'll start; what does he want?"

"The Swordsman or Patrick Bateman?" Spike said, grinning.

"The Swordsman."

"Just checking. Revenge." Clearly, Spike wasn't that far from the truth. People, and especially police, want to believe a killer hates someone, or a lot of someone's, in order to kill them; to be that violent. For The Swordsman, though, it wasn't exactly revenge, but what could be more accurately described as payback,

payback for the bullying he suffered as an unpopular, probably chubby loser kid. What was scary to ponder was how long would he keep killing. Until there was no one left? After all, the reality was he was only one unstable man with an extremely sharp blade.

"Revenge? Revenge on who?"

"Everybody."

"Everybody? That's kind of broad."

"It is what it is," Spike said with an I don't give a shit, shrug, and look, on his expressive face. And he didn't.

"Okay then, why?"

"Word is evidently he's always been something of a loser. Bullied when he was a kid and this is his way of proving everybody wrong."

"Sounds like he's still a loser to me."

"Maybe so, but everybody don't be like you, Reef."

"Thanks, bruh," Reefer said sheepishly, ignoring Spike's street English, but accepting the what seemed like a genuine compliment eagerly, nonetheless. "So, anyway, all we gots to do is run down every creep who's ever been bullied; find a thug who is motivated by revenge for that bullying, and we'll have our man."

Spike shrugged again and said, "Well, when you put it like that…"

Reefer said peevishly, "how would you put it?"

Spike shrugged again. A man of few words, why speak if a gesture would do. Taciturn could well be used to describe him. And churlish. Or less literarily than churlish; permanently pissed off.

Reefer liked the way Spike's compliment made him feel, at least. Like he was practically a respectable citizen. And if he could be of help with apprehending The Swordsman after almost single-handedly apprehending The Unholy Ghost, he could rightfully be justified in feeling good about himself.

They approached the site of the former legendary rock venue, CBGB, now John Varvatos Fashion. Even Spike and Reefer knew the iconic acronym had stood for country, blue grass and blues even though none were their preferred music genres, and that the notorious club was considered by most to be the birthplace of punk rock—and indisputably, the Ramones, Blondie, Television and Talking Heads getting birthed, and playing their first gigs there.

Spike said, "We probly should oughta get back to work. You know how it be's." Reefer had the canting thought that The Swordsman, the sick son of a bitch, probably listened to Psycho Killer by Talking Heads to get him in the mood for his brutal attacks.

"Yeah, man. But take it easy on the peoples." Spending only a few minutes with Spike, the polar opposite of his mentor, Bookworm, linguistically speaking, it didn't take long for Reefer to fall back into street speech. The argot of street thugs everywhere.

"I'm with ya."

They parted and Reefer strode off, not ambulating, toward the nearest subway station for what hopefully would be a quick train ride back to the Bronx.

Once on the train, the car rattling loudly, rocking side to side under their feet, the yellow tiles of the tunnel speeding by, the track spitting sparks, he phoned Bookworm.

"Spike says he's a stone-cold killer. Said he wants revenge for being bullied when he was a punk kid."

"I don't have any sympathy for the son of a bitch, then."

"That's what I thought.

"So, see you in the a.m., my place, and we'll catch this asshole, posthaste." Bookworm liked using the cop terms when he got the chance. It made him feel official.

Chapter Twenty-Five

"Coffee's brewing," Bookworm said to Reefer when he sat down at the kitchen counter.

He'd picked up Cubano at the bodega around the corner. He preferred its rich dark flavor to that of traditional Brazilian. "I'm out of Irish whiskey, though," he said somewhat ruefully, but without spewing Irish curses.

"I'm cool," said Reefer. And doubtless, he was; cooler than the other side of the pillow. Indeed, most people would hope they could get caught up in his reflected coolness.

"Okay, so what we gonna do?

Reefer said confidently, "We gonna find the son of a bitch. Shut his worthless ass down." Proving once again, the more time he spent with Bookworm the more loquacious he became.

And it made Bookworm proud.

And the student seemed to be enthusiastic about impressing the teacher. Polishing the metaphorical apple.

"Well, I think we should head over to Brooklyn, where the most recent murder occurred; see if we can get anybody to tell us anything different than what they told the police." Bookworm always had an idea. "Maybe they will if we lean on them a wee bit. We can be pretty scary to white folks that don't know how nice we are, you know. We can even tell 'em we're cops. They'll believe us. We look honest. And Detective Rossi'll back us up."

Bookworm knew that typically there wasn't much of a link between a serial killer and his victims, unless it was extremely thin; thus making it a crime of caprice and opportunity. And it made the murders much more difficult to solve. And like when Bookworm happened to see a vic with someone who turned out to be the Unholy Ghost shortly before she was murdered, they knew it would take someone knowing something and informing them, or dumb luck... or both. Unlike in more common single homicides when the killer is almost always a family member or someone close to the vic.

"Dope," said Reefer agreeably. They did look honest. At least in his mind. But he was feeling more like a good citizen with each passing moment. In fact, it was undeniable that, as the rest of the country was experiencing a decline in righteousness, Reefer was perceiving personal growth in the coveted quality.

***

"No time like the present," said Bookworm, making the easy decision to go there presently.

"Let's do it," said Reefer, in the moment and ready to find the killer. They chose to take Bookworm's SUV, a late model silver Infiniti QX, a huge, luxury SUV Bookworm had bought secondhand with low mileage and was like new and meticulously clean—in fact still emitting the new car smell, though it was beginning to be supplanted by Bookworm's new signature go-to fragrance, Versace Eros—to get all the way to the Coney Island area of Brooklyn and if needed, to follow up on any leads they might get. It was easier than taking the train. And far more pleasant. The QX's a/c worked harder to keep the interior pleasantly cool in the nascent summer at the shore. That's New York for you. Air conditioned all summer; heated all winter. Few moderate days.

Traffic is never good in the Big Apple but it still was not as hellish as it would have been during the morning, or evening, rush hours. In fact, by New York standards it was positively scant. Scant and almost pleasurable.

For all the difference between Manhattan and Coney Island it might seem one was leaving forever, to never return; but knowing that you were is what made it seem not quite so surreal as that.

After a few minutes driving Bookworm aggressively punched the steering wheel with the heel of his palm and swore, "damn. Hope this doesn't take too long. I forgot snacks."

Reefer glanced at him, confusedly.

"Some Reese's or some pretzels would have been good. Oh well; means we'll have to luncheon late or have an early dinner. I suppose it doesn't matter what we call it. 'Course the city's paying, whatever we call it. How's that sound, Reef?"

Reefer nodded approvingly. At the same time he chuckled inwardly at Bookworm's word. 'Luncheon'. He wouldn't dare chuckle aloud. The unveiled barb would be sure to hurt his sensitive feelings to the depths of his cilia. Reefer thought the lavishly comfortable SUV was an extremely cool vehicle.

In fact he thought the drive really pleasant indeed, since traveling by motor car was a treat for him as opposed to his usual mode of transport—the train or hoofin' it on his own two quickly wearing out feet. He ratcheted his seat back for comfort. The truth was, in its simplest terms, he would have thought any motorized vehicle was cool.

That was the first thing he wanted to do with the money the NYPD was paying him. Purchase a car. A convertible. Any convertible. Like many New Yorkers he thought of a convertible as a brand. A used one would be more than fine. He only wanted wheels. Since he had to walk or take the subway everywhere he went any old car would be an upgrade over those somewhat more than a little less than desirable modes.

Unless he could somehow come up with the dollars to buy a red Ferrari. Then he could be the African American Magnum P.I. private detective. He knew that that was more than a little less than likely, of course, since, it went without saying he'd have to get liability insurance, apply for a driver's license and most important of all, learn to drive. A stick. And as unusual as that sounds to most people, millions of relentless New Yorkers, whether by choice or circumstance, do not drive.

Bookworm wore a black concert t-shirt from 70's soul music super group, The Tower of Power, with the somewhat more than a little deep question "What Is Hip?" The title of one of their well-known bangers, emblazoned across the chest in a white mishmash design; slim fit faded black denim designer jeans and expensive Adidas running shoes completing the holistic look of the casual outfit.

Reefer looked positively preppie in a pink Izod shirt, khaki cargo shorts that showed his skinny calves which made his feet look big, and Teva strap sandals. He kept the harsh sun's rays off of his shiny head with a teal-colored Polo logo ball cap. He would have worn a skull cap, but it wouldn't portray the right look with the preppy look of the Izod.

But he was still more than a little twitchy because of his anxiety. And his nervous feet exposed due to the open-toed sandals, it was obvious that Reefer's toenails could use some trimming.

Their dress meant they both would fit in perfectly with the Coney Island beach crowd, where unlike in the city proper, most people didn't wear black year-round. Even the odd ones like the annoyingly strident fire and brimstone Baptist street preachers, the jugglers, authentically costumed belly dancers and the Uncle Sam wearing extremely tall red and white striped trousers on ten foot stilts, matching top hat, bright blue formal jacket with a waistcoat of the same bright blue with white polka dots, and large red drooping tie, an unlit matchstick standing against the salty sea air, he bracing himself high off the ground against the stiff gale that flapped banners and flags. They loud enough to be a distraction to all; the wind won't stop. The scent of the radiant sea and salt embracing them all. Even though Coney Island was built for leisure, few people shambled or sauntered there. Most appeared to be advancing as if on a mission.

A modern-day Will Smith and Martin Lawrence in the popular comedy-drama detective movie, Bad Boys; their companionable debate rages on as to which one is the six-foot-two Smith and which one is the five-seven Lawrence.

If Bookworm's toenails had been visible one would have seen that it would have been highly likely that he had had a recent pedicure; buffed, no polish. Likewise, his fingernails were perfect. Not too long-just a sliver of white showing at the tip of each. And no ragged cuticles. Only because there's a Vietnamese-owned nail salon, the best kind, in the old but spotless lobby of his building, and after his last girlfriend, Alia, told him his toenails scratched her legs in bed he'd been getting mani-pedis fortnightly ever since. The things we do for love; or at the very least for sex. The nail salon and the Starbucks were the only businesses he frequented in his building. Bookworm liked Starbucks' blueberry muffins; thought they were nice and crumbly. He thought it was cool having a Starbucks in his building, but not nearly as cool as the one in midtown's Park Central Hotel that was in the space formerly occupied by the barbershop, where in 1957, Albert Anastasia, a made man in La Cosa Nostra and after Louis "Lepke" Buchalter, the second head of Murder, Inc., was himself shot down and killed by two masked la Cosa Nostra gunmen nattily attired not in cheap suits wrinkled at knee and elbow, but expensive well-cut suits and gray wool felt hombergs with pinched crowns, purchased at F.R. Tripler and sporting lightweight black leather open back gloves on their gun hands, who rushed in, shoved the barber out of the way and started blasting away from six feet with ten shots from their cold black steel .32 and .38 revolvers.

His body was riddled with both calibers and blood from those wounds covered every surface in the shop. Although Bookworm wasn't even born when the shootout occurred, it was part of the historic and virtually unbelievable legend of Gotham's mob crime history and lore after venturing far from their beginning, their birth, bootlegging during prohibition, and therefore well known to natives. Before many of the bootleggers went on to found famous legitimate businesses like 21 Club and Toots Shor's the world famous eponymously named night club by the former bootlegger.

Of course none of today's Starbuck's that were in virtually every block in the city were as cool as any of the long since gone original Chock Full o' Nuts locations. Rossi liked their yellow and brown signs and coffee cans better than Starbucks' green and white logos, besides.

Although he had to admit he thought Starbucks did a better job of hiring quality people and training them up. And of course both of those coffee purveyors had more personality than the McDonald's that also occupied a space in practically every block of the city. And their decaf was as good as their high test. Which was really good. Or any bodega where you could get a Yoo-hoo in a glass bottle. Then you had something.

Being desultory at best but in no way nebulous, Bookworm and Reefer had somewhat less than firm plans for the afternoon. They had no plan but they did have a method—a method born of madness, maybe, but also of years of law enforcement experience. Work, and question, episodically, until they stumbled onto…or into something—hopefully not shit—had been their goal.

Though highly likely that it wouldn't be an exhaustive investigation, it would be a good start. Not much of a plan, but not as incoherent as a rhapsody, and it wasn't like they were going to totally blunder around trying to annoy people. Much less than that they would even make an effort not to be impolite.

If anyone had asked skeptically if they were cops Bookworm told them they were investigators, private. He embraced the gig enthusiastically and leaned into the role convincingly. And seemed amused with himself while doing it. He had decided it wasn't that much of a stretch. They were private citizens and they were investigating. Ergo…

So, after trudging around a wee bit—it was really too warm to do a lot of trudging—and speaking with the victim's neighbors, a few resolute interrogatives and a little threatening—they really didn't have to do much threatening, just had to look like they would—besides, Bookworm almost always preferred tact and guile to violence; almost. Although they always allowed themselves at least a little puckishness mixed with the guile—and learned that the last place anyone had recalled seeing her was at a low rent Mexican restaurant called The Taco Shack.

The neighbors had been pleasant; none refusing to answer questions or even appearing as if they wanted to refuse. Bookworm didn't take notes because he had a near cidetic memory, and besides that, he would be unable to read his iPad's screen in the harsh sunshine.

Besides, anybody with half a brain could see they weren't cops.

And not like some cops who look like tv show cops, which is even worse than looking like authentic ones. The pre-M*A*S*H Harry Morgan and Jack Webb of the dry-humored Dragnet, the serious Mike Conners of Mannix fame, the hilarious Leslie Nielsen in the equally hilarious Police Squad!, are extreme examples of Hollywood's perception of TV cops.

The Taco Shack wasn't hard to find from the vic's neighborhood; a short distance down the main beach road. The macadam, the crumbling tarmac of the asphalt two-lane road, probably laid during the fifties, was presently barely paved, beaten down, and could use some resurfacing. Rough even in the smooth riding luxury SUV.

Along the beach side hung an aged sagging power line, on the shoulder opposite the beach ran a rusty ancient railroad track, now all but abandoned except for when Coney Island businesses needed restocked or resupplied. Or delivering boardwalk entertainment venues' newest circus animals. The consistent groan of the steel rails under the weight of million-pound trains barely remembered.

A sunlit day at the seashore and it was beautiful. The white sand beach stunning; the capricious surging waves, sojourners crossing the Atlantic, after traveling more than three thousand miles from France and Spain, couldn't wait to kiss its dulcet crystals.

As he drove, Bookworm said, "it certainly is a fit day for the beach." And they absolutely would enjoy the change from Manhattan. None of the usual living New York flotsam and jetsam. No panhandlers accosting them. No hookers on every street corner; very pleasant, very pleasant, indeed.

Without looking at Bookworm, instead, staring straight ahead, Reefer said, "I don't do sand."

Bookworm jerked his head around disbelieving what he'd heard, and stared mouth agape at his friend like he was bedbug crazy, all the while trying to refrain from crashing into the car stopping short in front of him to make a turn across traffic.

"What can I say?" Reefer said, with young honesty. "I don't

like it to get in my…uh, orifices."

Bookworm suppressed a not unkind laugh, but was impressed that Reefer knew the meaning of the word orifice.

He continued straight a wee bit further, then made a sharp right turn into the white shell parking lot, the tires crunching them loudly, heard as much as felt even in the air conditioned quiet. Parked away from the front door next to a sign that designated employee parking and pulled nose-in to a white-painted wooden fence that housed a large pine green metal dumpster that was overflowing with restaurant trash, and spoiled and rotting food detritus. Not a pleasant smell in the warm weather.

They hoped that in the early afternoon on a weekday that someone would be working now that had been working Sunday evening. Next door to The Taco Shack was an old roadside garage, a place to get one's Ford station wagon repaired from the days when a trip to Coney Island was a family vacation trip; next to it sat a small empty gray cinder block building.

A for lease or sale sign taped in one of the windows. Paint the gray cinder blocks pink and hang pink and white striped awnings over the windows and it would make a helluva cute coffee-pastry shop. Of course it wouldn't be nice enough for a Starbucks. It would have to be an independent. Or leave the blocks gray and open a karate school. If one could afford the rent for a karate studio at the pricy seashore. As it was, it was nothing but a vacant disused building. Wishing to house a hoped-for new business.

Out of the SUV first, practically at a run, Reefer set the pace across the parking lot, his Nikes crunching the white and gray shells and Bookworm a half-step off his left shoulder in an easy lanky lope. Pure economy of motion. Reefer must have been craving some Mexican food. The bracing sea breeze was salty fresh and cool.

Inside, the place was a typical Mexican bar and grill; kind of dark, but over decorated with a light, rustic wood with accents painted in the colors of red, green and yellow, then lacquered. Cone-shaped straw Sombreros with colorful hatbands hung on shiny teal-colored walls. What one wouldn't expect to see in a Mexican restaurant was the accompanying assortment of mounted fish from the sea on the walls. Including a huge glorious blue sailfish. Not exactly what one would expect in a genuine south of the border restaurant.

The air conditioning was keeping the deep interior cool. The back bar, open to the patio, would be warmer. Brick walls that fell short of the ceiling divided the dining area into different sections and separated it from the bar. Once inside though, given that it was such a pleasant afternoon they decided to sit on the patio side of the al fresco bar.

Open to the sunshine and ocean breeze it would be far more enjoyable than the oppressively low-ceilinged café. Working as contractors on this case was good, since they could get away with having a couple of Margaritas during daytime hours.

They sure as shit couldn't do that if they were actual paid employees of the NYPD. Even if they weren't given to being bibulous. And that aside, Margs and soft-shell tacos beat the hell out of coffee and donuts. Even fruit-filled ones with sprinkles. Bookworm would have to remember to tell Detective Rossi that. He'd probably think it was funny except for the part about insinuating he liked donuts because he's a cop. Unless you wanted one for dessert; but at a Mexican restaurant you could always have a chocolate cheesecake burrito if so desired. That kills. Blows fruity donuts away—even with sprinkles.

A cute young—no more than twenty-two—Mexican, or possibly Filipina bartender with a life-altering butt, wearing little makeup, a thin gold chain gracing her fine delicate neck, dark-framed glasses, and a light floral scent perfume with a hint of spice-like cinnamon, not pepper, greeted them. She had a smile that could brighten the dark side of the moon and introduced herself as Krystle, which was the same as Crystal in Tagalog, and asked if she could help them.

Due to Spain owning the Philippines for more than three hundred years, most people from the island country were half

Spanish, so one could easily think that they were Mexican. And not only that, her given name, Krystle, sounded like a Filipina name. The word that came to mind to Bookworm was delectable, but he decided against playing his trump card, flashing his incredibly bright smile, at her or she would ignore all of the other customers. And that wouldn't be fair to them. And he knew their souls weren't connected anyway. It would've only been physical. Not that there was anything wrong with that. Reefer thought she was en fuego and would be chatting her up already if he weren't completely focused on the job at hand.

It was obvious to anyone paying attention that she knew she was cute and it was highly likely that she used it to her advantage in maximizing gratuities. Not that anyone could blame her for that, though, since most servers were near venal when it came to tips. Not as bad as workers in the sex trade, but still venal as hell.

Bookworm and Reefer both politely ordered Margaritas on the rocks. Truth be told, Bookworm believed Mexican food and Margs to be existential. He hoped that these would be pretty damn good. Of course he thought the worst one he'd ever had was pretty damn good. He only wished the Marg was the special soup of the day. He could really get into that.

Reefer felt that being in the setting where the unsuspecting young woman met her killer was a little unsettling. And he'd have to remember to light a candle for her at mass Saturday. He wasn't pious enough to know it would help her at this point, but he knew in his heart it couldn't hurt. And in that was all he needed.

Nothing but the cry of forlorn seagulls could be heard over the crashing surf and the terse but nevertheless refreshing sea breeze.

A casually-dressed altogether anything but mad-looking Caucasian man in his fifties, his russet hair turning to listless gray, sat at the other end of the bar tapping on an iPad's necessary for a writer, Apple keyboard. He looked up from where his stubby fingers danced uncharitably, doing what was asked of them. A white cloth napkin was tucked sloppily into his unbuttoned collar, his lips pressed together fiercely, probably chewing the inside of his mouth until he could taste the coppery blood. He paused to gaze at the truculent blue ocean indifferently. The look on his face altogether satisfied, and anguished.

The common look of a writer; not unintelligent but not altogether clever. He probably popped Prozac like cellophane-wrapped after dinner peppermint candies; a hoped-for cure for disappointment. As long as it worked he would be able to look forward to his palmy days instead of living in his current meat and potato days.

Bookworm charitably thought that the man was probably writing the next great American novel. His Magnum opus. One could only hope it wasn't a metaphorical Sturm and Drang— Bookworm never had liked that shit—or worse, a metaphysical one.

While enjoying the salty ocean breeze and a Margarita for inspiration. It's a perfect setting for it Bookworm had to admit to himself. It, writing, wasn't the man's life's work—not yet, anyway, but someday soon it would be and he would live for it. It and nothing else. Indeed, to most writers, nothing else but writing mattered or even came close.

Bookworm recalled from his college literature classes that all writers fall into one of two camps. Those who outline, and those who fly by the seat of their trousers. The second of those obviously being way cooler. From seeing this guy, Bookworm could tell there were two other camps. Those writers who look cool and those who don't. He surmised that this guy was an uncool-looking outliner. However, he assumed that the man would be interesting to talk to since a novelist would have to be have loads of knowledge of a number of esoteric subjects from all of the research required to write good fiction.

After pressing the key with a period on it to end a graph as aggressively as one would rend a sheet of paper from a typewriter he raised his eyes from his artful creation to stare lyrically at the belligerent blindingly bright sea.

A plate of empty half shells that formerly were possessed of raw oysters, along with a small bowl of spicy cocktail sauce was pushed to the side. A bone-dry Margarita glass, but with salt still encrusted around its heavy glass bowl, stood guard over the desiccated shells. His hunger and thirst pleasantly slaked for now.

A beautiful summer afternoon, Bookworm thought, but he still preferred New York's colorful crisp autumn days. It was quiet except when it wasn't. Wind of sky and ocean surf conspiring.

"Were you working Sunday evening when the young woman who was murdered was here?" Bookworm asked speaking in a practiced professional clipped cadence while performing an unrehearsed flip of his wallet to briefly flash his Triple A card. He knew she wouldn't give it more than a cursory glance.

Looking at her closely, Bookworm could tell she was definitely Filipina. He'd dated one of the beautiful islanders while at university. And he'd been quite besotted with her. If he hadn't taken care with the wine they might've married. The dangerous power of the grape. He still thought of her whenever he caught the scent of her preferred fragrance, Viktor & Rolf Flowerbomb. And he recalled her confidence, and how it smelled. He was happy he could still remember her face. That he hadn't drunk too much alcohol, certainly not enough to even partially anesthetize himself, or done too much of anything else to blur her image.

But now there was far less of the illegal anything else since he was getting older and helping the police, besides. It bothered him that he might someday forget her face, because for a while he had thought she was the one. Admittedly, for two semesters he'd been helplessly taken with her. And he mostly drank beer these days, unless he was hanging out with Rossi, when red wine was typically involved. He thought he must be turning Italian. And he thought the idea of that was hilarious—changing race. And he knew all Filipino women could cook. A well-earned international reputation as the best cooks in the world. And he was sure the bartender could probably cook the hell out of some adobo chicken, the signature dish of the Philippines.

"No, but Seabass was. I can ask him to come over if you'd

like," she said, still smiling. Reefer thought he'd like to see how she looked unsmiling. To see if she were still as cute. And he knew he'd be able to wipe the smile off her face. He had that undesirable knack with young women.

"If you don't mind," replied Bookworm, kindly.

She set the giant-sized Margaritas unintentionally, but sloppily before them, sloshing a wee bit appropriate of a refreshing tv commercial on the napkin of each and handed them dog-eared stained yellow cardboard menus, flimsy from use and age, brushing Bookworm lightly and intentionally with her hand when she placed the menu gingerly before him. A warm comforting touch. The scent of her blossomy perfume lingered even as she began walking over and saying something to a brother with a shiny skull similar to Reefer's, minus the ink; not as tall as Bookworm, not as short as Reefer.

Wearing dark aviator-style shades indoors, the brother looked like a previous generation Isaac Hayes. Somewhere between thirty and fifty; so split the difference and call it forty. He had skin the color of dark ale.

He was eating delivery pizza like men do when they haven't been house-broken and taught better manners by a good woman, from a shallow white red and green flat box the name of which Bookworm didn't recognize, meaning it wasn't from a national chain pizza store. New Yorkers wouldn't be caught dead eating chain store pizza.

A local slice joint was the only acceptable option for a fresh hot pie. He probably ate it the same way at home, except for standing over the kitchen sink. His slice folded in half, bone to point like all native New Yorkers. Probably nothing left but bones rattling in the carton.

Reefer guessed that the employees couldn't eat Mexican every meal. It looked like a double pepperoni with extra cheese slice; and ironically, in New York; it was Chicago style. And drinking coffee from a warm gray stoneware mug. Caffeine and carbs—all a working man needs. And chewing at least somewhat gracefully around a wooden kitchen match clenched between his slightly crooked but nevertheless ultra-white teeth.

He chewed on it not idly, but with a purpose. Looked like he was brought up learning to take care of his teeth, but without the benefit of braces. His parents probably couldn't afford them. On anyone else the kitchen match look would have had an over the top affectedness to it. Attempting to be Tres cool. But on Seabass it was perfect and not only that, something you'd expect.

Four different things in his mouth at once. One for eating; one for drinking; one for smoking; and one for chewing nervously, or out of habit. Mouth multi-tasking. They both glanced toward Bookworm and Reefer, then looked at them askance before the brother snuffed out his cigarette in a dirty large margarita bowl glass—looked like a non-filtered Chesterfield from the measure of the acrid smell and the crumpled hard pack he flipped toward the large green lidless barrel trashcan. Probably used an old school worn brass Zippo lighter to set it on fire. He was that cool. There was nothing daft about him.

Apparently he liked his nicotine unfiltered; drained his coffee mug in one long slug, then sauntered over, oozing cool without effort, picking his steps insouciantly in his flops stained with God only knows what, since he was a bartender. Deft and dexterous in his walk. On the typical for most bars, perforated black rubber mat.

He probably drove a sports car. He knew what time it was. He had most likely practiced the walk like an actor practices an entrance. Nobody could be that cool unrehearsed. It wasn't possible. He'd practiced it; critiqued himself and practiced it some more. If he were in a cool contest it would be his intent to win, and win big; to crush the competition. And it would be no contest.

He wore a bright green tanktop that read Taco Shack with a local artist's rendering of the shack, in white. His bare right arm showed a raised Omega Psi Phi tattoo. Visual scarred evidence that he was more than a lizard brain or a mouth-breather.

Even if he weren't a member of the esteemed fraternity but had the painfully acquired design only because he liked it he'd have to be able to think on his feet if someone questioned him about it. Again, proof of not being a lizard brain, Yet all humans had been for more than six million years. Or maybe even worse-a cow's slow brain. Most likely the dumbest creature on the planet. Fortunately for meat-eaters the animals didn't have to be clever to be good steaks.

He dried his hands on a forlorn formerly white ragged towel, and bit the head off the kitchen match, before spitting it over the bar and onto the stone patio even though the ginormous plastic trash can was right in front of him. But spitting it in there wouldn't have been nearly as cool.

His gaze forthright as he extended a man's who'd known real work overly large misshapen bony fist as he walked, and said, "I'm Sebastian," without mumbling even with the various items in his mouth and a bewildered expression. "I know…right? I don't look like a Sebastian. But when you get right down to it, does anybody? But you can call me Seabass, or even Bass if you like. Everyone else does. I work by the sea, you know. It seems to fit me better; don't you think."

When one was as cool as Seabass one didn't need a nickname other than who you are. Certainly not a Muslim nick or a need to become a newly minted Muslim. And he was definitely cool…and Seabass, besides. His voice soft. Not hostile but discordant, although it mightn't have been had the subject been not so unpleasant.

The tonal quality what one would expect from someone his size; not overly deep, not high. A full-throated lyric baritone. An octave and a half below a perfectly precise middle C. His farseeing crisp light mixed green eyes were clear and deep. Even though Bookworm had never seen a look like that before, he would have described it as smug.

He leaned close enough that Bookworm and Reefer could smell somewhat more than just a trace of the stale coffee on his breath, still. At this point it wasn't apparent whether the brother would turn out to be friend or foe. His face gave nothing away.

Bookworm extended his own fist vertically to bump Sebastian's and said, "John. Pleasant weather." That was the extent of Bookworm's idea of small talk, of which he wasn't a fan anyway.

Indeed, the ocean breezes coming off Manhattan Beach typically kept the temps barely touching the balmy seventies even during the depths of summer. Different from the city. Bookworm could sit and listen quietly comfortable longer than anyone Reefer had ever seen. Bookworm used his Christian name rather than his nick because if Seabass was less than comfortable with his own legal name he really wouldn't want to hear he was talking to Bookworm. Although John had thought about legally changing his name to Sir Bookworm and was still trying to decide.

Of course, he didn't want to sound audacious or like an asshole of the first order with Sir as his given name. And throwing his patriarchal name to the wind would ensure just that. But he liked Bookworm as a middle name. Yet, truth be told, he was only trying to be nice with the pleasant weather comment because it was expected. Because most people, especially New Yorkers, prefer the warm temps of summer.

When summer came around Bookworm missed the snow, brought as it was on the north wind by the hounds of winter. And he liked Sting's ode to winter's rule of the same name. He even liked January-cold, which in New York City was worse than January-cold in most other places. When the hoary snow was grayish-black with grime and piled high by the street plows and melting dirty gray mounds piled up between cars.

It was in his soul, no, a part of his soul. He felt sure that old man winter's rule energized him and tended to bring out the rascal in him, causing him to get into mischief, or just a wee bit of hijinks, and if he thought about it, what was wrong with anyone getting into a wee bit of mischief…or hijinks. A rhetorical question if ever there were one.

And at its simplest, it seemed to him that there was a refreshing reminder of life in the promise of winter's frosty chill more than in that of summer's heat. That and a resurrected winter's gravitational pull on Bookworm, undeniably bringing and once there, keeping him home.

Even Brooklyn's own much-loved Simon and Garfunkel sang about New York City winters in their mega hit, *The Boxer* with the line—"The New York City winters aren't bleeding me, leading me, home." Even though most people get it wrong. The song is not New York's soundtrack; New York is the song's soundtrack. The only thing he didn't like about winter was the weather forecasters' predictions of snow. Interrupting broadcasts, music, news programs, interrupting every goddamn thing to tell everyone that an avalanche was on the way when everybody knew it already. It just annoyed the shit out of him.

The only part of summer Bookworm could think of that he liked was that he didn't have to worry about Christmas Eve's sepulchral ghosts. No mere imps, those, but honest-to-God hair-raising phantoms. They of a winter's night, coming out when it's dark and snowy, late on Christmas Eve. Rising in the frozen sky, lured by the quiet hush of falling snow and the sounds of magnificent church choirs singing transfixing Christmas Eve carols. Everyone knew of the disembodied demons, in fact, they inspiring an album by Trans-Siberian Orchestra, The Ghosts Of Christmas Eve. Those incorporeal ghosts of the world, and of Christmas.

And even though he was a reader and not just of popular fiction, but of the literary classics, he had to admit he was a big fan of Christmas music, especially the Celtic band The Pogues' *Fairytale Of New York*, and Christmas movies. His favorites being the Home Alone films and The Santa Clause trilogy; and even Christmas with the Kranks, but at least it was based on the great John Grisham's novel, *Skipping Christmas*. So, that was his justification, at least in his mind.

The only thing he liked better about Christmas than those movies was walking around Manhattan and buying a small white sack of hot roasted chestnuts at one of the street vendors and placing it in his coat pocket where he'd tuck a hand to keep it warm until he decided to dig in to the hot wintery treats.

A real fan of Christmas, Bookworm wasn't one of those people who thought Christmas was a day; he knew it was a season, like any of the four others, it lasting, at least in his mind, from November first to the first weekend of February, ending after the big game was won on Super Bowl Sunday. Indeed, he got his money's worth when it came to Christmas.

The thing Bookworm missed most about winter though, in addition to fruitcake that is, were the Christmas taverns. Traditional dark dive bars, but at Christmas gaily decorated with shimmering-colored lights and a brightly illuminated tree and they were magically transformed. And if he had too much to drink in a Christmas bar then winter's exhilarating edgy cold could bring him out of its effects when he exited said bar. And he loved picking out his own blue spruce at one of the many sidewalk tree lots that covered the city during the season and carrying it home over his shoulder. It felt positively *A Christmas Carol* like.

But what he missed most of all were the street bums singing Jingle Bells at the tops of their inebriated lungs, all the while drinking from their bottles of cheap port wine wrapped tight in brown paper bags which they'd bought at downtown drugstores with begged change.

While the rich men bundled in their black wool trench coats silk scarves wrapped around their necks and drank bourbon or rye from fancy silver flasks concealed in their fancy cloaks' deep pockets. Only to last them until they returned to their posh eight figure townhomes in a gentrified Harlem for a proper hot seidel of Tom and Jerry; only tippled at Christmastime, and to read A Visit from St. Nicholas, more popularly known as The Night Before Christmas. Now, that was a New York Christmas to get emotional about, for you. Like one in a Runyon short story. And not something one could get from summer's warmth.

Bookworm knew many people would think him crazy, but he even liked how his fingers ached from the bleakest depths of winter's hiemal chill. Most New Yorkers thought the city's hawkish winters were dismal. Bookworm thought them life-affirming. They made him feel alive.

Indeed, they made him feel most alive when there was unfeigned concern about freezing to death in the city's drafty winter canyons. He loved wearing winter coats, mittens, and scarves to keep that from happening. Besides, he thought it was a good look for him. Not a look just anyone was able to pull off—winter wear. It took that certain something not everyone had.

He loved the flowers on the purple cabbages that shop-owners planted all over the city that thrived in the brumal winter months. He was glad though, it wasn't March, it as cold as December, but with none of the holiday fascination. He even liked the sound of steel tire chains on yellow taxis crunching against frozen pavement. It was a comforting sound in his mind. It was only the vehicles' smell that was bad; winter or summer, they usually smell of bodily odors mixed with industrial cleaners in a vain attempt to wipe out the other. Fortunately for him he didn't have to take taxis often.

Furthermore, he thought autumn, given all its colors of a rural New Jersey vegetable stand, had the most personality. Indeed, in a high school class it would win most genial student. Moreover, winter would undoubtedly earn most serious; summer, most carefree, and spring most delightful. Even though he wasn't a fan of the season that most New Yorkers looked forward to gleefully after winter's harsh chill.

Sebastian, obviously not one given to being a chatterbox, didn't reply to Bookworm's casual observation with regard to the weather. Of course working there at the ocean's edge, standing in the bar looking out toward the azure blue horizon as he delivered drinks to patrons seated with their backs to the sea, he probably was accustomed to the typically clement weather.

To be sure, New York's weather was capable of becoming schizophrenic in a minute, a proverbial New York one, but most of the time it was entirely predictable. Hot summers and cold winters, and the in-between seasons benign, leading to one of those other two.

Seabass probably didn't even notice the weather any longer. Indeed, the only thing unpleasant about the Long Island shore during summer that Seabass could discern was the plethora of mosquitos and other somewhat less ferocious winged biting parasites but nevertheless just as annoying simply by virtue of their presence and persistence.

Reefer, in his way, remaining cooler than ice, and even less of a fan of small talk than Bookworm, and never one to waste words, slurred, not in small part due to the Margarita, "sup."

To the east, over the Atlantic, the sky was cerulean. To the west, far beyond Long Island Sound, the grim dense onyx clouds were turning to black ink; a silent jagged streak of lightning ripped angrily across the dark sky. Not heat lightning, even if it was hot enough for it, but a snarling thunderstorm. The electrical flash had been accompanied by the resolute sustained rumble from ill-tempered temporal heavy clouds oppressively low on the western horizon like a heavy dark dish, a foretaste of a pelting rainfall on the maw of an irate Herculean summer storm, the angry teeth of a tempest roiling and rushing to intrude on the heat and cool the unsuspecting waiting summer day. No cloudlets, these; serious boomers, they were. To rattle windows and teeth equally.

Appearing vexed by the sound of his own words, and with a garrulous snarl on his lips, while looking to the ocean searching for answers he wouldn't find instead of directly at the brothers as if not looking directly at them was an intentional dis, Sebastian said, "I understand you want to know about the events of Sunday evening." It was obvious to Bookworm and Reefer that he was more a little less than giddy about discussing it. And not sure why they should want to know.

"If you don't mind," said Book, reading the brother's face and demeanor and determining it would be easier to get what he wanted by being courteous rather than being vituperatively Bookworm. And getting information was more important than getting into a pissing contest. Although he would undoubtedly win one with the massive power of the NYPD force backing him up.

"I have to ask. If for no other reason than my own idle curiosity. What's your interest in the case? Other than, like everyone else's; morbid nosiness."

"We're investigators. Contracted to the NYPD. And if you don't buy that, would you believe that we're Guardian Angels. I'm Curtis Sliwa. Don't I look like him? Even if I did leave my red beret on the shelf in the hall closet at home," Bookworm said smart assedly.

Only in the fairytale Bookworm was concocting on the fly could a dark-skinned African-American brother look like a pasty-skinned white guy almost twice his age; Sliwa who hoped to be the first Republican elected mayor of New York City since Bloomberg. Not very likely in what some very elderly senior citizens still call Tammanyland due to the site of the Democratic Headquarters downtown in the mid-1900s. Back before New York ever thought about electing Republican mayors. Not a LaGuardia, a Giuliani, or Bloomberg among them. "Sorry. But just between us girls; being a smartass is my one major character flaw. I can't help myself.

"Actually, I've always thought of myself as a younger, tougher Hawk from the Spenser books and the tv show. But then I think I'm better looking than Avery Brooks, although I do wish I were as tall as him," he said with a grin, referring to the over-the-top uber-cool actor who portrayed Spenser's sidekick, Hawk, on the tv show and in the made-for-tv movies. Sometimes it *was* true Bookworm couldn't help being a smartass. Fortunately, at least for those around him, those times weren't that often.

"Yeah, you look like you're NYPD," Seabass said sarcastically, while choosing to ignore the Guardian Angels comment. He was not the type to quail at anything. "Do you have any proof?"

"Okayyy," Bookworm said, reaching slowly, and theatrically with all the gravitas of which he was capable, for his wallet.

"I really wish I had a cool gold shield in a leather case to flip open and flash, you know, but maybe this will do the job, at least," he joked, "and that's really the point, isn't it," as he pulled out an aged business card, an informal imprimatur with stains on the white linen with the blue and gold embossed NYPD shield, Rossi had given him as a "get out of the slammer free card," so to speak, but not literally, since the detective didn't want Book getting into any trouble; with Rossi's name; title, Detective First Grade; and cell number on it. He really did wish he had an official I.D., but Rossi's business card would have to do. Bookworm had had it in his wallet for what felt like ages but had never felt the need to use it before now.

"Call him," insisted Bookworm.

Reefer was impressed; he'd never even seen it before, much less seen Bookworm rely on the implied power of the more than forty thousand members of the NYPD, or even one pissed off Italian detective. They paused in their back and forth, while a clangorous overloaded oil tanker plowed the maudlin sea lumbering against the ocean's insistent current, making its way southwest to New York harbor, past France's gift to the United States, the Statue of Liberty, on July 4, 1881, green with verdigris, Lording over all of New York Harbor and the traffic therein, then north to various ports up the mighty Hudson, formerly known as the Broad River. Its diesel engines fading as it moved further down the shore. Or it might take the shortcut up the East River, cut through the Harlem River to the Hudson, and then continue upriver. Depended on if it had any dockings south of where the Harlem River punches into the steady current of the mighty Hudson. At least the Harlem was free of its wintertime hazardous blocks of ice.

"I'm just glad it's you annoying him in the middle of a big murder investigation, and not me," Bookworm added with a shit eating grin while surreptitiously winking at Reefer.

Reefer thought the offhand comment was hilarious. And tried with difficulty to contain his laughter.

They both knew it was improbable that the bartender would have a congenial convo with Rossi. It was apparent to anyone who knew him how antagonistic he could be. But at least it was better for the receiver of his ire to get it over a phone than in person.

Unable to be affected by his repellent facial expressions. Of which there were many. It wasn't that Rossi was perpetually cross; it just appeared that way.

And while Seabass was on his phone with Detective Rossi, Book and Reefer took a look at the menu while sipping eagerly from the large Margaritas.

They knew the tacos would have to be good. After all, the restaurant included the most traditional of Tex-Mex dishes in its name. They wouldn't do that unless they were confident of their taste.

"Now that's something you don't see in every Mexican restaurant," said Bookworm.

"Octopus tacos," he continued, always adventurous when it came to food. "I guess because this resto is on the ocean. They probably caught the poor tentacled little creatures, bless their tiny little octopus hearts, themselves." He knew that that was unlikely but he thought it was something fun to ponder. He also assumed that deep fried and drenched in taco sauce and swaddled in soft flour tortillas of course, with rice and beans on the side would make them at the very least, edible.

Reefer made a sour face and said, "I think I'll stick with the fried chicken tacos."

Wimp," said Bookworm, throwing shade in his friend's direction. Or as it would have been described in New York City generations past; giving him the business.

Then, almost as an afterthought, Bookworm said, "You know what would be good? Lobster tacos. Man, that would be the bomb diggity."

The server returned to take their order, and by then Seabass had ended his call.

Knowing that Detective Rossi could be somewhat more than a wee bit less than affable when the mood struck him, which trended toward quite often, Bookworm asked, "How'd it go?" Sardonically hoping for the worst for the bartender, and actually surprised that the man's ears weren't bleeding from the dressing down that he knew the somewhat a little more than the naturally abusive Rossi was capable of administering. That it would be somewhat more than prosaic.

"Fine," he said.

"You don't look like it was fine," Bookworm appraised churlishly.

"Okay, so what do you want to hear? The detective said I should answer any and all of your questions to the best of my ability, tell you everything you want to know, and if I didn't believe him, I could talk to his lieutenant and if the lieutenant couldn't convince me then he'd be more than pleased to get the captain on the line. That's about the time I told him I was losing my signal." The bartender said, a sour look on his face and unhappily wagging his phone at Bookworm.

The look on Bookworm's face showed that he enjoyed the hell out of that. It sounded like something Rossi would say. The thought occurred to him that he might even have to use the detective's battered business card again sometime. Especially if it were going to be that much fun every time.

Reefer was doing all he could to keep from busting a gut laughing, and was barely succeeding.

Seabass raised his shoulders trying to show an air of confidence after the verbal beat down with which he'd just been administered. "So, what can I tell you?" he asked more than cooperatively, the previous tenseness abated. He'd made the decision he wanted to do all he could to win brownie points with the world's largest and best, police force. And that he had nothing to gain by being cagey.

"Was she with anybody, talk to anybody, hook up? You know." Bookworm started with the basic, and most obvious questions. Typical cop questions; the kind anybody would know from watching tv police dramas.

"She talked with this one dude who approached her."

"Did you know him? Or recognize him? Seen him hitherto Sunday?"

"Never seen him before that I can remember; but I've only been here about a year."

"An obvious question, but not for nothing anyway; what'd he look like?"

"Hard to say. He wore dark sunglasses, looked like Ray-Bans, might have been knockoffs; he didn't look like he had money, and a ball cap. Like everybody. Like nobody. Like me. Like you. Like ten million other faceless New Yorkers. Average height, average weight, fallow skin, average hat size, average shoe size. Like he was trying hard not to be noticed. Too hard. And that's why I noticed him. He never looked directly at me; not even when he was placing his order. A little unusual; you know what I'm talking about? Most people look you in the eye when they're giving you their order."

Bookworm thought Seabass sharper than he let on if he knew the extravagant word, fallow. A contained man, he spoke deliberately and unemotionally, even if the obviously concerned look in his eyes showed that he cared. And Seabass' somberness was suitably unfelicitous for the events he described. Indeed, he was surprisingly acute in his awareness. Everything about Brody had been average; not good if one's trying to be noticed, say by the opposite sex, but quite good if one's a serial killer trying not to be noticed by law enforcement.

"What kind of hat? You know; sport, team, work logo, fancy fashion designer? You know. What kind?"

"Does that matter? A dark hat. A hat-hat. "

"I don't know yet. Just asking questions. Ask enough questions, it'll lead to more questions. Maybe you learn something. Keeping asking questions maybe something good will come out of it." Bookworm had heard Detective Rossi say that. Bookworm didn't consider it dogma coming from Rossi. But it was common sense. Being methodical. That was how Rossi worked, and so it made sense to his self-proclaimed acolyte. Bookworm knew that his friend was a human compendium of esoteric police knowledge and he could have worse mentors…on a plethora of subjects.

Bookworm had taken no notes during the questioning since he had an eidetic memory and could envision the answers when he wanted to recall them later. That ability had enabled him to read all of his textbooks the first week of the semester all the while at Princeton and never pick them up again and earn all A's in his classes. Hence, his nickname.

"Yeah, I hear you. Maybe it was a Yankees hat. Everybody wears a hat in the sun. It's hard to remember, but yeah, Yankees." It sounded like Seabass was buying into it; which was good since Bookworm had no idea where he was going with all this.

Krystle returned with their orders. Reefer wasted no time digging in but thought his fried chicken tacos were typical, pretty much the same as those at Mexican restaurants everywhere. No better, no worse.

"Holy guacamole, these are bustin', and they certainly can't be called samey," said Bookworm to nobody in particular, referring to his octopus tacos, while making a satisfied sound and thinking the Spanish language exclamation was apropos at a Mexican restaurant, "even if the tentacles are a little rubbery and chewy. Still it's gots to be better than soylent green," he said cracking an I know I'm clever smile. Obviously neither Seabass nor Reefer got his joke, since it got no reaction of any sort, negative or positive. Of course, given his predilection toward the written word, Bookworm liked the novel titled '*Make Room! Make Room!*',written by Harry Harrison in 1966 that the film was based on, more than the movie, of the name Soylent Green, even though they were both released before he was born. It introducing the idea of cannibalism to feed a world overpopulating and starving. Taking care of two problems at once—the overpopulation and starvation. In all likelihood, a less intrepid stomach would be bilious at the chewiness of the tentacles especially while thinking of eating Soylent Green.

Seabass continued, saying,"If anything, it was like the dude was doing everything he could to go unnoticed. Of course it's quite possible that I could be imagining everything after the fact."

"And yet, with the unfortunate fatal happenstance it's possible that you're altogether correct," Bookworm said around overly chewy toothy bites of octopus. Except when a bicuspid fell on the grit of a sand crystal. At least that was proof of their salty ocean freshness, he thought.

Then, while trying to remove an irritating grain of sand at the same time from between back molars, "One more thing. Was she typically a heavy drinker?"

"Two Dos Equis were her hard limit, unless it was one bone dry gin martini. Two fingers on the rocks," Seabass said, proud of himself for remembering a regular's preferred libation. "But never more than that, though. I never touch gin, myself," he added, "although I can drink the shit out of a vodka martini; or a gimlet; even better."

"So her judgement shouldn't have been impaired." It was a statement; not a question.

"Not in this professional bartender's opinion." Seabass's look was wan, or perhaps closer to solemn as he talked and answered questions. That was good. It showed how much he'd been affected by it.

"Sorry, one more. Did they leave together?" Bookworm's cellphone buzzed on the metallic bar. He glanced at it, didn't recognize the number; so he let it ring.

Seabass searched the pictures in his mind for a moment; trying to be sure he said it accurately.

"Not together, but at the same time."

"That's convenient." *And what I would do if I were up to no good*, he thought. Of course it went without saying Book could never bend to such a detestable deed. It wasn't in his DNA and he didn't understand how anyone could. They would have to be mad, even if not clinically diagnosed as such.

"Oh, and here's a personal observation. Nothing more. It probably doesn't mean anything. It's not like I'm a professional analyst; no more than any other bartender anyways." He chuckled at that since that's what people considered most in their profession. "He seemed to me, at least, passive-aggressive."

Bookworm nodded. He had agreeably asked questions and Seabass had responded-at least as agreeably as he was capable. And after a shaky start it seemed like they had reached a somewhat more than mere pleasant accord. Obviously, the dressing down Seabass had received from Detective Rossi had increased his eagerness to cooperate. Bookworm could tell that he was not given toward being mendacious in the slightest.

After finding out as much as they thought they were able, Bookworm said, "Thank you, my friend. You've given us some new things to think about. Or chew on…like these octopus tacos."

"Good, I hope it helps. This dude has gots to be got. She was a nice girl. It was unfortunate she met up with the wrong asshole. She was normal, very down to earth. It wasn't like she was a pagan. She wasn't wearing Louboutins or any other designer shit." No one could accuse Seabass or Sebastian of being diffident.

"I hear ya."

"And what I meant was, is most of our assholes are okay. They wouldn't dream of doing something like that." At worst dissolute; at best, amiable drinkers.

Indeed, Bookworm, with Reefer's attention, looked around the place and could see that nothing untoward was going on and it was unlikely that it ever did. It seemed to be just what it appeared to be; a restaurant for upper middle-class patrons serving south of the border food and a drinking establishment of common order.

Too bad they'd taken out their one security camera months before. But they knew most of their clientele. Most were regulars and management had made the decision that it wasn't needed.

Although he didn't feel compelled to say anything since they were working, Bookworm thought it would be nice to thank the brother for the info.

"Don't mention it. If that's all, I should oughta get back to work. Just remember me if I'm ever in trouble with The Man. And keep your heads down. You'll keep them longer that way." He grinned as he said it.

Bookworm let it pass without comment.

"Walaikum assalam," Sebastian said, too cool to say the wish of peace in its longer traditional manner, while patting his chest twice, indicating he was done talking.

He didn't look muslim. But he did look cool. And cool was way more important. And that would do along with the peaceful wish. And he looked pleased with himself. Hoped that he had helped. That he'd given them more than a skerrick of information that would help them. He hoped he'd help bring The Swordsman to justice; but only if the world was just. Righteous; hopefully. Deserved; definitely. Warranted; without question; blessed, for Someone Greater to decide.

Bookworm saw his Muslim wish and raised it by saying "dosvedanya," really hoping he'd have a nice day, since Seabass had been helpful. Sebastian rolled his eyes theatrically and gave Bookworm a halfhearted fist bump. He knew without a doubt from first glance that Bookworm didn't look Russian.

Bookworm and Reefer finished their tacos and decided against a chocolate cheesecake burrito or even a lighter but just as tasty flan, instead, raising two fingers toward the server to signal their wish for a second round of Margs for dessert. The decision whether to have dessert or more alcohol was always a challenging one, one made with careful consideration, but they were young and decided they could handle the second round of huge Margaritas.

Drinking quickly before the ice could melt in the heat of the patio. Unconcerned about brain-freeze since their margaritas were on the rocks instead of the frozen concoction.

The occasional bouts of Margarita brain freeze from the the icy creations was the only thing Bookworm wasn't crazy about. Margarita brain-freeze—he thought it sounded like the name of a crazy-costumed female Batman nemesis. She'd probably be a more badass adversary even, than Catwoman. Would most likely have the power to freeze your brain from a distance with rays shooting from her eyes.

Each thought they could get accustomed to working like this. And on the city's dime, no less. Rossi had said beer and bagels were on them. Good thing he hadn't said anything about margaritas and tacos. Although they were sure that if he'd thought of it he would have. Oh well—what he didn't know…

An ambulance siren wailed in the distance and even though he wasn't Catholic, Reefer made the sign of the cross in the event somebody needed a prayer. The way he was taught in his church. And sardonically wished that someone would say a prayer for him when it was needed; although hopefully not soon.

Customers began to ready themselves to leave, and with them the fading buzz of animated conversation making the sound of the surf and wind even more pronounced. It competing likewise with the sound of traffic on the beach road out front.

The margaritas had served to take the edge off the hot summer day, and in that they had served their purpose.

Bookworm decided it was probably a good time to start back to Manhattan. The previously full parking lot was trending toward empty now. The ocean air pleasantly odorous with with the fragrance of salt and early summer blossoms. As they walked to the car Reefer spotted a homeless man lying in the shade of an old tree at the side of the seashell parking lot; a rusty shopping cart with his belongings comfortably close. And on a capricious whim, Reefer began to sprint articulately, head down like a fleet NFL running back on a straight course across the seashell parking lot toward the man, the pace set by his pumping knees and skinny calves driving his small size nine Teva rubber-toed sandals—not exactly made for running—rapidly into the white shells while unzipping his cargo shorts patch pocket one-handed and digging into it as he made his way.

Bookworm thumbed the key fob unlocking the driver's door and unchecking the alarm simultaneously.

Reefer reached the reposing figure, unsure if the person were asleep or passed out. Uneager to startle him in either case, Reefer spoke softly and gently, like speaking to a baby, "Sir? Sir," to rouse him. From trodding the city daily, Reefer's breath wasn't even increased minutely from the forty-yard dash he'd made without hesitation.

The man stirred, shook his head and groggily raised up.

"What? What?" He mumbled confusedly. Fireflies flashed their bulbs proudly in the veil of softly swaying summer trees above the simple scene.

The poor tortured soul smelled of sweat, filthy clothes, urine and cheap red wine. Reefer leaned over, took the man's hand gently and palming a bill to him, said, "Bless you, sir."

Bookworm flipped on the stereo and fondled the volume control, then started the engine and turned the a/c on high since the blazing afternoon sun had made the SUV's interior unbearably hot and the leather seats borderline intolerable. Then he snapped the seatbelt securely before he revved the big SUV's engine aggressively for cooling power and watched from the driver's seat as Reefer showed that his street hardness was eclipsed by the tenderness of his heart.

Acceptance and loyalty were what worked always for Bookworm and Reefer. No matter what else they had, there was always that. In that, they were perfect; not because of their positives, but because of their negatives, their flaws. Their flaws made them perfectly human.

And that was one of the reasons they were brothers. Neither would ever wrong the other. No Mending Wall needed. Elysium— only mortals related to the Gods and other heroes could be admitted there. Later, the conception of who could enter was expanded to include those chosen by the gods, the righteous, and the heroic. It was Bookworm's intent to be one of those. And although he wasn't on the precipice of being ordained a knight, nor was he a seventh son of a seventh son of a seventh son, and certainly had no halo confirming his status of being ready for sainthood; at least not as of yet, but it was thought by some that the screws with which it would be plumed to his skull had already been attached. And thus, preordained.

And like the gods, he hoped then to be able to choose some who might join him. And Reefer's kind gesture proof that he would be most deserving.

They both knew that street without heart was untenable or worse, even for those for whom the street was their genesis, or more than that, their soul.

But just because they were kind it didn't mean they were feckless.

Chapter Twenty-Six

Driving west toward Manhattan into the late afternoon sun, the road shimmered in the heat rising from the aged concrete. The bright orange burst through heavy dark clouds disrespectfully and reflected off the mirrored skyscraper windows of lower Manhattan, and while alternating between slanting trapezoids of bright sunshine piercing from the canyons and gloomy dark shadows cast from tall buildings. Bookworm, breaking local law by talking on his cell phone while driving, past a fallow former vacuum cleaner factory of aged once-red brick, not quite, antediluvian in appearance, revealing its age, even revitalized as expensive condos that looked alive only in winter when wisps of woodsmoke curled from its discrete chimneys that were tumbling down in its previous life, and relayed to the detective what Seabass had told him.

The vacuum cleaner condo building wasn't of the brutalist architecture, but it was brutal to look at and ironic at the same time because the employees that had spent a lifetime working there would never in their wildest imaginings be able to afford the million-dollar-plus buy-in it would take to live there. Bookworm figured he could get away with the small cell phone indiscretion by telling any prowl car cop who might stop him that he was talking to Detective Rossi. If that didn't sway the officer he knew Rossi would take care of it for him.

After being brought up to speed, Rossi asked, "so what d'ya think?"

"Inconclusive," Bookworm said, "but my gut tells me that the guy she talked with at the bar is our man."

"Cool. Let's work it, then. We mustn't be irresolute."

"Irresolute—good one. If it was him, make no mistake about it; he's one wily son of a bitch."

Cutting off the call with Rossi, Bookworm turned to Reefer, and said, "you gettin' hungry? How about some fried chicken?" Bookworm wasn't really hungry, but since it was on the NYPD, why not? It was a rhetorical question.

"I'd rather have fish."

Bookworm snorted loudly as a substitute laugh. "We're a couple of real brothers, aren't we? Fried chicken and fried fish. All we need is some hot sauce. But that's okay. I know a place." In truth, neither of them ate much fried food or they would be unable to stay as lean as they did, but Bookworm did know the best Jewish diner in the Bronx; which would be called a deli in Philly, where they'd put their eponymously named cream cheese on every sandwich.

He knew the diner because it was in the same building next door to the best newsstand on the upper east side and on the other side, his acupuncturist and herb specialist, Dr. Man.

He got a kick out of her name because of it being the same as the name of Bruce Lee's first kung fu teacher. And he would have never suspected that such a petite little Chinese woman could inflict on him so much pain. That unpleasant experience a necessary consequence of his injuries playing college football.

He needed to call for an appointment, dreading it already. He usually could hear anguished screams from other patients as he walked down the hallway before even entering her office. And how she'd say, "oh, that was a good one," if she caused him to flinch in pain. And he hoped people eating in the diner weren't able to hear the disturbing screams. They could certainly ruin one's appetite.

The eating establishment catering to lovers of everyday food was an altogether perfect example of the prototypical New York City diner, the heavy smell of cheap steaks, with but six cheap small white plastic and chrome tables set with plain but sturdy silverware, an aged white Formica topped counter that would seat only four, with the prices of the honest everyday meals for everyday painted in broad strokes in the large undraped plate glass windows, where you could sit at the real honest-to-God age-worn Formica-topped counter or a table to eat, next to other average people, if it wasn't too crowded, while Muzak, out of place in the frosty ancient eatery, played music from an era back when the diner was new and have your order taken by ay stained apron-covered, white uniform wearing gaunt but not yet wizened grandmotherly looking waitress wearing all older folks favorite sneakers; formerly white but now diner-dirty New Balances, a black plastic nametag reading Mabel pinned to her flat chest, and a stiff cardboard hat bobby-pinned to and perched on the uppermost heights of her gray bouffant-like hairdo, further adorned with two pencils crossed in a bun, like the ones she'd been wearing for over fifty years since back in the day when a bowl of soup and a cup of coffee followed by a huge slice of delicious apple pie topped with a square of yellow cheddar cheese could be had for eighty cents. It was still the cheapest place in town, but not like it had once been—and before the order was shouted to the most gregarious Jewish owner-cook through the silver aluminum shelved pass-through window to the kitchen located just below the menu hand-lettered on an aged multicolored dust-powder covered chalkboard on the wall above. Jewish food wasn't all they had though. One could indulge in real spaghetti from Italy, if they had a notion, or bangers and mash or Shepherd's pie from Ireland, or the aforementioned American fried fish or chicken.

"This place you know; does it have hot sauce?" Reefer didn't make a habit of being skeptical of Bookworm's knowledge of the city or it's many places in which a meal could be had, but he had to be sure.

"For fried fish?"

"Yeah."

"Yeah, I'm sure it does. But you know, if you haven't had it before, they have Filipino catsup. You oughta try it. They make it with bananas in the Philippines. It's gas."

"Catsup made with bananas? I think I'll take a pass." Reefer was incredulous at the idea.

"But, let's do it," he said, then, "you know, we be sounding a lot like Hawk on that Spenser TV show.

"The books were better," Bookworm reminded him with a sniff of self-righteous indignation. Truth was, he preferred the detail, imagery and carriage that reading called to mind that no actor, even the great Avery Brooks, could recreate. Or else it would be an actor's creation and not one's own mind and that would miss the whole point entirely, in his view.

"Have to take your word for it."

"But together we're tougher than Hawk, and smarter, and funnier and better looking, besides. Nothing against Hawk, of course. I'm just saying."

They found themselves in a surprising amount of inbound traffic. It didn't phase Bookworm, however. A surprisingly adept driver for a native New Yorker, since by the very nature of it it meant he didn't get that much practice; even if he did say so himself. Most likely couples going to dinner at Masa, Gramercy Tavern, Eleven Madison Park or any one of the other Michelin-Starred restaurants. No stodgy food, any.

And maybe take in a show on Broadway. Or if so inclined, to dance the night away at whatever boîte en fuego was the current place for beautiful people in the know.

At least those who don't rush home to use their latest generation iPad or iPhone to post pictures of their dinner on social media. Only because doing it while still at their table was considered bougie. But even with a serial killer on the prowl, for the most part New York was safer than ever and people felt safe coming back to the city; even at night

Neither Bookworm nor Reefer had ever been to a Broadway show. A shame for young men born and reared in the city. Bookworm was fairly sure he'd enjoy it though and kept telling himself he was going to go to one. Or even see one of the literary theatrical productions on the outdoor stage at Shakespeare In The Park, in Central Park. But not now.

There was work to do; a killer to catch. Life is short. The Bard would understand and appreciate Bookworm's sense of priorities. No matter what one's beliefs, priorities were as important in the twenty-first century as they had been in the sixteenth century.

Chapter Twenty-Seven

The Swordsman thought he needed to step up his game if he wanted to be the country's, possibly the world's, most prolific serial murderer of all time, or even New York City's most prolific, Joel Rifkin, the infamous killer of what is believed to be seventeen women, most of them prosses and sex workers. Of course he had no idea what number he would need for the U.S. record, since all serial killers tended to embellish their numbers when faced with imminent execution, since at that point it no longer mattered.

And yet there was virtually no chance at all that he could approach the numbers of some of the world's most prolific killers.

The hundreds attained by certain Colombian killers, or even the multiple dozens of those by U.K. and Eastern European psychopaths. By comparison, U.S. serial killers were positively pedestrian. He didn't know the reason for that unless it was that U.S. law enforcement officers were, in general, better than those of other countries and were apprehending murderers before they were able to get larger numbers.

And yet, that was his biggest problem mostly because of his choice of a weapon. It made for slow, tedious, albeit more enjoyable—for him at least, not the victim—kills, instead of being faster with a firearm of some sort. But using a sharpened blade was also what served to cause him to be somewhat more than a little terrifying.

Wednesday evening and the night was hot and humid, but The Swordsman was cool; or at least he thought so. A night in Times Square terrorizing rowdy partying tourists was just what the doctor ordered. His own devil's playground, him playing the role of the unholy specter. He wore his usual simple disguise of a ballcap—on this night the bright blue with red trim of the New York football Giants rather than the dark blue of their New York mates, the Yankees—pulled low over his eyes, and sunglasses, even though it was past twilight and nearing full dark. The fleeting thought entered his mind that maybe he should get a New-York-Jets-forest-green ballcap for a different look than the blues of the Giants and Yankees. But because they suck so bad, and he was afraid of the personal embarrassment and the ruination of his image, he didn't know if he had the stomach for it. Being a serial killer or being a Jets fan; he wasn't sure which was a more horrendous and altogether shameful fate.

But then he'd been considering adopting the head-to-toe black attire of a depressingly dressed Hasidic Jew and it would be all but guaranteed he'd never be recognized as a young blue-collar goyim, or gentile.

The thought of he, a lapsed Roman Catholic and serial killer, pretending to be Hasidic, to keep from being apprehended by what would more than likely be Irish or Italian Catholic cops was beyond hilarious in his twisted mind and would make an entertaining movie, he was sure. And it fitted with his own twisted rhyme and reason for doing what he does. And it reminded him more than a little of a scene from *The Saint*, the mid-twentieth century black and white tv drama series that, because of his young age, he'd seen only in reruns.

Being out and among the throngs of Times Square caused it to occur to him how New Yorkers liked to pretend that they didn't like tourists or at best begrudgingly accepted them, even though everyone knew that tourism was by far the city's most lucrative industry at more than forty-seven billion dollars for the most recent year; inclusive of Wall Street and international business of which it wasn't even close.

Barely dark and the welter of streets and sidewalks were packed. People were doing more than merely ambulating. They looked, gazed, breathed in and enjoyed every minute of the somewhat more than slightly visceral experience.

Every ethnic group in the world represented within a few small blocks. The wealthy and inconsequential side by side. They were all inconsequential to The Swordsman. Men in their Ermenegildo Zegna or Brioni suits, and Berluti Scritto sharkskin slip-on dress shoes, most wearing Breitling or Patek Philippe wristwatches that were worth more than Brody's car, all the time thinking they were the cat's ass. The women dressed not for their men, but to impress other women in Gucci or Armani outfits probably purchased at the uber expensive Bergdorf Goodman, with red lacquered-sole Christian Louboutins or Manolo Blahniks—never knockoffs for them, even if no one would know the difference, and Boadicea the Victorious perfume at almost thirteen hundred dollars for a 3.4 ounce bottle—fortunately for Brody he wasn't near enough to them to smell it; it would most likely turn his stomach, make him profoundly sick if he did—on their way to the newest Broadway musical, where they'd tipple a dram or two of brandy from the dimly lit theatre's cocktail bar until showtime.

Unless they imbibed in Ketel One Vodka martinis poured from dripping wet frost-covered silver shakers.

It was too warm for them to be dressed that fine, but in their minds they were pulling it off. Barely-dressed but finely made-up hookers on the prowl; tourists, probably staying at the Marriott Marquis right in the center of Times Square even though there were newer and more exclusive hotels now, since it opened, and because they couldn't afford a room at the Plaza even if they could have gotten a reservation as unlikely as that was, dressed like what they were, complete with Fanny packs and Zagat's in hand searching for the newest starred restaurant popular with their alike friends because they'd heard that all the beautiful people swear by it; even though it was unlikely that they had a clue as to what fine dining was, or who the beautiful people were, and smelly downtrodden homeless begging for handouts or at least looking at all the passersby with puppy dog eyes, trying without success to look if not deserving at least not undeserving; a difficult ambition, without a doubt.

People, male, female, young, old, all races, anyone who needs a job that pays minimum wage, handing out fliers that end up littering every inch of every sidewalk, advertising…everything, anything, that you could possibly desire which can be found in the streets of Mamhattan; and at least one fatalistic serial killer, all rubbing shoulders. All represented, except for the possibility of Sting's *Englishman In New York* from the song of the same name, in his bowler hat and walking stick in hand. There were however, in his place the men with the ever-present straw-colored Hasidic Jew-fro pressed down by the typical black wool felt wide-brimmed fedora. They, dressed in all black suits with all of the fingers of their hands covered in diamonds but instead of fedoras, half of them wearing their ubiquitous yarmulkes, most of whom worked in one of the nearby gemstone merchants in the diamond district of midtown west. The area cleverly, but somewhat less than kindly referred to by some as Jew York. Mixing with the ones shunting rolling rack of dresses. Giving that large area the look of a shtetl. The only setting where you could see more Jewish folk was at the shul. Or at the mikvah where Hasidic men stopped for their daily immersion, twice on Friday, in preparation for the sabbath. Their rebbetzin waiting patiently for them at home. While they kibitzed with each other in Yiddish and greeted everyone who graced their stores of jewels with a Yiddish blessing even though they eyed them cautiously through the plate glass doors before buzzing them in through the locked security entrances.

The practice started from the time they worried about the Italian mafia robbing them. Then showing the treasured guests huge perfectly cut sparkling diamonds on small wavy black velvet lined trays under the subdued but direct lighting. And certainly the last of those present, which would frighten the others literally to death if they were but aware of his presence.

The main reason Brody recognized the designer outfits is because of the stay-at-home suburban princesses he met when working on the air conditioning units in their abhorrently expensive outré East Hampton mansions, who were already dressed to meet hard-working hubs—the poor schmucks—for dinner at the latest hotspot Manhattan gourmet resto where dinner with expensive Chardonnay, and a side of roasted chestnut stuffing, except when it's not close enough to Christmas, and either beluga caviar or beef carpaccio appetizers or both to start, if they even eat beef, with which they would undoubtedly know the correct fork to use with each course, and all before dessert and espresso, which in total, cost more than Brody made in a week, which hubs would undoubtedly pay for with his platinum American Express; unless he'd already upgraded to the black card.

The underpaid loser, but movie-star-beautiful hostess, who isn't qualified to do anything else, would undoubtedly, greet them with air kisses on both cheeks, sniffing the perfumed air caressed by the expensive fragrance around the woman's neck, newly beginning to wrinkle, for which hubs was already paying for Botox treatments, which are an absolute necessity among the middle-aged female Hampton's set, all the while lying sweetly to her about how lovely she looks.

Then, after they're seated she would stop by their table, the coveted four top which they are allowed because of the insane amounts of money they spend there, with two fresh flowers in a ridiculously expensive purple glass bud vase lovingly placed on an immaculate white table cloth, to say hello again and then, have a complimentary bottle of ridiculously expensive highly communicative and resplendent Chardonnay sent over to them. Ensuring herself a lovely cash bestowal for her thoughtfulness.

The very thought of the whole scene making him want to heave. He'd have more respect for them if they went to Nathan's on Coney Island for takeout hot dogs or even to the largest and one of the oldest Chinatowns in the U.S. in downtown Manhattan, and ordered carryout authentic Chinese food and ate it at home from the little white cardboard cartons with red Chinese characters decorating them that unfold to make primitive plates, with genuine chopsticks made of wood, complete with splinters. But never ebony ones. They'd have to be a shade of tan, a common wood color. Not that he was autistic and therefore the black ones offensive to his brain. It was just personal preference. Or they could even eat the rice with their fingers the way it's done in Southeast Asia. But that would work only if it's thick and clumpy. He knew that was the way they did it from his time spent in that part of the world when he was in the army. And only if they ate it plain. Never to be eaten with any of that sriracha sauce shit. And the same way, never to use the new plastic chopsticks, even if they were the same color and did last forever, then forever more in a landfill.

Although it occurred to him that chopsticks could make fine weapons of murder. The thought crossed his mind that he might have to try them sometime. One in each eye of some sad victim. Leaving them protruding. The reason being not to prevent a permanent retinal image imprint of their killer like the theory some believe that occurred before death. For him only because he was evil and he thought it might amuse him. He'd have to decide though; plastic or wood, plastic or wood. Perhaps one of each, to determine which he prefers, for future reference.

And unknown to Brody the wooden version of the implements was mass produced in the small town of Americus, Georgia, at the only chopstick factory in the Americas, at the rate of four million sets per day of which almost one hundred percent were shipped to China. It was a fact, as hard to believe as it sounds, over a billion Chinese people use Georgia-manufactured chopsticks daily.

The lights of Time Square illuminated the nascent dusk. Only to remind people of their purpose. So no one think them fey. Still early for summer. The large digital clock visible on The Times building had just ticked off eight thirty-seven. One could taste the heavy muggy air. The buzz of it. Actually, it was more than a buzz, a sensation never felt before, by anyone…on this planet. But then, were they? Really? A theoretical depth virtually no one ever considered lest they not like the answer they encountered.

The center of the universe looked like what one would think. Especially to the first-time visitors from Toledo, Baton Rouge, and Jackson, MS. The gaping wide-open mouths and gawking stares told you which ones they were. Of course, they had to be from somewhere. Everybody's from somewhere. If only the world.

To the Swordsman it was nothing more than mere killing fields. He was grateful for the scores of tourists unawares.

Most of the visitors looking for Times Square fixtures, the

muscular Naked Cowboy or the green-painted and topless but green-draped Lady Liberty either of whom they'd pay five dollars to be in a picture. The first, Times Square's original performance artist and serious bodybuilder, whose more common name, Robert John Burck, wasn't really naked but wore tighty-whiteys by his official sponsor, Fruit Of The Loom, with Naked Cowboy imprinted across his posterior and his matching white leather hand embroidered cowboy boots and coordinating cowboy hat and a strategically placed acoustic guitar on which he played country tunes popular even in New York City. Dressed skimpily even on the bitterest days of winter while singing for tips. But he couldn't really be considered a busker because the Times Square performances had been his daily full-time job for more than twenty-two years, except in 2010 when he considered running against Barack Obama for president representing the Tea Party movement and that took time away from his regular income producing pursuit, rumored to earn him consistently one hundred, fifty thousand a year and producing a net worth of four million dollars. Proving that his bachelor's degree in political science from the University of Cincinnati was worth it.

The Swordsman wasn't paying attention to either of the Times Square celebrities, however, as he was focused on finding his next unsuspecting victim. But first he wandered inside the open doors of one of the twenty-four-hour souvenir shops for a fresh pack of cigs. *Shout It Out Loud* by Kiss blasting away from speakers they hoped some sucker would buy, even though they'd been blaring loudly 24-7 for too many years to remember. And were the staticky type that comes with old age and overuse because of it.

Resupplied with his preferred legal drug, he walked slowly, chain smoking, while leaning over and cupping both hands around the nicotine delivery systems to protect the precious flame from the gusts between the tall buildings, to light the next one off the one previous. Clouds of steam billowed up from small steel grates where the homeless typically slept to warm themselves by the steam that rose from New York's otherworldly underground of iron pipes.

Brody would have to stop smoking before he picked out a target. No way he could pick up someone with class whilst smoking like the proverbial Christmas chimney.

And most were unsuspecting; especially the most annoying ones from Gary, Indiana or Sheboygan, Michigan, gazing skyward, ignoring everything around them. Thinking to themselves; "That could never happen to me." But, night falling, staring open-mouthed toward the miasma of undulating fog obscuring the upper floors of buildings and the sudden burst of Times Square neon as far as one could see.

Fortunately for the Swordsman, in a city of roughly more than ten million people plus tourists, visitors and people traveling on business more than doubling that number it was highly unlikely that he would bump into anyone that knew him.

The temperature was surprisingly pleasant for early evening in late June in the confines of the city's sheer anachronistic old school skyscraper-walled canyons and valleys. None of the glass and steel ones that don't fit in with their older brothers. But wait until August, before autumn would arrive changing everyone's opinion of New York for the better.

Kids were everywhere, acting as if they were adults. And compared to their counterparts in the Midwest or the south they probably were. New York would make you grow up fast, whether you wanted to or not.

The Swordsman paused to watch a street artist doing a pastel drawing of a tourist seated in a folding chair in the middle of the world-famous intersection. He could remember the time when you could drive through Times Square, before the city made the decision that it would be better used as a pedestrian plaza.

The artist's assistant, a cute young brunette trying to rustle up new out of town clients, asked the Swordsman, unaware of her possible danger, if he'd like a portrait. Her looks and over the top personality made her perfect for the job. And although his ego thought it would be cool to have an original one-of-a-kind portrait of himself, the serial killer he was knew it would be unwise to put himself on display in that manner. Either posing in front of a large crowd or the permanent record. Even if he was wearing a fairly nice, albeit sort of dated red chambray shirt that would look good on canvas.

Even he was smart enough not to wear his work shirt with the company logo above the left pocket when he was on the prowl. Didn't want to make things too easy for those law enforcement assholes.

Instead, it was easy for the Swordsman or anybody to get lost in the mass of humanity that is Times Square.

A first-time visitor couldn't imagine the lights, the action, the noise, the din, that was Times Square twenty-four, seven, 365. It would be unnatural if it weren't.

The Swordsman's biggest challenge would be finding a secluded spot to do what he hoped would present itself presently. And in such a large crowd there would most likely be more than a scant number of suitable possibilities.

That and avoiding the large contingent of uniformed and plainclothes NYPD officers that were a constant presence doing their best to keep Times Square safe for all; New Yorkers and tourists alike. The Swordsman just thought they were a pain in the ass.

In fact, as he walked, he passed two horse patrolmen sitting astride their magnificent mounts at the curb, one, older, looking like he didn't have a care in the world with his forearms crossed over the saddle's pommel, the younger of the two officers sitting at attention astride the huge animal with his right hand at rest but ready on the butt of his holstered weapon. Without looking directly at them, he muttered under his breath, "assholes," not meaning it in the nicest possible way, and kept walking.

Unlike the typical profile of many serial killers who are, Brody wasn't a police groupie and couldn't understand why anyone, serial killer or not, admired police. He thought they were all pieces of shit and was pretty sure that most of them got into law enforcement because they liked hanging with the criminal element but didn't have the guts to be thugs themselves. And he certainly didn't want to hang out with any of them like the almost legendary Wayne Williams, the Atlanta Child Murderer, narcissistically claimed, or the equally infamous Burbank, California killer, necrophiliac and cannibal, Edmund Kemper did, going to the local cops' favorite dive bar, The Jury Room, and befriending them and drinking beer with them. Audaciously showing little respect for their abilities to stop him showed the extreme level of his hubris. Playing a dangerous but nevertheless exciting game of hide-in-plain-sight. But Brody had his own problems.

He was someone's, maybe a lot of someones, living, breathing nightmare, and he had to live with that, which was surprisingly easy to do.

Easy because he was bereft of the usual human qualities of empathy, sympathy and caring. Easy because it was almost like he was completely uncivilized. But he thought he was better than others because it wasn't like he was killing people by running them through with a Narwhal tusk the way the last heathen serial killer did in New York the year before. At least he had that working for him.

And besides, all he was attempting to do was honor Charles Bukowki's famous line in his poem *Alone with Everybody*; the graveyards fill. That his unstated to anyone else, goal; to fill the graveyards. Which made him a poet of sorts. And it wasn't like he had enmity for any particular type. He just loved the shit out of killing people. Playing God in his own sick way.

"Fucking cowards," Brody added as he continued past the mounted officers. And without guns they wouldn't be jackshit, he thought. But as long as they were there, a presence, in sight, nobody would assault anyone, or rape anybody, or jack a tourist, or rob a business. And that was all they could do. Try and stop crime on their small piece of turf in Times Square by their presence alone; by virtue of being seen by people who didn't wish to run afoul of them.

Two obviously well-fed fat pigeons were laying siege to and fighting over the disgusting remains of a Starbucks apple fritter someone had discarded in the gutter. They were lucky the feral rats from down in the underground tunnels, which they'd left abandoned to the Mole People of New York hadn't gotten to it first. Or maybe they had and that was why it looked disgusting. Just for shits and grins the Swordsman clapped his hands at them in a vain attempt to scare them off. But they did startle a moment later, when the sky, brocaded with ponderous clouds, the deep-throated thunder sounded long and loud, and they skittered away to the safety of the tunnels that were thought of as their home and away from the human intruders.

Like the pigeons, The Swordsman was snapped back to reality by the ear-piercing clap of thunder. "Concentrate," he chastised himself aloud. Thinking too much about his next kill. Just let it happen. Mind wandering again, he noticed on one of the flashing lightbulb news by the minute billboards next to one advertising sodas and cigarettes on a high building, told everyone, locals and tourists, alike, whether they cared or not, that the Yankees were leading the Angels five-four in the fifth inning.

Of course the Yankees are baseball's most popular franchise, with fans the world over. So, in the international epicenter of Times Square, it was highly likely that there were somewhat more than a few folks who cared. Brody counted himself among them as one of the blue-collar faithful of the Bronx Bombers, influenced as he had been by his dad and gramps. And if it were called because of weather with the current score, they'd record a rain-shortened win. He couldn't recall whether the informative billboard belonged to Fox News Channel or NBC.

The same as every night, Times Square was aswarm with throngs of people, but not like it would be on a Friday or Saturday evening. None of the usual weekend Times Square bacchanalia and drunken revelry.

Although less than crowded it was intoxicating for Brody even if he was a native New Yorker. Watching the throngs of tourists, however, caused him to wonder how many of them had tickets to see Saturday Night Live. Everybody knew it wasn't the same since the days of the Blues Brothers, Chevy Chase, Eddie Murphy, and the other greats. And he'd heard how surprisingly small the stage actually was but he'd really like to see it in person sometime, even if the show sucked compared to the old days. Or Late Night, but it wasn't worth a shit anymore since David Letterman retired. Everybody knew that that asshole, Stephen Colbert, couldn't carry Letterman's jockstrap. But he was sure tickets would cost way more than he could afford anyways.

But if he could find a tourist or a businesswoman alone maybe she'd take him back to her room at The Plaza, which takes its name for the Grand Army Plaza with its continuously flowing fountain in the center of 5th Avenue and mere steps from the hotel's grand entrance, the grand dame built on the site of the perhaps even more gallant, Savoy, and or the Pierre; the regal twin neighbors on 59th St, also known as Central Park South and Billionaire's Row. That would be cool, unaccustomed as he was to propriety. And it would help him to take his mind off his financial limitations.

Brody had never stayed at either one of the iconic hotels. He thought he'd like to get a haircut in the hotel's barbershop; probably by an effeminate young man named Pierre or Jacque, who would be anything but indifferent, if he could afford one in what was sure to be a swanky salon. And that was doubtful. He hand-smoothed his unruly hair with the thought of it.

The staff would greet him courteously, as if he were someone important, and probably pour him a drink while he was getting a trim. Bourbon, vodka, rum. Or perhaps a glass of French Chardonnay; a lovely white Burgundy. Or get him some drugs.

Whatever his heart desired; but he'd stopped doing drugs. He only smoked a little grass every now and then. Grass didn't count. Everybody knew it wasn't really even a drug. In fact he'd grown so accustomed to it it didn't even affect him anymore. They'd probably send someone to get him a beer from the hotel's dark lounge, or to a street dealer they could trust for some good quality grass. Not like the crap he usually smoked. But just for their upscale clients. One could dream. And, if he did get a trim, then he could do her in luxury before he really did her in luxury. Who knew? With a classy haircut it might even be that he'd appear to be a real human being; not just living in his own head, existentially, even to himself. Especially to himself, since he didn't abide anyone else judging him.

But even if he could afford a pricey salon 'do with all the extras he didn't know if he would, because he'd been thinking about dying his hair blonde or letting it grow out. He thought he'd like a look similar to Jared Leto's when he portrayed the serial killer in the movie *The Little Things*. Brody thought the long haired look would work for him, too, since they were both blue collar workers, and serial killers. Although Leto's hair was pretty damn long and he might not be able to pull that off while working a 9 to 5 gig. He'd probably have to pull it back in a man bun to keep it from getting in his way at work or during his extracurricular activities. Tying it back would probably work for protecting against leaving DNA evidence also. Of course, Jared Leto tied his back too, when he's playing with his band, *Thirty Seconds to Mars*. Otherwise, it probably got too hot when he's moving around on stage.

In that case, if not that long, at least as long as John Wick's, er, Keanu Reeves' hair in the newest John Wick movie.

Of course he'd have to grow a somewhat scraggly beard too, to copy either look. And it was highly likely that his boss would say to hell with that and fire his ass—the asshole, and that would suck; emasculating a grown ass thirty-five-year-old man and army veteran. And at the same time thinking how cool technology is that he'd already watched both movies on HBOMax, even if it was on his cheap ass phone's shitty little cracked screen from when he'd dropped it too many times while he was working.

At least it kept him from having to scour New York for a still operating video rental store since they were closing at a rate faster than when they opened back in the eighties. And then have to worry about returning it on time. And having to pay a late fee. Or spending even more money at one of the city's ridiculously expensive multi-screen theaters, which he certainly couldn't afford to do on his meager wages and would be unwilling to even if he could afford it.

Moreover, it was a matter of principle with him not to let any of those rich assholes get any of his hard-earned greenbacks.

Brody needed to find a restroom soon to take a piss or else he'd need to duck into an alley to relieve himself, which he wasn't above doing. It being a much better option than pissing his pants in the middle of Times Square.

Of course as hot it was and as much as he was sweating he might never piss again. It unfortunately reminded him of the time he spent in Kuwait after he was conscripted by his family history into the army. A hundred- and-twenty-five degrees Fahrenheit in the shade if…you could find any. But like the old joke goes—but it's a dry heat. Like that makes any difference. And the other old joke—it's better to be pissed off than pissed on.

His goal now, though, was to focus on finding a victim. It didn't matter who. Male, female, young, old, anyone. He hated it when he got like this; his need overpowering everything else. Including his usually uncommon common sense. That's when it was possible he might do something stupid; something that could get him caught.

The portended torrent the thunder boomer promised arrived throwing its weight around assaultingly. In a matter of minutes the streets and sidewalks of Times Square were awash, reflecting shinily what one might think were all the neon colors in the world. But at least he wasn't hot anymore. Just wet. A wet Philistine hitchhiker moving guide-less through the galaxy that is Times Square. Doing his part to hasten the destruction of the planet.

And what better place to do that than Times Square?

And if he thought about it that sounded rhetorical even to him. The center of a metaphorical universe, neither as honorable as the west side, it the home of the World War II Intrepid Aircraft Carrier Museum parked on the Hudson River piers, nor as indecorous as the East. While in his head a bleak to anyone but him noir music soundtrack played on a continuous loop. The soundtrack of his existence.

On the one hand, it would be hard to pick up a female victim while soaking wet. On the other hand, if he did manage to get lucky, once she realized what was happening, and began to sob, no one would be able to see her tears in the Manhattan rain. And that was the bitch of it for her. And his saving grace. And he knew that that attitude wouldn't be considered enlightened, but he just considered it gender honesty. And as Polonius said with a shrug in Act I, Scene III of *Hamlet*, he thought…This above all to thine own self be true… Brody wasn't aware of the saying or from where it came among Shakespeare's most noteworthy works, or even know that it was from Shakespeare, or the rest of the famous saying, but he was pretty sure that the first line was the most important part of the soliloquy most famous; to him at least, anyway.

Truth was however, he had lost hope, in himself, in the world, in his place in the world. As it was he was resigned; to what he is, to what he would ever be. And in that there was no hope. And that's why he was resigned to his future, or his lack thereof of one. No hope and resignation; a vicious, endless circle. And he accepted that with somewhat more than a little reluctance.

There was noise, lots of noise, in the shiny glittering Mecca that was Times Square; that looked like a Hopper painting. There was the rhythm of the city, the energy of Gotham. Most New Yorkers considered it nothing more than white noise. A background sound to aid them in sleep; if indeed they heard it at all. Without noise the city didn't run. Without noise it just was. And it always was. But the noise is the proof. It's hard for one to discern the individual sounds.

There's always the confection of sounds. Those of unmuffled archaic V-8 yellow taxi motors, at least an equal number of Ubers and Lyfts; too many of those on the streets but at least they drove all of the gypsy taxi companies out of business and that pleased everybody. Horns blasting, echoing off the concrete, buses pulling away in low gear, the ear-piercing wail of police car sirens, unrecognizable but nevertheless loud music from storefront doors flung open wide and never to shut, people laughing, talking, swearing, the shriek of screams, those of joy and those of surprise, in different languages and accents; shoes scraping on the sidewalks. But taken altogether, it was just noisome. The never-ending symphony of the city. Like the sound of a million discordant, or worse, dissonant, voices. None of them individually distinguishable. And why would you want them to be? Together, they're only the sounds of the universe. A universe the center of which was Times Square. That universe ill at ease with itself. And that was okay. Why wouldn't it be? That was a rhetorical question of course. One for which that there was no answer; rhetorical or otherwise. Once one grew accustomed to the noise no one wanted quiet ever again.

Thinking himself a gourmand, but only in the sense of one who enjoys eating big but not necessarily gourmet, Brody proceeded to walk down Broadway's east side sidewalk south to the McDonald's sitting next to the Times Square Visitor Center in the literal center of Times Square and the metaphorical universe, to get a Quarter Pounder with cheese, large fries and a vanilla shake.

As it turned out however, he was ravenous and decided a Quarter Pounder with cheese and a Big Mac with all the trimmings in addition to the fries and shake would be just what he needed. He could eat the shit out of some McDonald's even though the well-known menu items in the city cost correspondingly more than in smaller U.S. towns because of the astronomical rent in New York. Indeed the company had to make up the difference somehow. But Brody wasn't monomaniacal about the fast-food restaurant. Likewise, he could also eat the shit out of a Burger King Whopper, or even an Arby's roast beef sandwich on occasion. It depended on his mood and which he had last eaten.

He considered himself lucky for he had a high metabolism and did manual labor besides, because he could seriously overdose on some fast food and not give a second thought to his weight.

Brody took his two sacks bursting at the seams from the considerable amount of junk food outside to sit on one of the long granite benches the city had installed on newly-constructed raised concrete islands where there had once been traffic lanes in one of the busiest intersections on the face of the earth making it a pedestrian plaza.

He wiped off the stone wet from the rain with a couple of the napkins of which they always put more than you need, in the bag. Or at least Brody needed since he usually used the sleeve of his shirt. Keeping an eye open for opportunities should they arise, but at the same time not wanting anything to interrupt his dinner. I think therefore I am. He knew someone, somewhere, at some time, had said that. In Latin. Probably a Roman, in Rome, but perhaps among conquered regions, millennia before. But at the moment all he was thinking about was food. Because for The Swordsman there was no past; no future. Only the moment. That's not unusual. He wasn't clever enough to think deep thoughts, to live anywhere but in the food.

And in the moment, while he was consuming the food, likewise, the food was consuming him, or at least his focus.

His mind wandered as he dug rapidly cooling fries out of the white sack logoed with Golden Arches and red print. After two or three fingers full he wiped his greasy fingers and his greasier mouth on his sleeve. They had put plenty of the cheap paper napkins in the bag but it didn't occur to him to use them. Why would he change a lifelong habit now; unless he were trying to impress some chick. Of course, if she were impressed by him not wiping his mouth on his sleeve, or knowing which fork to use for each course, then he wouldn't want her, anyway, except for killing.

With the gently arriving dusk the rain had stopped but still a mist worthy of London's most notorious areas of the unusual, or of macabre stories by Poe or the recently deceased great Carlos Ruiz Zafon, warm penumbras of darkness appeared around the ever so slightly dimmer neons of the city's center, its heartbeat of activity.

Indeed, he considered deeply. Inept, ineffectual, incompetent;

Brody wasn't sure which word best-described the piss-poor job the NYPD was doing in its attempt to apprehend him. Maybe that was it; piss-poor. Whichever word described it best, he was glad for their incompetency. They certainly weren't as ubiquitous as they might wish the citizenry think in their efforts to stop urban crime.

And he wouldn't be surprised to hear they introduced a deus ex machina to help solve the murders or to distract the public from their lack of success, whichever was most apropos. At this point, like most other killers before him, Brody was starting to become confident that law enforcement would never catch him. That they were inferior to him in all ways. It seemed to him that an elaborate ruse based on pissing on the public's collective leg and calling it rain was in the works. Even so, he had not been in contact with the NYPD in a dangerous game of cat and mouse that follows the examples set by many other killers, who, being narcissists and thinking themselves cleverer than they actually were, liked to prove it by attempting to outsmart law enforcement one-on-one.

The most notable of those, Edmund Kemper from Burbank, Ca, the six-foot, nine-inch murderer known as the Coed Killer, who murdered ten people between 1972 and 73 and liked to hang out at a bar popular with police to drink beer and talk with them in an attempt to learn what they knew about the killer, they unaware that the killer was sitting there among them. Until he actually killed the teenage baby sitter for the family of one of the cops he charmed with his outgoing personality. But as long as the NYPD kept those ViCAP sons of bitches from the FBI from getting involved Brody felt like he had a better than fifty-fifty shot of evading capture.

Suddenly he thought about the large vanilla shake sitting on the bench beside him and needed to start on it before it melted away completely in the humid warm dusk. A mom with her little shit of a kid, a probably five-year-old little boy sat down on the bench near to him. The kid being an annoying little ass, alternating between staring at him, and his food.

He wanted to tell the chick to control her goddamn kid. But he decided to leave well enough alone. Of course he could have straightened them both out, but he knew that wouldn't go over well in overcrowded Times Square. She had no concept of how lucky they were. If in fact, she had known who he was she would have been as nervous as a Thanksgiving turkey during the third week of November.

Perhaps picking up on something detestable adults wouldn't notice in their bench neighbor and doing as kids are wont to do, the annoying child stuck his thumbs in each ear and wriggled his fingers at the dangerous man. Little did the child know how dangerous the gesture was, as Brody glanced around to see if anyone was paying specific attention to him, and noticing no one, flipped the little bastard off. It didn't feel as good as killing him would have felt, but it was satisfying, at least for the moment. And it didn't bother him in the least. As he was most assuredly an equal opportunity asshole. The only thing that mattered in his twisted mind was that the recipient of his ire deserved it. And right then, at that moment, the little shit deserved it. He wished the little shit would just leave him the hell alone since it was hard to concentrate on his thoughts and his food while being stared at.

Chapter Twenty-Eight

Finished with the cheap and unhealthy dinner and feeling the need to relax in a cool setting, and since it was directly across the broad center of the world known as Times Square, he decided to visit the Marriott Marquis' eighth floor lobby lounge for an adult beverage. Who knew, maybe he would encounter someone who couldn't resist his charm. In that there was always hope.

As he knew it would be, it was much cooler after stepping out of the hustle and bustle of Times Square into a different hustle and bustle of Times Square's metaphorical universe on the the hotel's eighth floor. People shopping in the hotel's many boutique stores, eating sumptuously in its main restaurant and waiting to meet friends while staying in the center of everything. And he felt immediately cleaner away from the heat, dirt and grime of the world's most famous street eight floors below. Not that his lack of cleanliness bothered him except that it might keep him from being as successful in finding his next opportunity.

He sat at the dark marble-topped hotel piano bar adjacent to the dining room and close enough to get caught up in the smell of and the reflection of lights in the heavily lacquered shine of the beautiful ebony Steinway baby grand, manufactured right there in the city, sitting but a few steps away. He thought the opulence was a waste on most of the redneck assholes from Iowa, South Carolina and Arkansas who were undoubtedly staying there; but he wouldn't mind killing one or two of them if he got the chance. That's not unusual. That would give them something to tell their friends about back home, he thought. Except that they'd be dead. He cracked himself up sometimes.

And although he was certainly capable of, and did, on occasion, hunt humans, in truth, was a capable hunter, many times, in such a target-rich environment such as the beautiful hotel lobby, victims were almost certain to fall into his proverbial lap. Or his clutches. And so, thinking tangentially was not a requirement when it came to finding his next victim. Moreover, wasn't death ubiquitous? And inevitable? And inescapable? A ubiquitous, inevitable and inescapable conclusion to this time capsule called life. That was rhetorical. Of course it was. And in that event, so what if he were only hastening someone's inevitable and inescapable grand finale a bit; so what, so what, indeed. Plainly he could see what he does as nothing but a quickening of the supreme ending. An abstract and at least a little naive vision of existence and its ultimate conclusion, undoubtedly. But until and unless it happened he always wondered if and hoped there would be blood.

In a setting such as this was when he was at his best. He could be friendly, warm even, but only if one were exceptionally aware and an astute judge of character would they see that the warmth was just skin-deep. It didn't reach his eyes.

His steely light blue eyes that were perennially deadly. That was physiological and something that couldn't be changed along with the halfway pleasant manner of which he was capable when he tried. At the same time he found being even halfway pleasant laborious. He'd much rather be his usual self, which if he were to be honest, most of the time, was an asshole. Still, it was much easier for him.

So everyone must be prepared. In their own way, whatever that means. To them.

And most of the time when The Swordsman killed he did so so exquisitely the victim didn't even feel pain. If they did, most of the time, he felt like he had screwed up. He wasn't always successful in that noble goal, but the truth was he tried his damndest. And it wasn't that he didn't want them to feel pain, it was only that he considered himself an artiste and an artiste should be able to perform his skill, his art, in this case to kill, without inflicting needless pain. At least in his twisted mind. And with every killing he became more confident; it dawning on him that with each killing he became as self-assured as serial killers in novels. And he hoped that he could inspire writers, novelists, to use his deadly artistry in future stories.

Brody ordered a beer—and he found it a touch unbelievable

that in such a fancy setting they didn't even have domestic. He had to order some fancy-ass Dutch beer for twelve dollars a goddamn mug, which pissed him off even more. You'd think an American hotel in the theoretical capitol of the United States would at least have his usual Bud Light Draft tall boy or a nice ice-cold Lite beer from Miller. It was a disgrace in his mind. Might as well be drinking some girly-shit white wine. The country was going to hell faster than one could even think possible. What was a fine true-blooded American man supposed to do…or drink? It was a rhetorical interrogative. And without an answer, a red-blooded American could die of thirst, and that wouldn't look good on any bartender's resume.

A moment later, a not particularly striking, but rather plain brunette woman, of no more than her late thirties, the type who typically responded well to his overtures, dressed casually for walking midtown's fashionable streets and laden with shopping bags from her trip around the borough sat down the bar a way, and he gave her an over-the-top cool acknowledgement with a nod and a subtle naughty boy smile. He had mastered the art of various smiles because he never knew which one would work to disarm a victim, so he had to be practiced in them all.

He was happy to see her, the act renewing his faith that there were in fact real humans in this theoretical universe of Times Square. She smiled back tentatively with her mouth and a little more than somewhat severely with her eyes. Probably nothing more than a reflexive act akin to pulling a bedsheet up to cover your shoulders.

A fan of old movies, Brody thought she looked the part of a visiting ingénue from out of town, in a 1950s era black and white New York City based film. Probably made by famed director John Cassavetes and starring the inimitable Rod Steiger.

Her slight gesture taken as encouragement, at least in his eyes, was all it took for Brody to slide his all-too-pricy bottle of Dutch hops down the shiny bar, adjusting the insatiable hori hori knife in his waistband at his back with his other hand as he did, to move a couple of stools nearer to his neighbor who had suddenly become a target unsuspecting. As he did he casually glanced her way again as if by accident, as she gave him a lingering glance he interpreted as feigned coyness before turning away. Ah, playing hard to get, he thought. Or highly more than likely, pretending to. When, in her mind she was attempting to do anything but encourage him. It didn't matter. She would still be his. It was just a question of how and how soon.

His heartbeat quickened. It usually did at times like these.

He could feel more than hear the basso thump-thump deep in his chest. Even as he looked at her he scanned the hotel lobby entire. Being aware of his surroundings was how he both kept out of trouble and located additional victims. Then he turned his careful gaze upwards forty-four floors, past all of the hotel's room floors looking below to the eighth-floor lobby atrium, to where the hotel's revolving restaurant, The View, called the rooftop aerie home aptly named because the only time it didn't have a view was when the top of the hotel, in fact New York itself, even the winged statue of the infernal appearing Mercury atop Grand Central Station, was shrouded in dense ethereal fog.

A musician most likely awaiting his hoped-for Broadway call, wearing black polyester trousers and a long sleeve white shirt with ruffles, with skin the color of café au lait and near waist-length orange dreads much like suspected drug dealer and rap superstar, Fetty Wap, looked quite colorful and appropriately began to softly tinkle the eighty-eight keys. He rocked his head and grinned like a Cheshire Cat in the dark-framed and dark-lensed sunglasses, an indoor indication that he was blind as a bat.

One less pair of eyes for Brody to worry about remembering him and describing him to the NYPD. The orange dreads appeared to be weighing heavily on his head and neck. His songbook consisted mostly of 50s era jazz and pop standards. It was a manner fitting for the dramatic setting. His sick and twisted soul nevertheless old, Brody thought if the musician had had a horn player and drummer sitting in on Dave Brubeck's all-time great jazz standard, *Take Five*, it would be the perfect backbeat for the early evening in the classy setting. And he wondered, wondered why they didn't make music like that any longer. Jazz had so much more soul than anything else, before or since, in his mind. Though his was an old soul.

Brody took a serious drink of the fancy lager and the price of it caught in his throat causing him to blanch.

The dim light was classy and appropriate for the magnificent lobby and in sharp contrast to the neon-bright overwhelming darkness of Times Square, outside. Not the darkness of night, but the darkness of Gotham. The bleakness. The darkness that is always a part of the city; in truth, one of the elements of the city.

There was nothing temperamental about the darkness. It was always present. It was left to the individual as to whether they would choose to accept it or not. It was inconsequential to the darkness whether people accepted it or not. The darkness frightened some; for others it was a part of, or they a part of it. Like The Swordsman. It a part of The Swordsman's tortured soul, a welcome presence during the light of day or to cause the night to be darker; at least psychologically.

He had grown accustomed to it. Like the mighty winged gray stone gargoyles and their cherub friends perched on the cornices of the same color on tall aging buildings were accustomed to it. Their penetrating untiring eyes keeping watch over all. Even when Manhattan slept. More than merely coexisting with the darkness, The Swordsman had embraced it; undeniably, earned its respect, made friends with it, and it with him. What else was there to do?

Although Brody listened to some hip hop, Fetty Wap included, he thought that romantic soft music might better serve to aid him in picking up a woman who was destined, nay, preordained to become his latest victim. She wasn't aware of it yet, or certainly she would have already made her escape.

The Swordsman tilted his mug containing the pricey but nevertheless welcome foreign ale toward her neat martini—he had no way of knowing if it were vodka or gin, and nonchalantly, choosing his words carefully, as if he didn't have many to spare, said, "come here often?" He mistakenly considered that it was a clever line to use on someone who, sitting in a luxurious hotel bar in an international city, might be from anywhere in the world and visiting for the first time. Even if he unknowingly mispronounced "often," saying it with a hard "t." Too unsophisticated to realize his mistake.

"Actually, no. I've never even been to New York before," she said in a Midwestern non-accent, before adding, "Oh, you were trying to be funny. Sorry; I didn't get it at first."

The look on his face was one of feigned dismay before he said, "and here I thought it was one of my best lines."

"I hope not," she said meaning it, showing a strong sense of deportment, while looking as if she only wanted to be left alone. She didn't look like she cared one way or the other if it was one of his best lines. It was obvious to The Swordsman he would need to tone down his personality.

He knew it could be overwhelming at times, and it appeared that he needed to dial it back to whelming only, lest he run the risk of turning her off. Good thing he wasn't having coffee and a cruller. The deadly combination of caffeine and sugar would really send his personality over the top; possibly making it too much for her to handle. That's not unusual.

Oh well, just a woman with an attitude, anyway, he thought, and smiled insolently. And that would only serve to make him want to do her even more than he already did. And make him enjoy it even more. The takeaway here being it doesn't pay to be an asshole. Or a bitch for a woman. It would be obvious to anyone paying attention that no one ever taught her that she should remember her manners and shouldn't be incautious, especially when visiting the naked city.

Alas, she had never learned one of life's most important lessons, judged so by numerous generations of people before, and it was about to cost her dearly as she was getting ready to have a date with murderous mayhem.

She began to dig, head down in her handbag; then raised up, and with a concerned look, said more to herself than anyone, "oh dear, I seem to have misplaced my room key. I bet I left it on the counter in Century 21."

Seeing his opportunity, Brody said, "can I be of help?"

"I don't see how, but I'm sure I can get another key at the check-in desk." She said softly, pointing vaguely in the direction of the long counter on the other side of the large lobby.

"Allow me," said Brody, recognizing the minor inconvenience as an opportunity and starting to rise.

"It's nice of you to offer, but they won't give it to you."

"Oh yeah, that's right," he said, not really knowing it but trying to fake it, since he didn't have experience staying in high-end hotels.

And, with that in mind, she eyed him somewhat skeptically.

He wasn't paying attention to her look, however.

She said, "you could keep an eye on my packages, though, if you don't mind."

"It would be my pleasure."

"Aren't you sweet?"

"Not really," he was unable to stop himself from saying while chuckling to himself.

But, by then her heels were clicking across the hard marble lobby floor leaving him to check out her ass while she walked away without a care in the world, other than getting another room key, toward the check-in desk, and she never heard what he said.

Yep, things are looking up, he thought to himself. He took another hesitant sip of the expensive beer that was beginning to grow on him as he watched her across the huge lobby as she gestured excitedly to the desk clerk.

She returned a moment later and sat down to finish the pricey cocktail that was getting warm.

"Thank you for keeping an eye on my packages," she said between delicately feminine sips.

"My pleasure. I'm honored you entrusted them to my care,"

Brody said, knowing he was laying it on thick. But he had already decided that that's what it would take with this chick. And he was disrespecting her already, in his mind. Steeling himself mentally, and psychologically, for what he hoped he was about to do. He was always ready physically. That's why he worked so hard at his laboriously intensive job; to stay physically in tune and always ready.

Mostly to herself but still where Brody could hear it, she said, "It's going to take me at least two trips to get all these packages up to my room. Maybe three."

Never one to be diffident, Brody offered his services again. "I can help you."

"I don't even know you," she said, "I can't let you come up to my room."

"I'll stay outside. Besides, I think I proved myself. Showed that I'm…trustworthy," he said, his most genuine smile gently caressing his face.

"I guess you're right," she said hesitantly.

"Good. It's settled, then," he said thinking, *that was almost too easy. I must be getting better at this shit.*

And,"I guess I should introduce myself properly. I'm Todd, Todd Murphy." And with much more ease than a novelist comes up with names for characters he had a new name. He hoped he wouldn't forget it before he was done with the task at hand.

"I'm Sheila Jones."

A classically boring midwestern name with no imagination he thought. "Pleased to meet you, Sheila Jones."

"Likewise."

After paying their tabs, since he had acquiesced to it and because he had ulterior motives of which she wasn't aware, he willingly allowed her to load him up with armfuls of bags and packages, causing him to resemble an unenthusiastic but nevertheless willing packhorse. Similarly, she was weighed down by the recently acquired plastic card room key.

From the piano bar they trudged to the circle of eight glass elevators, one of which that would whisk them to the forty-fourth floor, where her room on the south side of the hotel gave her a magnificent view of the new World Trade Center and Lady Liberty in the bay beyond, a silent sentinel standing guard over New York Harbor as she had since 1885. Her friends in the Midwest would be insanely jealous and never forgive her for not inviting them.

On the elevator, surprisingly with but two others on it, he dropped one of the multitude of packages. Burdened as he was, Brody waited for her to pick it up. He thought that was the least she could do. He leered at her ass happily as she bent over to retrieve the dropped package, her unaware of his leering or the peril she was in.

The lift stopped twice, releasing the others before it came to a firm stop on the forty-fourth floor.

She exited first and turned left, then left again. Laden as he was he hoped it wasn't a long trek to her room. Unfortunately for him, it was on the the east side, the opposite side of the hotel from the elevators, that were centered more toward the west.

At last it seemed, they made it to a door she seemed to like. She wielded the credit card sized key to buzz the door open and even though he was energized by what he was fairly sure was about to happen he resisted the urge to rush in overwhelmingly and allowed her to begin taking the packages from him. It wasn't empathy that made him wait; he just thought it the smarter thing to do.

A moment's hesitation and uninvited he followed her in, letting the door close behind him. The look on her face showed it wasn't what she was expecting.

"I guess they don't teach you to be as careful in the midwest like they do in New York," he said with a sneer.

Sheila covered a startled gasp with her hand and the smell of fear suddenly made its presence known in the cold room.

The delicate white hand covering her mouth didn't do anything to deflect the devastating right cross Brody planted square in her perfect porcelain white well-maintained teeth, or to stifle the strident scream while his vicious baleful eyes stared into the dark depths of fear in hers.

Without her even having a chance to feel a cryptic sense of peril the punch was true and collapsing in a heap, she hit her head on a heavy white nightstand and fell unmoving to the green carpeted floor. Her chest still, he checked her neck for a pulse and got none. Clean and done. Too clean. He didn't like it that clean. Even if she was deader than shit, it didn't give him the same thrill. The Swordsman was known for his gory murder settings. He unkindly yanked off a large turquoise nugget ring she wore, as a souvenir-memento. Admiring it later would remind him of the powers and control he possessed over his victim.

Bloody scenes were sort of his artistic calling card, so even though she was dead and growing colder by the minute he withdrew the ugly hori hori knife with the fake gemstones from where he'd concealed it in his waistband and plunged it into her formerly beautiful and breathless chest over and over again; tugged it out to a sucking sound leaving a gaping hole, and began to saw raggedly through her neck and sever her trachea, almost beheading her. She wouldn't be any deader, but at least he could feel better about his deed. That's not unusual.

And even though she wouldn't bleed after her heart stopped when her head hit the nightstand there was still plenty of blood and gore around the wound to her throat, enough that when her body was discovered no one would even notice the beautiful downtown Manhattan skyline through the drawn drapes on the large south-facing picture window. Although the north side of the nondescript unknown building across 45th St, always devoid of sunshine, was mildewed and in need of a pressure washing.

At the very least the Swordsman thought most people were vapid; at the most, most were stupid. None as clever as he. At the same time happy that enough of them were or he wouldn't be as prolific as he was. And the goal of every serial killer who had hopes and dreams was to be the greatest of all time. Of course that would only be temporary until the next greatest would come along to break records.

In his final act he ripped a large shiny diamond stud more than a carat in size from one of her ears as a souvenir and stuck it in his mouth for safekeeping. Its blood covering it from ripping it from the lobe tasting warm and coppery. The room was a now a particularly terrible mess and he actually felt sorry for housekeeping having to view what for most people would be a disturbing scene; Brody excepted. It certainly wasn't their fault that things worked out the way they did. Of course they wouldn't be turned loose until after NYPD investigators finished their once…or twice, over. Now to make his way from the room and the hotel while attracting as little attention as possible.

That meant one of the glass bullet-shaped elevators was out.

Brody opened the door slowly and cautiously and backtracked the direction they'd come, but instead of turning right toward the elevators in the center of the hotel's fifty-two story atrium, he turned left toward a corner where he'd seen the steel door with a crash bar with red lighted letters above it reading EXIT.

He wasn't looking forward to descending fifty-two stories. *It's a good thing I'm still young and in good shape,* he thought to himself. Even the walk down fifty-two floors would be a challenge for most people. He got his good physical condition and maintained it from hard work. He wouldn't dream of going to a health club like all the white-collar assholes leaving their corporate boardrooms to come and pretend to work out like you typically find filling up the places.

The heavy door squeaked noisily from disuse when he opened it and slammed shut behind him. So much for not drawing attention. The stairwell smelled of chipped scuffed concrete, steel and dust. Twenty minutes later he made the eighth-floor lobby and opening the door slowly and stealthily, taking a quick glance around the huge room before quickly emerging. He felt at least somewhat comfortable entering onto the still lively floor even at the late hour. And his knees would appreciate the break offered by the elevators.

He strolled insouciantly, carefree even, feeling good about himself-probably a challenge to pull off after what he'd just done.

The glass bullet elevators in the center of the huge luxurious lobby were about sixty feet away. He would feel even better in the lone security of one of those glass enclosures. At least no one could arrogantly and aggressively shout "stop; you're under arrest."

Three others followed him onto the one he chose before the door closed. The silence in the enclosure was deafening and made him wonder…wonder why normal folks don't talk on elevators. Like men wouldn't dare to speak to another man in a public restroom.

On the street level, for once a uniformed doorman didn't offer to get him a taxi, distracted as they were by the intrusively loud arrival of the NYPD, as three prowl cars, sirens wailing like a pack of angry wolves, and with the same level of gravitas, jerked to a stop at the curb next to a no parking sign on the 46th St. side of the hotel.

Brody kept his head down making out like he was an uninterested New Yorker who had witnessed the scene countless times, while resisting the urge to run, striding forward, a man on a mission attracting no unwanted attention.

The mist hanging low on Times Square was even heavier than it had been earlier. In the damp cloud his exposed skin was wet and he felt a slight chill in the midsummer night.

Walking in the mist his collar turned up against the cool, he might have been London's legendary Jack the Ripper, also known as the The Whitechapel Murderer, but he was The Swordsman and proud of it he was. He had to admit he dreamed of being as prolific as the infamous Jack and hoped history would recall him as respectfully for it.

As he walked he thought about it more. An interesting thought regarding legends is that they become truth…based on legends. He thought how he had learned to look at life in the shape of life—because life was determined to do what life was going to do. We could choose to accept that and go along with it or choose an alternative way. And his life's desire was to help people with that. His turpitude being limitless.

He took the subway from the Times Square station, and passing through Penn Station, as he rode he worried. Worried that someone would remember seeing him with Sheila and describe him to police. Of course he always did what he could to prevent that. Wore a ball cap and in addition never looked anyone directly in the eye. And he knew most people were so wrapped up in their own meaningless and mundane little lives that they never paid attention to anything going on around them. After getting on the number four line at the downtown station riding comfortably west toward Brooklyn he stopped his worrying until he was disgorged along with the throngs of Brooklynites.

It had turned out to be a productive evening even if it had started slowly and methodically. And it was only Tuesday so who knew what the next few days leading up to the weekend might hold. He didn't dare to think. If he did and if he knew the term he would have understood that his avocation, as well his life, was kafkaesque.

Chapter Twenty-Nine

"Our guy struck again," Rossi said after Bookworm answered his phone.

When he got nothing but dead air, Rossi asked "Are you there?"

"I'm here. I'm just at a loss as what to say. I was hoping he was on a break. Maybe a permanent one. When? Where? Who?"

"I hear you, but no such luck. Furthermore, you got to get this guy. Earn the big bucks the city's paying you." Even Rossi chuckled at that. "A woman, last night, early evening, actually, in a room at the Marriott Marquis. A tourist. Left her a bloody mess. No witnesses-eyeball or earball. Found by housekeeping."

"Sweet Jesus on the Cross. That will put a damper on the tourist trade." That was not what Bookworm had wanted to hear.

"Tell me about it. So anyways, you and Reefer get over there post haste. Unis from midtown west are already onsite. I'll clear it with the sergeant in charge."

Bookworm knew Rossi was serious when he used police terms like post haste. So he likewise was brief in his response.

"10-4. Talk soon."

He cut off the call and keyed in a number he knew from memory.

"Reef, we're up," he said."

"Where?"

"Meet me at the Marriott Marquise, post haste. Eighth floor lobby."

"See you there."

As it turned out, with both of them in need of their morning injection of caffeine, and without it being planned, they unintentionally met in the Starbucks on the south side of the building, just outside the hotel's main entrance and after getting their drinks that couldn't be more different—Bookworm an overly sweet Cinnamon Dolce Latté and Reefer an unsweetened coffee black—they rode up on the elevators together to the eighth floor lobby where they transitioned to one of the glass-enclosed bullet elevators to the forty-fourth floor where Detective Rossi had told Bookworm they'd find a beehive of activity. And where he'd cleared it with a sergeant on site for them to be there.

They rode in silence each of them guzzling their hot but different coffees as they did, in the ascending glass bubble that showed the lobby falling away in all its marble and granite glory. Arriving at the floor needed they exited the lifts and tossed their empty cups into the first trash receptacle they passed.

"Who the fuck are you?" The man wearing a uniform with sergeant's stripes questioned splenetically, and with more than only a hint of attitude when Bookworm pushed open the heavy door. Rossi had phoned the midtown west precinct in which the Marriott Marquis was located to find out who the supervising officer on site was.

"Bookworm and Reefer," replied the first, "Detective Rossi should have called you about us.

"Oh yeah, you're the goddamn CI's. That's all I need. Fucking civilians fucking up my fucking crime scene." He obviously didn't want them turning it shambolic, and seemed to think of them as his crucible. Bookworm stared at him seethingly while biting his tongue, and Reefer's red-eyed glare was even worse.

But Bookworm decided to consider it no more than havering and even so, the mean-spirited comment made him even more committed to he and Reefer getting their private investigator licenses and opening their own detective agency. Hopefully they'd get more respect as private investigators than by being mere lowly informants. And for good measure, they could legally carry guns, if they did. And carrying guns was always a good thing.

Nevertheless, the sergeant stepped aside acrimoniously so they could enter his crime scene and said, "Don't get big heads. I'm only allowing this because from what people tell me Rossi is a better than passable cop. So this is for him."

Bookworm was reluctant to accept the somewhat less than sincere passage, but for Rossi's benefit and in hopes of catching the killer on his behalf, he decided they should and so he stepped aside without saying a word and let Reefer enter first. Along with the sergeant were two uniformed officers, two crime scene investigators, and a three person forensics crew with their ubiquitous silver aluminum cases.

Controlled chaos was the only term Bookworm could come up with to describe the scene where a mutilation had occurred.

Their startled eyes grew huge at the scene before them, as it wouldn't have been possible for Bookworm and Reefer to make it any worse since it was already a disaster. A literal blood bath, overturned furniture and scattered clothes everywhere they looked. A grotesquerie they couldn't have imagined in their most frightening nightmares.

After seeing all they needed to see Bookworm and Reefer took their leave without a word to the sergeant. A brief ride on one of the unique elevators and they were back at the eighth-floor lobby ready to begin investigating. They started at the concierge desk thinking it would be his job to notice anything and everything going on his lobby.

Without saying who they were they explained that they were investigating the murder to a uniform wearing middle-aged Latino who said in broken English he had seen her at the long check-in desk late the previous afternoon.

They strode to the counter with a purpose and without introduction, boldly asked the desk manager what he recalled about his interaction with the victim.

He spoke proper English. "I merely gave her a replacement keycard for her room since she thought she had left hers on a counter at Century 21. It's right on the other side of Times Square, you know. Then I watched as she walked over to the piano bar." He gestured toward the other side of the huge lobby. "She was quite the looker, you know. Then she got some poor schmuck—probably her husband—to carry all of her packages, loaded his poor ass up; it looked like she'd been shopping and they walked off in the direction of the elevators."

"What'd he look like?" Reefer asked.

"Too far for me to see any clearly defined features." "Not even with these things," he said taking off his glasses. "And my counter was getting backed up with the late afternoon check-ins, besides."

Bookworm and Reefer thanked him for his help but they would have to return at five o'clock when the bar would open for the evening.

***

Bookworm and Reefer felt like they had just left the hotel as they emerged from the elevator into the luxurious lobby. At 5:15 they could already hear the piano player entertaining the happy hour crowd, and walked directly in the sound of the music. The lobby was comfortably cool after the humid warmth of the city.

They spoke first with the bartender who'd been working the previous day. Fortunately she had been scheduled again. She told them that he was drinking a Dutch beer and how he had been dressed. Not at all proper for such a fine place was what she'd said. They also questioned a cute young server who couldn't add anything of significance. She probably couldn't have added anything with a calculator.

A moment later the blind African American earnest piano player paused between songs and grinned, saying, "What? You aren't going to ask me what I saw? I'm hurt. Excuse me, I'm Antigone. Yeah, I know; my mom was a Sophocles fan. Lucky me." He spoke in a voice grandiloquent and gestured with brio. He wouldn't be described as handsome as his chin appeared unfinished.

"Charmed," said Bookworm; because what else would one say to someone named Antigone.

The looks on Bookworm's and Reefer's faces would show a sighted person that they thought he had lost his mind. He removed the black horn-rimmed Ray Charles-like dark shades and insouciantly slid them aside and said, "what? These? These are a prop. Nobody is impressed with a musician who can see. But a blind one; now that's cool, then you got something. Probably even get me some sympathy tips. You know what I'm talking about; think Little Stevie Wonder, Ray Charles and my personal favorite, Blind John Davis. But I wonder why the blind ones are all brothers. What's up with that?"

"Edify us, then," said Bookworm, putting his vocabulary on display.

"Beg pardon," said Antigone.

"So what did you see?"

Antigone interlaced his fingers and stretched his hands backwards cracking his knuckles, readying his hands for his next number. His nails were perfect. He obviously got regular manicures. A must for a piano player since people were watching his hands constantly. "A white dude, didn't look particularly menacing. In fact, looked quite benign more than anything else— about thirty-five, longish brown hair under a dark blue Yankees cap, slender, five-ten. Clean shaven. Cocky smile. What else you want?" Antigone was able to acquire more detail about him because the man had ignored him, thinking him blind, and unable to see him and therefore not a threat to him, where he avoided anything direct from the others.

Bookworm turned to Reefer and said, "Who does that sound like?"

"Dude our vic was last seen with at the Mexican resto at Coney Island."

"Bingo."

Feeling like they'd accomplished something they thanked their new friend, Antigone, for the info and left in a better mood than in which they arrived. Then, after making their way almost to the elevators they changed their minds and decided to circle back to the bar and have an ice-cold cocktail or three and listen to Antigone tickle the ivories for a few. A pleasant way to spend a hot summer early evening. Certainly better than dealing with the crowded midtown sidewalks…or worse, the stultifying and sweaty subway or equally as bad buses.

***

While they chilled over chilled mixed drinks with fancy names and colorful little umbrellas in them and listened to Antigone Bookworm pulled out his cellphone and dialed Detective Rossi.

"Sup," answered Rossi.

Speaking quietly so as not to disturb the others enjoying Antigone's stylings, he said, "Apparently the man that was chatting her up in the piano bar looked like our person of interest in the Coney Island killing."

"Get the hell out of here. Now that's something we can work with."

"I thought you'd like that."

"Yeah, talk to you tomorrow. We need to get the department artist to talk to your witness, see what he can come up with; then we gotta discuss where we go from here."

"10-4." And with that terse cutoff, Bookworm beat Rossi to the punch with the cop lingo.

Proud of himself, he turned to Reefer, grinned, and said, "That's a first. I got him that time.

Chapter Thirty

At ten the following morning Rossi, Bookworm and Reefer met at the Starbucks that was in the space that was formerly occupied by the barbershop in the old Park Sheraton Hotel on 7th Avenue at 56th Street where mafia boss and cofounder of Murder, Inc., The Lord High Executioner himself, Albert Anastasia, was executed by two masked gunmen while getting a shave in October of '58. The Starbucks was centrally located for each of them and Rossi thought its infamous history made it an apt location.

Glad to see his friend and LEO mentor, Bookworm glad handed Rossi enthusiastically while clapping him on the back. Reefer did so less enthusiastically but only because he's Reefer. Rossi didn't take it personally.

After greetings, Rossi said, "So can you meet our artist at the piano bar this afternoon? Introduce him to the piano player?"

"Of course we can, but he won't need our help, or interference. Antigone is a very worldly and companionable gentleman, and will be happy to help the NYPD."

"I'm sure you're right, but since you all already have this close brother connection that only you brothers can have it can't hurt to keep that going." And Rossi winked as he said it in an effort to get Bookworm's goat. "And moreover, this guy isn't what you would call the epitome of cool, so you probably need to be there to translate brother-speak for him."

"No problem. We'll be there. NYPD is picking up our bar tab, right?"

"This time. But don't think it's gonna become a habit. I know how you guys are, you know."

Bookworm and Reefer appeared downhearted at Rossi's response.

"Well," Bookworm said, trying to sound forlorn, "you can count on us anyway."

Rossi didn't bite. "Oh, poor things."

***

They walked into the piano bar just before five while Antigone was warming up. "This is becoming a habit," he said.

Bookworm gave him a thumbs up.

A moment later the artist arrived, a sketch pad under his arm, and came straight toward them. Bookworm knew it was him because he looked like a cross between a sad eyed scientist with the escapist look of an artist. Exceedingly thin and rapidly retreating dark hair with a sad excuse for a goatee. And apparently Rossi had told him who to look for. The tired looking man nodded at them then sat down and they introduced themselves.

A busboy clearing tables of glasses looked like he should be in or recently got out of the joint.

Bookworm then walked over to the piano where Antigone was still warming up and told him why they were there as he glanced over his shoulder at the sketch artist.

"I can take a break in forty-five minutes. Can I come over and us talk then?"

"Sure, we're on your schedule. By the way, you want a beer, anything?"

"Thank you, but I don't drink. "However," he said with a little boy's up-to-something grin, "if you've got a little weed…".

Bookworm thought not unkindly, typical musician for you. He hoped this plan would help or otherwise he knew that Rossi would be forced to call in VICAP, the FBI organization for analysis of serial killer evidence. And once they were called, the Feds would take control of the case.

As Bookworm returned to the table Antigone began to play *Wichita Lineman*. His talent on display, anything but banal. Unless the relaxed commonality of the song was one of brutal banality.

Bookworm thought the popular country song sounded a little out of place played on the beautiful Steinway and in New York City.

***

After a set that Bookworm thought improved after *Wichita Lineman*, even though Reefer didn't like any of it since his tastes ranged from Lil' Wayne to Sugar Hill Gang among other hip-hop artists, Antigone joined them. But even though Reefer wasn't familiar with the tune and didn't care for it besides, his head bobbed to the beat. He couldn't help himself. Indeed, that was what you'd expect; Reefer being Reefer. And that explained a lot. Bookworm noticed him doing it, looked his way and grinned. Reefer stopped immediately.

Bookworm introduced Antigone and the sketch artist and left them to do their thing. The artist delicately withdrew a pen with multiple colored ink cartridges from his shirt chest pocket and began to draw on the tablet. A simple but surprisingly lifelike form began to take shape. Narrow face, longish brown hair sides and back, dark ball cap covering the crown of the head. Unlined face, even a sparkle in his eyes. The last detail; the Yankees iconic NY appearing on the front of the slouch cap. The artist cum scientist didn't take for granted the gravity of what he was called upon to do, but the artist in his soul just enjoyed the hell out of creating art; even the serious art of killers, rapists and the like.

A fast-working artist, thirty minutes after beginning he displayed the drawing and Antigone excitedly exclaimed, "That's him; that's him."

Glancing at the artwork Bookworm said, cleverly, "he looks pretty sketchy; pun intended." Then he picked up his phone from where he'd laid it on the four-person hightop and called Rossi to tell him what they had, and Rossi said, "then I'll get it to Sharp, excuse me, Lieutenant Sharp, to get it on the tv news asap. Hopefully in the early morning. And then get it in the local rags' afternoon editions later. Where do you want to meet to give it to me?"

"We're in the lobby bar. How about here? Nice music. Ice cold adult beverages?"

"Sounds good. Give me an hour."

"You got it. We'll be in the piano bar. Sitting in front of the huge ebony baby grand. You can't miss it."

They both clicked off the call without another word.

***

Bookworm and Reefer drank fancy Dutch beers and Antigone sipped a Coke Zero Sugar on the rocks in a tall glass while they waited patiently for Detective Rossi's arrival. Reefer's fingers did an anxious tap dance on the tabletop. After the better part of an hour they watched as Rossi got off one of the elevators looking beat, his tie loosened and his suit rumpled, and dragging his feet soundlessly on the shiny dark marble floor and walked in their direction. No Beau Brummel was he.

Before getting there however, and after passing the large gift shop on his left without its New York City souvenirs and treasures enticing him to enter he ducked into the mens' restroom.

Five minutes later he stopped at the bar and glanced at a cocktail menu before asking for a proper Manhattan, though with rye instead of bourbon, and on the rocks instead of in a martini glass, unknowing how a man could drink a whiskey sour, before walking to the glossy wood hightop bistro table for four and noisily sliding over a barstool to join them, and glad-handing everyone. Bookworm said jokingly, "I hope you washed your hands."

Abashed by the remark, Rossi gave him a dirty look while sipping the Manhattan disinterestedly, although if he were being honest he'd have to admit to himself the offhand comment was pretty clever. "So let's see whatchu got," Rossi said. Then he took a healthy swallow of the rye that warmed him comfortably on its way down. This was a very informal meeting with serious ramifications. But in such elegant surroundings with the view of the hotel interior rising forty-four floors from the eighth-floor lobby with alcoholic beverages flowing and even mixed nuts in a small bowl on the table it was relaxing and in fact felt more like a group of old friends catching up over happy hour, a modern reflection of one of C.S. Lewis' more well known sayings. Most of the several cocktail tables were occupied by two, three, or four people; and the more alcohol they consumed the louder their conversations grew.

Knowing he'd see Detective Rossi at the precinct in the early morning, the sketch artist slash scientist handed the sketch off to Bookworm's safekeeping and proceeded to take his leave. He flipped it over from where it lay on the table for the big reveal.

The only server working, with the longest tattoo-covered legs and wearing the shortest shorts any of them had ever seen, made her way to their table and said, "My name's Moody. Can I get anyone a fresh drink?"

They chuckled like they didn't believe her, and Reefer said, "Seriously. You expect us to believe that?"

"Seriously. That's my Christian name. My given name. My mom said it was that or Memry. I prefer Moody. Of course, I admit it has grown on me over twenty-three years. In fact I've kind of grown accustomed to it."

Having just arrived and barely started to sip his drink, Rossi waved the nearly full glass her way and said "I'm good."

Bookworm and Reefer, having been there longer, nodded.

"What do you think?" Reefer asked Rossi.

"About her name? I don't care what she says. I'm not buying it. Even 60's hippies wouldn't hang a handle like that on a kid."

Then, knowing what Reefer was asking, he picked up the drawing and tilting it this way and that, studied it carefully. A self-satisfied broad Italian smile appearing on his face as he said, "Thank the good Lord he wasn't wearing a balaclava. This is our man. I can feel it in my bones that this is our big break, and unless our plans go awry, with it we shall begin to disentangle our killer from this particularly vexing mystery," sounding like the narrator of a Poe novel, showing off his vocabulary since it tended to be somewhat recherché to most people and he didn't often get to use it unless Bookworm was around, before taking another swallow of the expensive rye that he had never tasted before.

"God only knows we need a break. And by God, we're going to get him with this instead of the case dying of the terminally long eventually fatal illness of nothing occurring." Rossi wasn't one to speak obliquely and he didn't think of his measured response as hackneyed. If anything it only sounded as if he were trying to convince himself, but he was sure of it because he could feel it in his ganglion. The sensation in his central nervous system told him it was so.

After another icy Manhattan Rye for Rossi and two more expensive Dutch beers for Book and Reefer they decided to call it a night.

Chapter Thirty-One

Exiting the Marriott Marquis onto the brightly lit Times Square sidewalk teeming with throngs, Rossi said, "youse guys want a Nathan's hotdog? I'm buying…or at least the city is." Sometimes Rossi couldn't help his native New Yorkese coming out.

Bookworm answered with alacrity, "I'm all in for some Nathan's."

Reefer, being Reefer, and maybe suffering from his namesake munchies, said, "I dunno, maybe; depends on if I can have some onion rings…and a Ghirardelli chocolate shake."

After pretending to think about it before finally coming to the decision to acquiesce, Rossi said, "I think the city can afford that."

"Then, let's do it," said Reefer, just as enthusiastically as Bookworm had, with a huge smile.

A block north and on the other side of 8th Ave from Howard Johnson's orange and blue restaurant they entered the famous chain fast food restaurant's colorful Times Square location. The small space was almost full but they managed to find a table for four and quickly decamped. Their eyes adjusting from the dark of night to the neon light and bright colors inside. Paint and decor the bright colors of mustard and ketchup and containing an aroma of fresh onions and beef hotdogs and corndogs cooking, it was a culinary feast for the senses. Sixties era beach music played on hidden speakers.

After getting their orders and beginning to chow down like they had never had a meal before, Reefer said, "this is bustin'.

Rossi said, "if bustin' means good, then I agree. Nothing more American than hotdogs from Nathan's. The only way it could be any better or more American would be if we had beer." In place of that adult luxury he guzzled a large Coke.

Bookworm grinned up at him, and said, "true dat."

Rossi looked at him skeptically but knew he was only momentarily slipping into the street lingo like he had to do from time to time to keep his rep from becoming tarnished too badly by his immense Rutgers vocabulary.

Even though he agreed about a beer, Reefer was too busy eating to say anything.

"So what do you think?" Asked Rossi.

"About what?" Asked Bookworm while Reefer nodded wonderingly.

"Do you think we're going to get the son of a bitch?"

"No question about it," Bookworm said, "The only question is when."

While they ate and discussed the as of yet unknown suspect it began to drizzle. A warm comforting summer rain, though; not like the misery of a New York rain in winter.

Discussing possibilities, game plans, strategies and such, finally, like it was a revelation, Reefer said "I guess first thing tomorrow I should oughta check with Spike and his boys, see if they hear anything new. You know Spike already told me the man just likes the hell out of killing people. Thinks it's fun as shit. It's not like he gets pissed off because Mickey D's runs out of fries so he kills everybody in the place or because he doesn't like the smell of somebody's aftershave." Spike had given Reefer info that had proved instrumental in them catching the Unholy Ghost less than a year before. Reefer hoped he might have some new info that might help them this go 'round.

After deciding on at least the parameters of a plan Rossi told them about his idea for retirement, moving to Long Island, and buying a small house with a swimming pool and acquiring a restaurant and bar. Bookworm thought it sounded like a grand idea. Reefer couldn't wrap his head around being old enough to think about retiring and then actually doing it.

They finished their food, cleaned the trash from the table and getting up to leave shoved their chairs back noisily on the tile floor. Their table wouldn't be free for long since Nathan's was full with people waiting for tables.

Rossi returned to the counter and ordered two corndogs to go with packages of mustard ketchup and sweet relish

Bookworm said, "Sal, you got a new dog you're taking that to?"

Rossi ignored the frivolous comment.

Once outside Rossi said, "Hold up," and walked over to a wet miserable-looking man sitting on the sidewalk with a stump of a leg bent under him and one good leg sticking straight out to the side. The hand-lettered cardboard sign sitting in his lap read 'homeless vet, please help.'

Rossi handed him the Nathan's bag and a huge toothless smile creased the grateful man's face.

"Oh my goodness, this is just like Christmas before…before. And mustard and ketchup, too," he said without finishing, tears spilling from his eyes. The three friends overcome also by his unashamed show of emotion.

As they walked away, Reefer, still moved by the scene said, "I wonder why some people ignore the homeless."

Rossi gazed at the downtown Manhattan skyline, thought a minute, and said, "Some people draw the drapes on their minds so they don't have to see.

Reefer nodded at the deep response.

Then, Rossi said, "how about that beer now, before we call it a night?"

"Where?" Bookworm said, suddenly interested.

"Langan's Irish Pub. Left at the next corner, then, less than a hundred feet on the right. "Coldest Guinness in midtown."

Bookworm looked at Reefer's nodding head and said, "we got time for a Guinness."

"Good. It's settled, then."

A typical look for an Irish pub, every surface polished dark wood and the bar running down one side was probably fifty feet long, so it could seat a lot of thirsty micks.

The rain had picked up and along with that the streetlamps and stoplights had been knocked out and fog was settling in and none of them had been prepared for it. Nothing to do but shove their hands in their pockets, hunch their shoulders and tilt their chins as if to head-butt the dark rising storm and move swiftly forward in soaked shoes and socks as sodden as their clothes, as best they could past sluicing gutters. Alas, it was rain with no soul; a lonely soulless rain. And thankfully no glassy sheets of slippery ice like there would be if it were the dark of winter; although a cold winter rain could provide healing. They would make it to Langan's without getting too drenched.

Walk wasn't accurate; since they ran, jogged, double-timed it, whatever you wanted to call it, actually some of each, all the while slipping and sliding, struggling for traction and trying their best not to fall on the pebbly-slick, dark sidewalks and Rossi, who outweighed them by at least forty pounds, doing his best to keep up with his thinner and younger companions. So much for that. Some folks, like them, were trying to rush to get out of the rain. Others, old and young, slim and heavy, weren't even attempting to hurry; having already given up on the futility of their efforts to stay dry. All of them proof that solipsism doesn't exist.

The blithe tolling of the bells from nearby St. Mary the Virgin Episcopal Church as they prepared to enter nevertheless made it feel like a solemn event. Stepping up to the large front brown-mullioned window that opened wide to allow fresh air into the long bar, Rossi said, "you know, this was Steve Dunleavy's favorite pub before he died. In fact I met him here, once. He always sat on the last stool at the other end of the bar."

Bookworm and Reefer responded with confused looks that belied their wish to look like they were in the know.

"Of the New York Post. From Australia. Some people say he's the greatest reporter who ever lived. And cops liked him because he supported cops. No, that's not true. He loved and supported cops. He never took shots at us in his reporting."

"Oh. Cool."

"Oh, yeah."

The lack of enthusiasm with which they responded rendered them unable to convince Rossi that they had any idea who he was talking about.

They entered the door and pulled out three barstools at the near end of the bar. Each of them ordered pints of Guinness.

After clinking their mugs, Rossi said, "here's to catching the son of a bitch post haste.

"I'll drink to that," said Reefer. He was in to helping the NYPD once again. And when Rossi used law enforcement terms like post haste it made it feel official.

They finished two pints each before calling it a night; then had to make another dash in the rain to the train station.

Standing in the Times Square Train Station and trying in vain to stamp their feet dry, Rossi counted out two hundred bucks in twenties from his wallet and gave it to Bookworm to share with Reefer.

"Courtesy of the NYPD," he said.

"Thanks, we like it when the NYPD is courteous," said Bookworm in his usual weak stab at humor, as Reefer stared at the bills and nodded agreeably.

"We'll talk tomorrow," said Rossi, and then, "Father," with a respectful tip of his head in adulation of the prelate in his collar, smiling and smoking a cigarette as he walked past. His teeth clenched the filter tip. He'd probably been to visit the nursing home in the neighborhood; checking on elderly parishioners. Serving communion to the relics. Then Rossi watched couples kissing…good-bye. It would probably be at least tomorrow before they saw each other again.

"Gotta run for my train. Ella will be wondering where I am." said Rossi.

"Us too, and tell Ms. Ella I said hi," said Book.

"Will do. She still talks about what a nice young man you are. And still refers to you as John, though."

Bookworm said, "She probably always will," and grinned as if to say 'and you didn't think she'd like me'.

And they headed off in different directions.

***

Brody's boss had seen the story and drawing also, and convinced as he was that the sketch bore more than just a passing resemblance, he wasted no time calling the NYPD. He was connected to the administrative department and it took more than only a few minutes to be routed to Detective Rossi, but after a series of buzzes, clicks, and periods of silence, the connection was finally made.

Detective Rossi said, "So you think the drawing of the suspect in the Daily News is an employee of yours'?"

"I'd swear to it, Detective."

"Well," said Rossi thoughtfully, "you won't have to do that unless there's a trial, but that's a good start."

"And to be honest, I've never really trusted him that much, but in this business you do the best you can when it comes to hiring employees. It's not like they're a lot of Harvard grads in the hvac business, you know.

"No, I guess not."

They made plans for Rossi along with Bookworm and Reefer to visit the man's business early the next morning before Brody would leave for the day. Unfortunately that wasn't soon enough.

With a long holiday weekend coming up Brody decided to take the rest of the week off. And since Rossi had nothing to go on except the company owner saying the drawing looked like Brody Rossi didn't have probable cause to do anything but wait.

Chapter Thirty-Two

On Monday on a long Independence Day Weekend Brody decided to do something a typical tourist would do and took the three-decker yacht cruise to Liberty Island to visit France's greatest gift to the States. He hadn't seen it up-close since a grade school field trip and he thought it was about time. Indeed, most New Yorkers rarely, if ever, visited any of the most important tourist attractions. They felt it beneath their sophisticated selves. The Green Lady, as most locals referred to her was because of the weather tarnishing the natural copper color; the same as a new copper penny turning green with age and time.

Brody wasn't actually looking for opportunities for mayhem, since as a professional he considered that he needed a weekend off, a respite. And with that in mind the yacht cruise to the island, the ensuing stroll around the island and climbing the tower the entire way to the torch were uneventful. The fresh salty sea air was invigorating, however, and evoked in him the motivation to pursue his intended, if self-inflicted, calling.

He sat on the largest second level, part of it indoors and part of it open air; the middle of the three levels of the yacht. The promenade deck providing it's partial ceiling above. The fresh ocean breeze was pleasant in the open areas. And then the unexpected but nevertheless welcome opportunity happened by in the form of a blonde in her late twenties or early thirties wearing a pair of painted on white denim pants.

As painted on as Olivia Newton-John's painted on black ones in the movie Grease.

Shiny black stilettos and a pink silk tank top completed the a little less than wholesome look. He followed her with his eyes until she entered the women's rest room he knew was a single stall from having already answered the call in the men's next to it, while a plan materialized in his mind's eye.

Envisioning how it would play out and waiting for the cue he needed to put his nascent plan into action he leaned insouciantly against the narrow strip of laminated wallboard between the men's and women's room doors and pulled his Giants cap tight over his sunglasses, knowing he could ditch the ball cap later, while listening carefully for the sound of the deadbolt lock of the women's disengaging. And while surreptitiously making sure to see that the one nearby security camera was currently pointed in a different direction, and confirming that the coast was clear with no one paying attention, using his martial arts training, he blasted the metal door open with a vicious front kick, stunning the stunning woman on the other side.

Fortunately for Brody, the yacht's loud diesel engines and the bay water's noise and other boat traffic rendered the abrasive noise of the door being kicked in unnoticeable.

He pulled his hori hori knife from its usual place and dropped to his knees to straddle her ribcage, before he slashed a deep gash across her throat. She gurgled loudly from the grotesque amount of blood. Even though she was dead immediately blood continued to gush and cover most of the small room's surfaces.

Brody touched two fingers to her throat just to be sure, felt nothing, then rose; straightening his clothes and composing himself before he moved as cautiously as he could to the door and trusting the gods and luck that no one was waiting to enter, opened the door but an inch, slowly and carefully, before committing to the inevitable decision to exit and opening the door wide. Then he found his way to an enclosed stairway to climb to the uppermost deck with his only goal being to distance himself as far from the bloody scene as he was able.

Brody was able to separate himself as much as possible from the insanity on the medium-sized yacht when the body was discovered. Without being conspicuous by his lack of interest.

And that was nothing compared to the maelstrom of blue lights and sirens that greeted the ship when it reached its usual mooring spot in downtown Manhattan's financial district.

Although it wasn't without challenges, Brody managed to disappear along with the ship's crew after docking.

Once on dry land it was much easier to blend in with millions of New Yorkers plying the sidewalks as he made the easy five minute walk to the nearest subway station for the short trip east toward Brooklyn and other points further east.

Detective Rossi was trying to enjoy the extended holiday weekend, but no such luck as the precinct switchboard tracked him down.

On his way to the downtown pier he tapped Bookworm's name on his phone.

Recognizing the name and number immediately, Bookworm answered, "Detective," formally, assuming it must be serious business on a holiday weekend.

"We got another one."

"Shit."

"Same thing I said when they called me."

"Well, you know what they say, good minds do think alike."

Detective Rossi chuckled and slapped his knee, smart-assedly even though Bookworm couldn't see it.

"Meet me at the downtown pier where the boat to the Statue docks."

"Will do. And I'll call Reef on the way."

Forty-five minutes later, Bookworm and Reefer arrived at the dock and followed the obvious crowd of law enforcement officers toward an equally imposing group already collected on the pier.

Rossi carried a copy of the sketch artist's rendering of the presumed killer. Upon questioning, several people said that the man had been on the tour boat. And since he knew a dozen witnesses would likely give you a dozen descriptions he didn't always have faith, but the odds of having two killers working in the city at the same time using the same method would be somewhat a little more than minuscule and gave him confidence.

After most of the afternoon spent interviewing New Yorkers who weren't excited about being detained, Rossi, Bookworm and Reefer set out on their renewed quest of tracking a killer.

The simultaneous thought occurred to them that if they fell in with the crowd leaving the dock that just maybe they might hear something useful. Rossi couldn't help looking like a cop. That's where being with Bookworm and Reefer helped since they looked like anything but cops. And anyone seeing them together just got confused.

Their secretive plan didn't work out the way they hoped, however. The smell of sweat engulfed them like a pungent stale cloud and all they overheard were complaints of sunburn.

***

Brody made his way to the lower east side to join the hundreds of thousands of New Yorkers and out of town visitors for the spectacular Independence Day fireworks display from barges moored in the East River, praying that he would come across an unyielding opportunity. If he were fortunate the evil specter of a two kill day might raise its head.

He was accepted grudgingly into an almost impenetrable crowd of nearly a million New Yorkers in lower Manhattan. It sounded like a million bees.

The crowd size in fact, made him question if he would be able to get another victim due to the lack of privacy to do what he needed to do. But it wouldn't be for lack of trying.

There *were* a number of narrow alleys in the South Street Seaport area however, and if he were to get lucky…well, one never knew what might happen.

Across South Street and on the opposite side of the seaport mall he saw someone that made him feel like his fortunes were changing.

A cute young woman, dark skinned with an Asian look to her; probably Blasian—or that could have only been wishful thinking on the Swordsman's part since he'd hadn't killed an African American Asian before—in her early twenties walked alone glancing nervously from side-to-side like she was looking for friends. He thought *I can be her friend; her very good friend. The last very good friend she ever has.*

The Swordsman crossed the street as quickly as he could against the crowd. He ducked into a filthy narrow nightmare alley that she would pass by momentarily. If he stood spread-eagle in the center he could touch both dirty brick walls with the palms of his hands. She walked by on the building side of a dumpster which helped to shield her from view from the largest part of the Independence Day celebrants and gave him the opportunity to formulate a plan and then put his sadistically aggressive move into action.

As she drew nearer, he jerked the horrifying hori hori knife from its usual place of keeping and readied the manifestation of evil he became, to pounce.

The Swordsman leapt from the narrow alley and grabbed her by the throat as she passed, stifling any sound she could make.

The shock and abject terror on her innocent face told everything anyone would want to know as he jerked her head back exposing her porcelain-like throat to his evil blade and into the blackness of the alley. FBI estimates show that the average person will come in contact with more than 30 killers in their lifetimes. Most of them as simple as passing on the street. That number was an average for the entire country due to an abnormally high number of the killers having been in California since FBI tracking began. Unfortunately for her, it was more than just a passing contact.

For the Swordsman however, it was a day of jubilation, a day to be celebrated; a two-kill day. But in the moment he needed to slip out of the killing place and furtively fall in among a passing crowd to avoid being noticed near the crime scene. He wasn't concerned with the CCTV cameras that peppered the city due to being able to get lost in the large number of people on the streets for the holiday celebration.

The fireworks were beginning and as they started to light up the nighttime sky recorded patriotic music sounded on huge speakers and the crowd of millions began to ooh and ah. It didn't seem real.

As the huge explosive finale began Brody thought about how he would return to Brooklyn. Watching the last of the show while trekking across the bridge would be spectacular, but he did have to be at work early the next morning and it would be a long walk. *"Working sucks,"* he thought. Instead he decided that the overly packed subway would be a better option even if it would be crowded with people he wouldn't associate with.

***

As usual Brody arrived at seven and was immediately summoned to the owner's small office. It was overly-cramped with a desk, something that might be called a credenza and three file cabinets since he didn't believe in computers.

The Italian detective he'd seen on local news and one of two youngish brothers-probably plain clothes detectives, he thought, occupied a visitor's chair while a taller one leaned cooly with his elbow resting on top of a file cabinet. It was obvious from the presence of those three that the jig was up.

Unnecessary introductions were made before the man's secretary entered the office. She passed too close to Brody and he grabbed her in the manner he'd put into practice many times and thrust the knife against the hollow of her throat.

"I'm walking out of here," he said as he backed slowly to the office door.

"No, you're not," Bookworm said while taking a step away from the file cabinet toward Brody.

While Brody was distracted by Bookworm Rossi drew his Glock and aimed it at Brody's forehead and said, "he's right. You're not."

Brody took another backward step and Rossi put three pounds of pressure on the dark gun's trigger. "Drop it or she's dead." Brody said before he took another slow backward step while applying pressure on the knife edge against her exposed throat as he did. The explosion in the small office was louder than the previous night's fireworks. The black hole in his forehead appeared instantaneously and pieces of his brain and skull, and blood decorated the wall behind him morbidly.

www.ingramcontent.com/pod-product-compliance
Lightning Source LLC
Chambersburg PA
CBHW050510260626
47157CB00004B/1271